LEGEND of the LAKE

ENDORSEMENTS

Legend of the Lake stayed in my hands from the moment I picked it up until I read the final line. The story is simultaneously heartrending and heartwarming—with relatable characters and an engaging storyline. Sheri Schofield tenderly showcases the restorative power of the Gospels, the encouragement of church fellowship, and the joy of pure love. *Legend of the Lake* is a book that inspires the readers to "go and do likewise" and love their community well, especially those who are vulnerable and on the outskirts of society.

—April D., twenty-two-year-old college senior and avid reader

I thoroughly enjoyed *Legend of the Lake*. It is a warm-hearted novel about people whose lives intersect in life's difficult places. Through its main character, the reader sees God's promise played out to redeem her as she deals with the death of her fiancé, her mother's betrayal, and a move to a Montana home that opens its heart to her.

—Rebecca Price Janney, award-winning author of the Easton Series, including *Easton at Sunset*

This heartwarming book highlights the power of God to redeem any situation when people turn to him in the midst of their problems. Sheri Schofield has used the paintbrush of engaging fiction to craft an unforgettable image of a community united to be God's instruments of life-affirming care.

—Rhonda Dragomir, author of historical fiction

LEGEND of the LAKE

SHERI SCHOFIELD

PUBLISHING THE POSITIVE
Plymouth, Massachusetts
A Christian Company
ElkLakePublishingInc.com

COPYRIGHT NOTICE

Cover and Interior Design: Derinda Babcock, Deb Haggerty
Editor(s): Peggy Ellis, Cristel Phelps, Deb Haggerty

PUBLISHED BY: Elk Lake Publishing, Inc., 35 Dogwood Drive, Plymouth, MA 02360, 2024

Library Cataloging Data
Names: Schofield, Sheri (Sheri Schofield)
Legend of the Lake / Sheri Schofield
p. 23cm × 15cm (9in × 6 in.)
ISBN-13: 9798891341456 (paperback) | 9798891341463 (trade paperback) | 9798891341470 (e-book)
Key Words: Montana; Pro-life; Christian romance novel; western ranch; small towns; escaping abuse; pregnancy support
Library of Congress Control Number: 2024931418 Fiction

DEDICATION

To Josh & Kirsten

ACKNOWLEDGMENTS

I would like to thank my dear friend and mother-in-law, Dollie Schofield, for her encouragement, for listening and commenting on the contents of this book as I worked my way through the plot.

Special thanks to my husband, Tim, who encouraged me to write, and who has provided all I have needed to move forward as an author.

I would like to thank my editor, Peggy Lovelace Ellis, for all her work in helping me present this book in the best way possible.

My publisher, Deb Haggerty, has been a huge encouragement to me as I have written. Thank you, Deb, for all your support.

Above all, I thank my Lord and Savior, Jesus Christ, for leading and inspiring me as I wrote. I can honestly say, "Jesus wrote the last line in *Legend of the Lake.*" I recognized it as soon as the line hit the paper. With his masterful touch, he pulled this book together in a way I never could have done on my own. *Blessed be the name of the Lord, indeed.*

PART 1

CHAPTER 1

Where is Konnor? He's already an hour late! Did his boss keep him late on a project again?

I turned away from the June sunshine spilling through the kitchen window and checked the scalloped potatoes and ham staying warm—I hoped not overcooked—in the oven. The scent wafting through the apartment made my mouth water. A tossed green salad chilled in the refrigerator. A cherry pie from the bakery down the street sat on the counter.

I looked out the window again. A tiny bit of anxiety crept into my heart. *He always calls when he expects to be late.*

We'd moved into this apartment in Medford a couple of weeks before—after we'd graduated from Southern Oregon University and found jobs in the area. Now it was the second week in June, and we had been too busy to connect with our new neighbors except to wave. Most of our friends had scattered to new jobs across the country. This was Konnor's and my first independent relocation, and we were just beginning to feel settled.

"I miss our friends," I'd told Konnor the night before.

"We'll make new ones, honey." He wrapped his arms around me and held me close. I smiled at the memory.

Footsteps sounded outside on the steps.

Finally! He's here. I hope he will like what I've made for dinner.

The doorbell rang.

He has a key. That can't be him.

I opened the door. Two uniformed police greeted me when I opened the door. They stood there, sober looks on their faces.

"Ma'am, are you Lily Mains?"

I caught my breath in apprehension. This couldn't be good. "Yes. Why?"

"I'm sorry to have to tell you, but there's been an accident."

His compassionate expression told me something bad had happened. I reached backward, searching for something to lean on. But there was nothing. One of the officers quickly reached out to support me.

"Konnor West was idling at a stop light, and another car coming from his left swerved into him. Mr. West didn't make it, ma'am, but he lived a few minutes. His last words were, 'Tell Lily I love her, and I will see her again if she believes.' I'm not sure what that meant. But ..." He shrugged. "These are the things he had with him in the car. He told me to give them to you." The officer handed me an envelope.

In shock, I reached out to take it, but my knees suddenly gave way. As I started to fall, the officer holding my arm helped me to the nearest chair.

"Let me get you some water," the other officer said, turning toward the kitchen. A moment later, he held a glass to my lips and told me to drink.

I don't remember much after that. Everything became a nightmarish blur. Konnor's brother made the funeral arrangements. My parents, Will and Margaret Mains, came from Santa Rosa, California, to help. Dad arranged for our meager possessions to be shipped to their home, terminated the rental agreement, and dealt with other necessary details. Mom led me to their car as we left.

I was home again in my familiar room where I had grown up. I lay on my bed, staring at the ceiling.

Then came Konnor's funeral. His brother stood with me by the grave. His parents, long divorced, were traveling somewhere, and we couldn't get in touch with them. They were not a close family.

Dad stood on my other side, his arm supporting me. I placed a rose on the coffin and said goodbye to my beloved Konnor. Grief washed over me. I could barely see to walk back to the car.

For the next couple of months, I worked with a temp agency to earn money for another apartment—my own. Just me. I drifted in a daze, living with my parents and letting Mom tell me what to do.

That was a mistake.

Mom was a controller. She had never approved of Konnor. She had wanted me to marry Dominic Jantzen, the wealthy heir to a fortune in my hometown, Santa Rosa. I'd dated Dominic in high school, but I wasn't interested in him. He was as domineering as Mom. Konnor was the only one I had truly loved. My sweet darling.

Now that Konnor was gone, Mom often invited Dominic to the house, and I was too broken to resist. I couldn't respond to him, either, though he waited somewhat patiently for a change. I heard Mom telling him, "She'll come around, Dominic. Just let her get over what happened."

She was wrong.

I couldn't forget my lost love for even a moment.

I'd met Konnor at Southern Oregon University at Ashland, which had a good art program and an interesting drama department known for Shakespeare in the Park performances every summer. Mom had wanted me to attend University of California at Berkeley, where Dominic was a freshman, but Dad quietly backed me on my choice to go north to Ashland. Mom was furious, but Dad said the choice was mine to make. He was firm about it. Though he rarely stood up to Mom, he was unmovable once he took a stand. I went to SOU that fall.

One day when I crossed the campus after guitar class, my friend Aaron, a student in my English class, called to me from a picnic table. "Hey, Lily! Come here. I want you to meet someone."

I toted my guitar case to the table and sat next to him.

"Lily, this is Konnor West. He does gigs around town. He needs a girl's voice in his band, and I thought you might be interested. Konnor, this is Lily Mains. You have to hear her sing. Lily, show him what you've got." Aaron grinned at me.

"Oh." I was startled. My face grew hot.

Konnor smiled, his blue eyes dancing beneath his dark curls. "Would you mind, Lily? I'd like to hear you."

"Okay." I pulled my guitar from its case. I'm not sure what prompted me to choose the song I did. Maybe Konnor's charm. I began singing.

"Black, black, black is the color of my true love's hair ..." then stopped, smitten with embarrassment. I felt breathless for a moment as I looked up.

Aaron stifled his loud howl of laughter.

Konnor's eyes widened for a second before he bit his lip, probably to keep from laughing, and said, "Keep going, Lily. You have a beautiful voice."

Looking down at my guitar, I began the old, traditional Scottish ballad again, with slightly adapted words.

> Black, black, black is the color of my true love's hair
> His lips are something wondrous fair
> The purest eyes and the neatest hands
> I love the ground where on he stands.
> I love my love and well he knows
> I love the ground where on he goes
> If he on earth no more I see
> My life will quickly fade away ....

When I finished, my eyes locked with Konnor's. I saw into his heart in that moment. The attraction was instant. Konnor later told me he fell in love with me as I sang that song. I know I fell in love with him in the same instant. We were opposites in many ways. His hair was dark and curly, mine was short and blonde with only a slight wave, like my dad's. Konnor was moderately tall, while my head barely topped his strong shoulders. He was outgoing and dynamic. I was quiet and reserved, hesitant to share my inner thoughts with anyone. Our instant attraction convinced me I could be open with him. Our voices, though, blended beautifully. Together, we sang our way through college, often performing as a warm-up band and to raise awareness of other campus events to attract crowds.

My mother had tried to talk me out of dating Konnor because he wasn't rich or socially connected. Still, we moved into a small apartment together our sophomore year of college without telling anyone for a few weeks, enjoying our life together without outside pressures.

After graduation, we found jobs in Medford and located another apartment closer to work. Konnor, who had studied architecture, worked at a local engineering firm. My major was in art with a minor in English, but I took a job as a salesclerk to bring in money while I put together a portfolio to submit to children's book publishers. I knew several years would pass before I would become established in my chosen career, but I was determined.

"Take your time, Lily." Konnor wrapped his arms around me. "I'm making enough to pay the bills. You'll find a place with a publisher, I'm sure. Your work is far above the norm."

Encouraged by his support, I relaxed and did some of my best work. Every day was a delight. I painted during the late afternoons after work, before Konnor came home, looking forward each day to our time together. Our joy lasted only a short time. By late June of the year we graduated, Konnor was gone—my love, my life.

Now nothing mattered to me. My paints, art paper, canvases, and easel lay abandoned in my parents' garage, boxed and collecting dust, along with my meager household possessions. Shattered by grief. I couldn't concentrate on anything. Tears came easily, often without warning.

Alone in my room after the funeral, I gazed at the garden behind the house where oak trees dressed in Spanish moss moving gently in the wind. I opened the envelope the police officer had given me, fulfilling Konnor's last request.

Keys, his wallet ... and a marriage license. I stared at it in shock. The paper was spattered with blood.

Konnor's blood.

Filled with horror, I dropped it to the floor, lay down on my bed and wept. We had decided to get married at the courthouse, but I didn't know Konnor had the license until that moment. Obtaining the license was the last thing he had done on earth and—his first step toward total commitment to me, to marriage, to a family of our own. Now he was gone.

Gone forever? No, not forever. Konnor had said we would meet again if I believed.

I remembered the day he'd come home from work, excitement in his eyes. "Lily, Aaron called me last week and asked to have lunch. He's back in town for a surveying job for a couple of months. During lunch, he told me he'd been studying about Jesus. He said Jesus was more than just a good teacher. He was the Son of God!"

I didn't hide my skepticism. Our college professors had ridiculed those who believed in God. They said God was a myth people invented to make them feel better about their lives, and Jesus was a good teacher, but people had made up a lot of myths about him.

"I know. I didn't believe in Jesus at first either," Konnor said. He shrugged. "But Aaron told me there's more proof Jesus rose from the dead than there is evidence Julius Caesar even lived. He was very convincing. I think he's right, Lily."

Konnor met regularly with Aaron during May and early June, fascinated by the topic. One night about a week before the accident, he said, "Lily, I believe Jesus is the Son of God. There's a verse in the Bible that says something like God loved us so much, he sent us his one and only son, Jesus. Anyone who believes in Jesus will not be condemned for the wrong things they have done but will live with God forever. It doesn't mean we won't die, but it means after this life, we will go to heaven. So, I've decided to follow Jesus. Will you go with me to a meeting next week to hear a speaker Aaron likes?"

I nodded. I didn't fully understand what he was saying, but I saw his life changing before my eyes, becoming joyful. I wanted that same joy.

One evening after work, Konnor said, "Lily, all that I've learned about Jesus and about his commands tell me

I should love others as I love myself. The Bible teaches couples should not become sexually involved unless they're married. Sex before marriage is not the way of true love. I realize I've been selfish toward you by not protecting you as I should. I love you, Lily. You know that. True love is more than a feeling. It is a commitment—a legal commitment which will protect our relationship, protect our future children, and guard our hearts. Since I love you, I want to make that commitment. Will you marry me?"

My heart pounded so loud I thought it would jump out of my chest. Was this really happening? Breathless, I nodded my head, barely able to speak. "Yes!"

We laughed in each other's arms and talked about our future.

"Do you want a big wedding, Lily?" Konnor moved back just enough to see my face.

"No. I dread being the center of attention. Besides, my mom will take over if we have a big wedding. Our special time wouldn't really belong to *us*. I want a quiet wedding. The courthouse would be lovely. Just the two of us. No fuss. Only commitment and love."

"Okay, sweetheart. Let's do that." Konnor kissed me and smiled.

My heart was full of joy at the thought of being Konnor's wife.

But he died. Now frozen in a state of shock, I stared at the blood-stained marriage license on the floor. Konnor's love reached out to me through the pain and shock. I picked up the license and clasped it to my heart. Tears poured down my face.

I will learn about Jesus too. That's what you wanted, Konnor. Then ... someday ... I will be with you again. That's what your dying words meant.

"Lily." Mom approached me in the kitchen one day in late August. "You need to pull out of this depression you're experiencing. Get back involved with life."

Mom was almost as tall as Dad, her dark hair beautifully styled, and her clothes were fashionable. Her very presence intimated me, but I knew I needed to stand up for myself now.

"I was almost finished with my art portfolio before Konnor died. I could start working on that again, but I'm not ready to get involved socially yet. It's only been two months since Konnor ..." I couldn't go on. Tears gathered in my eyes.

"Nonsense. The sooner you move on, the sooner you will feel better."

I shook my head.

Moving closer, she reached for my face.

I jerked away out of habit. When I was a child, she had grabbed my face or slapped me whenever I displeased her. She hadn't done either in five years, but I knew her habits and feared them. She had dominated my life until I'd left for college, dictating all that I did ... until I met Konnor.

Taking a deep breath, lowering her hand, rigid lips held her anger in check for a moment. Then she said, "Lily, you are not confident enough to find a good job and support yourself. This has been obvious ever since you came home. Artists need money these days to succeed. You don't have any. So, you will marry Dominic. The sooner the better. He has plenty of money to support your unrealistic art ideas."

I just looked at Mom, frightened at the violence emanating from her. "No."

"No? You think you know better than me? You cannot live with us forever. You are too quiet—too unsure of yourself—to be successful in the business world. You need to make a good marriage with a man who will support you. Dominic will do that."

I said nothing. My life with Konnor had been a reprieve from her domination. But here I was again, cornered by my mother, being pushed into something I did not want. This time, I would have to stand alone against her wishes.

"Dominic is coming over for lunch. I expect you to behave like a lady and be pleasant. Do you understand me?"

I just stared at her. *How could she do this to me? Doesn't she understand my grief?* My heart ached in mute agony. Her criticism of my personality and possibility for success totally undermined me.

Is she right? Can I succeed in life? Can I succeed without Konnor's encouragement and love? I feel lost and alone! God, if you are there, help me! I don't understand why you let Konnor die. I don't know what to do without him. Mom has belittled my abilities for so long. Is she right? Even if she is, that's no reason for me to marry Dominic. He would crush me. I just can't do it, God. If you are real like Konnor said, show me what to do.

When Dominic came, I did my best to be pleasant, but I cringed inside and drew back every time he reached for my hand.

His grey eyes would darken with anger each time. Would he revert to the abusive teenager I had dated in high school? He had hit me more than once when I had refused his physical advances. I sensed it was only a matter of time until his true personality emerged again. He and Mom had a lot in common.

After he left, the small amount of food I'd been able to eat rose up my throat. Going to my room, I sank onto my bed and pulled a soft blanket over me. I'd been feeling nauseous a lot lately. My eyes widened. *Could I be pregnant?*

Fighting the nausea, I climbed out of bed the next morning, splashed cold water on my face, grabbed a roll from the kitchen, and headed for my car. A few minutes later, I left the local pharmacy clutching a pregnancy test.

In my room a little later, the digital pregnancy test showed the result—pregnant. My hands went to my midsection. I took a deep breath. Suddenly, my mind awoke from its apathy. *No way will I yield to my mother's pressure to marry Dominic. I have hope now. I'm carrying Konnor's baby. Our very own baby.*

I sat on my bed, looking out my window at the mist swirling around the maple trees. I wanted to savor my secret knowledge for a while.

I need to make plans. I can't stay at home any longer. Mom will wear me down. I don't have enough confidence to stand against her for long. I know I'll have to make my own life somewhere else ... for my baby's sake. I can't bring Konnor's child into Mom's orbit. And certainly not Dominic's.

Should I go back to Ashland? I know I can find work there. No. Bad idea. Everywhere I looked, I'd see Konnor. I need to go where I can heal—concentrate on this new life inside me. I have no idea where that could be.

Two days later, I was no closer to an answer. I just knew I must move out of the house, away from Mom. I was about to pull my clothes out of the closet to start packing when Mom stuck her head in my room.

"Lily, come help me fix lunch."

I swallowed a sigh and followed her.

A beautiful bouquet of fresh, white roses served as an elegant centerpiece for the table, their delicate scent filling the room.

"Make some roast beef sandwiches. Use the hoagie rolls. I'll warm up some potato soup." She reached in the refrigerator for a large plastic bowl.

"Okay."

"Dominic and his parents are coming Wednesday evening for dinner." She dumped the soup into a kettle and turned on the heat.

"Again?" We didn't usually have frequent company. Dad's work at the bank kept him busy, and Mom was heavily involved socially.

"We need to get things going with the Jantzens. If you and Dominic get married next spring, we need to be planning things now." She rinsed the plastic bowl, left it in the sink and sat down at the breakfast bar.

"I'm not marrying Dominic."

Mom huffed impatiently. "We can talk about that later. You know you're going to. Right now, it's important we start socializing with them."

I drew up straight. "I'm pregnant." A surge of joy rose in my heart.

Mom looked at me, her face growing red with anger. "Get rid of it!"

Horror and anger swept over me. How could she even suggest that? "No! And I will *not* marry Dominic Jantzen!"

The dazed state I'd been in since Konnor's death disappeared. Now, I was a mother fighting for her child.

Mom rushed over to me, her face dark with rage, her black curls framing furious eyes. Towering over me with her superior height, she grabbed me behind the head and pulled my face close to hers. "Do you think anyone will marry you if you're carrying another man's baby? Dominic certainly won't. Yes, you *will* get rid of it. I will make an appointment for you at an abortion clinic, and you will go, and you will take care of this ... this *mistake*."

"No."

She slapped my face.

I just looked at her and inwardly shook. I was afraid yet boiling over with anger at the same time. But I had learned to hide my feelings well.

Dad, who had been reading the newspaper in the living room, strode into the kitchen and grasped Mom's shoulders. "That's enough, Margaret."

She jerked away. "Don't tell me what to do!" She turned to me. "This is not over, Lily." She stormed out of the room.

Dad sighed. "I'm sorry, Lily. I should have stopped her from hitting you." He pulled me into his comforting arms. I cried for a moment from anger and fear.

"Is it true? Are you pregnant?"

"Yes." I nodded against his shirt. "Dad, I can't stay here. Mom will wear me down. I cannot let her do that to me ... or to my baby. And I will *not* marry Dominic. He's abusive."

"I know." He stroked my hair, calming me. Too low for Mom to hear, he asked, "Lily, would you be willing to stay with a friend of mine, someone who will help you get through this pregnancy?"

"Who's that?"

I heard the door slam. Mom had left.

"Her name is Rachel Carson. She lives at Lake Thechihila in Montana. We grew up together." Dad ran his fingers through his dark blonde hair and sighed. He turned me toward his study. "Rachel is a gentle soul. You will be safe and happy there. I can call her and ask. Will you go to her?"

I had never heard Dad mention anyone named Rachel before. "Who is she?"

"She was a neighbor, a friend of my family. She lives on a farm near a lake. You will be safe with her. She is very hospitable. I'm sure she will want you to stay at her place."

"If you think she'll take me." I nodded, not sure about this, but Dad said she would keep me safe.

Safe. The very word comforted me.

"I'll give you the family van. We don't use it much anymore, and you will have a place to sleep whenever you feel tired while you're driving. The van is big enough for you to take your clothes, a sleeping bag, and your art equipment with you. It has good, all-weather tires, which you will need there. You can work on your art portfolio from Montana as easily as any place. I will not tell your mother where you're going. She would try to bring you back."

"Yes, Dad. Thank you. I'm afraid to stay here. Mom always gets her way. I'm afraid of her."

Sadness settled on his face. "She can be difficult. I want you to start tomorrow morning. Your mom has a hair styling appointment and a manicure scheduled for nine. Can you be ready by then?"

"Yes."

"I'll help you load the van as soon as she leaves. And Lily, go to the phone center and pick up a new phone today. Leave your old one here, or your mother will be calling you all the time. I'll call you on Wednesdays when she's playing cards with her friends."

"Okay. I'll take care of it."

Dad wrapped his arms around me and held me close. "I'll miss you, honey, but your happiness is all that matters now. You go to Montana and let Rachel take care of you."

I breathed a sigh of relief. If there was a God out there, like Konnor believed, I would have thanked him. Our family wasn't religious, and my college professors had mocked those who believed in God. Yet, I felt a strange sense of destiny and gratitude, as though someone greater than I were guiding me, helping me, opening the doors to freedom and safety.

Closing my eyes against the night, I whispered, "Wherever you are, Jesus, thank you."

The next morning, I stood at my bedroom window looking down the driveway, watching my mother's car vanish around the bend. In my hand was a note I had just written to her.

> Mom, thank you for letting me stay here for a while. You're right. I cannot stay here in your home any longer. I need to make my own way and make my own decisions now. I am leaving Santa Rosa. I need space. I will be in touch again after my baby comes. Please understand. Thank you for your kindness in allowing me to stay here these past two months. It has helped.
>
> *Lily*

CHAPTER 2

A tap sounded at my door. "Ready, Lily?"

"Yes, Dad." I put the note into an envelope, sealed it, and propped it up on my dresser. Opening the door, I leaned down for my suitcase.

"Let me do this for you, honey." Dad took the suitcase from me. "You bring some blankets and a pillow."

Together, we headed for the garage, where Dad backed the van out and helped me stow my things inside. A flock of pigeons flew up from the lawn, their wings beating at the air.

"You've loaded it!" I smiled, looking at a box of food and the cooler.

"Did you really think I'd let you go without being sure you had enough food?" Dad grinned. "There's milk, cheese, and orange juice in the cooler. I put a couple peanut butter and jelly sandwiches in the box along with some other snacks. Your art supplies are in the back. Now come back inside and have breakfast with me one more time before you leave."

Hand in hand, we returned to the kitchen.

"You left a note for your mom?"

"Yes." I told him the contents.

Dad nodded with satisfaction. "Good. Polite but firm, and it should stop her from trying to find you." He reached into his shirt pocket. "Here's the pink slip for the van. You should register it in Oregon."

"Thanks so much, Dad." I threw my arms around him in a quick hug and kissed his cheek. Tucking the pink slip into my purse, I asked, "Tell me about this Rachael Carson."

Dad had never said much about his life as a child and rarely mentioned Montana. I knew his parents had passed away, but not much else.

"Lily, you'll like Rachel." He forked a toaster waffle onto my plate.

"What's she like?" I buttered the waffle, poured the syrup, and plopped a juicy bite into my mouth, savoring the sweet syrup mixed with salted butter.

"We went to high school together. She's quiet and sweet, like you. She's about your height. When I knew her, she had long, blonde hair. She wore a braid that wrapped around her head, like a golden coronet." Dad had a wistful look in his eyes and seemed to be looking in a far distant time and place.

"I spoke with Rachel on the phone last night. She's looking forward to meeting you." Dad studied my face. "You will be happy there, Lily."

"Where in Montana does she live?"

"In a small town called Lake Thechihila."

"What? Te-chee ..."

"It's pronounced Teh-chee-HEE-la. A Sioux word meaning 'I love you.' We just called the town Thechihila."

"What a lovely name."

"Thechihila is a nice little place. I've written the address and marked Rachel's house on the map. It's on the passenger seat in the van. There are a few stores in town, a couple of restaurants, a group of cabins people can rent. There's a K–12 school, too, but not much else. Thechihila is in a wide valley in the Rocky Mountains. Rachel said they have a clinic now, for whenever you need to see a doctor or nurse. I haven't been to Lake Thechihila since you were a baby." He paused, looking out the front windows at the city below. "I grew up there. I miss it."

I had wondered why Dad rarely talked about his early life, but since he wasn't much of a talker—like me—I hadn't asked. He'd never said much about his family. "Do you miss Montana?"

"Yes. Sometimes I'm homesick for the ranch and the lake. I miss the smell of the pine trees when the wind blows." Dad smiled and looked down at me. "You go to Rachel and be happy. She will make sure you're okay. You can trust her, Lily."

"Thank you, Dad. And be sure you call me on Wednesday evenings. I will expect to hear from you." I hesitated. "Dad, I don't want Mom around my baby. I said I'd be in touch after the baby comes, but after what she said to me ..."

Dad wrapped his arm around my shoulder and led me outside. "I understand, honey. I'll come out there to visit you after the baby comes, but I'll leave her at home unless you decide otherwise." He handed me some cash, a gift card, and a gas card. "Take this too. There's two thousand on the gift card. The gas card is prepaid and should last you several months."

I tucked the money and cards inside my purse next to the pink slip. "Thanks, Dad. I'll be careful with my spending."

"I'm sending Rachel some money to help with food. She objected, but I think the funds will be helpful to her. I've also put enough money in your bank account to pay for what you'll need if you don't find work. There aren't many jobs at the lake. If you need more money for expenses, let me know."

"Okay. Thanks, Dad. That will help, but I'll try to find work."

"Of course. Remember, if you need anything, I'm always here for you. Oh, and here's Rachel's phone number in case you can't find her house." Dad pulled a notepad from his shirt pocket, scribbled down a number, removed the top sheet, and handed it to me.

"Thanks, Dad. I love you." I hugged him again, my heart brimming with love for my quiet, dependable father. He must know this Rachel very well if he could write her number from memory. I wondered about that for a moment. Who was Rachel? How close had they been?

I breathed in the scent of his Old Spice aftershave, something I knew I would always associate with him in years to come.

"I love you too, Lily. Be safe. Remember, I will call you every Wednesday evening after your mom goes to her card game. Don't try to call me, because she might see your number on my phone and pick up. Understand?" He kissed the top of my head and let me go.

"Yes, Dad." I slipped into the driver's seat, pulled the door closed, and started the engine. One more thing. I rolled down the window. "Um, Dad?

"Yes?" He stood there, sadness in his eyes. His sandy blonde hair was beginning to show his age. The loose wave across the front had some faint white strands in it which, in my own sorrow, I hadn't noticed before.

"Do you have any family at Lake Thechihila?"

"No, honey. Both my parents passed away before you were born. I had an older brother, Jared, but he was twelve years older and was in the military when our parents died.

He made sure I had enough to take care of myself and then sold the ranch when I went to college. That money paid my tuition." Dad bowed his head. "Jarod was killed in action the same year I left Lake Thechihila. I adored him. But he'd been gone so much, I was almost like an only child."

"Like me?"

"Yes, like you. But honey, you have me, and I will always be here for you. You are not alone."

I leaned forward and kissed his cheek, saddened by the look on his face. "You are not alone either, Dad. You have me too."

He smiled. "Yes, I do." He stepped back and watched as I put the car in drive and pulled away from the house.

At the edge of the driveway, I looked back. Dad was still standing there. I waved. He lifted his hand and watched as I pulled out onto the road. He looked so lonely.

This last week in August 2019 began my new life.

Will watched as Lily drove down the driveway and pulled out onto the road. He turned back to the house, his head bowed. It would seem empty now. Just a house now. Empty of the child he treasured. Inhabited only by two unhappy people. The pigeons settled back on the lawn as he moved away from where they'd been searching for bugs to eat.

Life hadn't turned out the way he'd hoped. Yes, Margaret was fascinating. He'd been drawn to her like a moth to the flame. She was exciting, alluring. Her father was a banker— an intimidating fact at first. He was only a country boy with no business experience and no sophistication. But her father had welcomed him into the family. Life had been wonderful, especially after Lily came along within a year of their marriage.

Margaret's dad had welcomed him into the world of banking immediately after he'd graduated from college. Life was full. But somewhere along the way, Margaret's sophisticated ways began to repel him. When Lily had announced she was pregnant, and her mother's response was to suggest aborting that baby, the bare threads of love he still felt for Margaret were ripped apart. How could she say that? His heart filled with fierce anger. He would protect Lily from her, no matter how angry she became. This was his *grandchild!*

Every instinct rose to protect the baby against this dangerous woman whom he suddenly didn't even recognize. He would have some choices to make soon, but he would have to step carefully. Margaret's father was still his boss at the bank.

His circumstances overwhelmed him.

Will's heart followed his daughter as she headed toward the place he thought of as home. The rugged mountains ... the clear, blue skies and lakes ... the old-fashioned houses along the shore and in the meadowlands. Homesickness invaded him for the first time since he'd left Lake Thechihila. Well, he would return when his grandchild was born. Maybe he would even stay there. He'd been crazy to leave.

He still remembered Rachel's eyes when he'd said goodbye for the last time. Her eyes haunted him.

Sunflowers nodded their heads in the breeze beside the two-lane country road that warm August afternoon as I turned off the highway toward Lake Thechihila. Sage brush dotted the wild grasses of the fields. Clumps of pine trees soaked up the summer sunshine, their resinous scent filling the air.

Only ten more miles. I wonder what this town will be like. What will Rachel think of me—with a baby on the way but no husband? Will there be other people my age? Will they accept me?

I looked around, taking in the scenery.

I do love the atmosphere. The blue sky, the sunflowers along the road, the silence. Not a person around. The open sky, the far-reaching fields, and the whisper of the wind caressing my skin … It's peaceful. Maybe I'll be okay living here. This is where Dad grew up. I wonder where his family home is. Does he miss it?

Thump–thump–thump–thump.

Uh-oh, flat tire.

I pulled to the side of the road. There wasn't much of a shoulder, so I couldn't fully park off the pavement. Climbing out of the van, I walked around to see which tire needed changing.

Right rear wheel. Good. At least it's away from traffic. Of course, I don't see any traffic at all.

I moved suitcases onto the pavement, so I could get to the spare tire and jack. Looking down at my aqua shorts and matching tunic top in multiple shades of blue, I shrugged.

So much for making a good first impression. I'll arrive at Rachel's house covered in dirt and grime. Oh well. That's life.

Cows came to the fence, curious at my activity. One, two, five, eight … they chewed grass ponderously, their bulging brown eyes fixed on me. The scent of pine mixed with their warm animal smell. A meadowlark's song drifted to me on the breeze.

Placing the jack under the frame near the wheel, I managed to raise the van high enough to remove the tire. But the lug nuts wouldn't budge no matter how hard I tried.

I sat back on my heels, defeated. Now what?

Just then, I heard a vehicle approach on the other side of the road and stop. A moment later, a young man who looked to be in his late twenties appeared around the end of the van.

"May I help you?"

"That would be kind of you." I stood and looked up into his face. Brown hair kissed by the sun framed a tanned, pleasant face with a darker brown mustache. He was tall with broad shoulders encased in a sleeveless muscle shirt above old blue jeans and leather sandals. Alone with a man I'd never met, standing between empty fields with no other person in sight, I crossed my arms nervously. It was true. I needed help with that tire. I moved away from the car to give him room to work.

"Thank you," I said, truly grateful for his help. I glanced over at his vehicle, a dusty pick-up truck with no passengers.

"You know, changing tires for a lady is one of the last dragons which we men can slay." He grinned. "I'll have you on your way in a jiffy." He removed the lug nuts with ease. "By the way, my name is Caleb."

"Glad to meet you, Caleb. My name's Lily."

"Hi, Lily." He grinned up at me then removed the last lug nut and pulled the tire off. Standing, he pulled the spare tire from the wheel well and rolled it over. A few minutes later, he finished and stood.

"Let me put things back into your van, Lily." He swung the flat tire into the wheel well, put the cover back over it, and stepped back, wiped his hands on his jeans, and reached for my suitcases.

"There you go," he said, placing the last suitcase in the van and closing the doors.

"That's very kind of you. Thanks."

"No trouble at all." He stepped back and looked at me, arms akimbo. "I hope you enjoy our lake."

"You live here?"

"Yes. I have a ranch just a few miles down the road."

"I guess I'll be seeing you around then. I'm headed for Rachel Carson's place."

"We'll be neighbors." He smiled. "My ranch is next to hers."

"Oh. How nice!"

"Rachel is looking forward to seeing you, so, I'll let you be on your way." Still smiling, he turned and headed for his truck, waving through the open window as he pulled away.

I wonder if all the people here are this friendly.

A few minutes later, I drove down the hill toward the town beside the lake. Dad said Rachel's house was the second house on the left, about a half mile from the water, and if he remembered correctly, painted white.

Lake Thechihila sparkled in the sun, a few boats bobbing on its surface, one speeding across the opposite side of the lake. A variety of trees edged the water and shaded the town crowded near the shore. Closer to me, I saw a white cottage surrounded by fruit trees and green meadows. A cow and three calves grazed in the field near a large, red barn. Was this Rachel's place?

Beyond it, on the righthand side of the lane, was a large log building with a sign out front announcing it to be the community church. Hidden in the trees past the church, the town rested peacefully in the afternoon sun, simple houses generously plotted with large lawns and colorful flowers showing here and there. On the hillside above the house, a herd of black angus cattle grazed along with three horses.

I slowed as I neared the driveway to the white cottage. Yes, this was the address Dad had given me. I turned in and drove slowly up the drive between the apple trees laden with ripening fruit and came to a stop beside the walkway to the house.

The front door opened. I would have known Rachel anywhere from Dad's description. Her blonde hair was wrapped around her head in braids with a fringe of short hair wisping over her eyes. She looked young and fit, dressed in blue jeans and a knit top. But if she was Dad's age, she must be in her early forties. She smiled and walked toward my car.

I cut the engine and climbed out from behind the steering wheel, tired from the long drive. "Miss Carson?" I queried hesitantly.

"Call me Rachel," she said, a sweet smile lighting up her face.

"Rachel." I moved toward her.

Hesitantly, Rachel reached out her hands, placing them on my shoulders. "Welcome to my home, dear." Her voice trembled slightly.

"Thank you, Rachel."

"Let me help you with your luggage." She moved briskly toward the van and pulled it open.

"I had a flat tire a few miles back, and your neighbor, Caleb, stopped to help me change it. He seems nice."

"Yes, Caleb is a good neighbor. Always helpful. I'm glad you've met him." Rachel smiled and reached for a suitcase while I reached for another.

"Your father said you're an artist?" Rachel's eyes sought mine for a moment. I noticed her eyes were green, with thick, dark lashes.

"Yes. I'm in the process of putting together a portfolio of some of my work. I hope to find a job illustrating children's books."

Rachel smiled and nodded. "Good. I've set up an art room for you. Let's put your luggage in your room, and then I'll take you in there so you can see if it's what you need."

"You set up an art room for me?" I could barely believe such thoughtfulness.

"Yes, Lily. At the end of the hallway, past your bedroom, which is right here." Rachel turned into a room decorated in delicate pastel colors, a small pot of pink African violets on the dresser. Flowered curtains hung on either side of the window, white sheers falling between them.

"What a lovely room!" I walked forward examining it. Homey, inviting, pleasant. A cool, earthy breeze blowing in at the window, billowing out into the room. "It's perfect." I turned and hesitantly hugged her.

She cleared her throat. "Come. Let me show you the art room."

I followed her down the hallway to the back of the house into a no-nonsense room with a northern exposure, perfect for painting. The walls were coral, giving a warm reflection to the room. The windows rose high, wide, and unadorned except for raised shades, with a view of the pasture and the hill behind it. A picturesque log house perched part way up the slope. An easel and a stand for paints stood in one corner of the room. An off-white canvas tarp lay folded on the floor next to them.

"It's all ready for you to start painting. And don't worry about getting anything on the floor. Linoleum wipes up easily, but the tarp will help keep it reasonably clean."

"Rachel, are you an artist too?" I asked, anticipating her answer. Only another artist would have known what I'd need.

She nodded. "Yes, I paint. Oils mostly. My painting room is right above this one. I don't have a lot of time to paint this time of year because of all the farm work, but come winter, I'll spend some time every day in my own studio."

"Where are your paintings?" I asked, eager to see what she had produced.

Rachel drew me into her living room and waved. "All the artwork is mine."

For the next hour, I looked at her work and studied her techniques while she shared various oil paintings with me. A closeness had developed between us by the time we were done. Rachel and I finished storing my art supplies in the painting room. Her casual acceptance and kindness helped me relax. I felt as though we had been friends forever, such was the sweet spirit between us.

Rachel glanced at her watch and turned toward the kitchen. "Time to start dinner. I've enjoyed talking art with you, Lily dear."

"Can I help you with anything?"

"Tell you what. You sit down here at the counter and tell me about yourself while I cook. Tomorrow you can help, but today, I just want to get acquainted. I'll put the kettle on for tea."

As Rachel peeled potatoes, chopped carrots, and put together a stew to simmer on the stove, I told her about my parents and Santa Rosa. Placing a plate of cookies between us at the counter, she sat across from me while I sipped tea and told her about Konnor and the coming baby.

Rachel nodded. "I'm sorry for your loss, Lily. Yet, you have a baby coming, a memory of Konnor to help you get through this. A baby is a precious gift from God. I'm glad you already love this little one. I will help you all I can, Lily." Her voice was firm, determined.

"Thank you, Rachel." I relaxed, basking in the warmth of the kitchen and Rachel's acceptance.

Looking out the window, I asked, "I see you have cattle and fruit trees."

"Yes. I milked the cow just before you arrived. I sell much of the milk to neighbors. The calves are for beef and taxes on the property. I keep one pasture for mowing hay for the winter to feed Daisy—that's the cow. The calves will go to market in October. I also have one pasture for growing alfalfa to sell. From the orchard, I make apple pies and applesauce to sell. There are Nanking cherry bushes out by the creek too. I make jam from them. There are chickens out back for eggs and meat. And I have a vegetable garden near the creek. Farming is a pleasant way of life."

"Busy too. Did you grow up here?"

"No, my parents lived in a small town without a high school. I came here to live with my great aunt when I was fourteen, so I could attend the local school. When Auntie June passed a few years later, she left this place to me. Owning it has been a blessing." Rachel looked pensive, a hint of sadness on her face. She smiled quickly when the timer went off. "Here. Take the hot pads and pull those biscuits out of the oven."

Later that evening as I lay in bed looking out at the starry sky, my heart, frozen since Konnor's death, began to awaken with a deep, abiding gratitude toward the God whom Konnor had discovered. Closing my eyes and giving a sigh, I whispered, "Thank you!"

Caleb Maxwell sipped a cup of hot coffee as he looked across the valley below his cabin, enjoying the early morning before his day grew busy. A school bus made its way up the hill to collect the local children after a summer full of swimming and playing. Very little else moved. Looking down at Rachel's house, he wondered how she and her guest were doing. Rachel had mentioned the young daughter of a friend would be coming to stay with her. She'd indicated the girl was expecting a baby, and her mother was pressuring her to have an abortion, but the girl wanted to keep her child.

Hearing a door slam below, he noticed Rachel coming out of the house carrying a big basket, Lily at her heels pulling on a jacket as she walked. The morning sun shone on the two blonde women moving together toward the chicken coop. Good. This girl would be helpful, willing to share the work. In his opinion, Rachel worked way too hard keeping up that farm. She needed some help around the place.

He'd helped Rachel occasionally as had his father. He barely remembered a time when Rachel wasn't there with fresh cookies whenever he'd accompanied his dad to help her with a fence that needed mending or when there was snow to move. When his dad and mom moved south to live near his sisters in Arizona, Dad's parting words were, "Caleb, you keep an eye on Rachel and make sure you help her when there's a need." And he had done just that. Some jobs needed a man's strength.

Rachel's warm personality and her natural beauty should have drawn a husband her way. Still, she remained alone, showing no interest except for kindness toward the men who would have liked to court her. Caleb was puzzled by her lack of interest. But he shrugged it off. This was Rachel's choice, her business. She always seemed a little sad, though she was quick to smile at others.

He sighed and drank the last of his coffee, its strong bitter scent filling the kitchen air. Time to get to work. He needed to move his herd of cattle to a different pasture today. Gage Bower was coming to help. Gage was the local Fish and Game warden—a church friend as well. Caleb appreciated his help. He wished he could find someone to work around the ranch regularly, but most of the young men left for college as soon as they graduated and never returned for work in the small community. He had to make do with whoever had extra time to assist him with the cattle. Now that he was thinking of expanding his business, he could see the worker shortage would be a handicap.

Clapping his cowboy hat over his head, he headed for the barn. He saddled the sorrel gelding, led him out of the barn into the warm summer sun, and mounted. Glancing down at the white cottage below, he saw Rachel waving toward him, inviting him to come down. He waved back, turning the horse toward her. His dog trotting behind, he cantered down the slope. Rachel had placed a gate between the two properties years ago as a convenience for his family, a shortcut to her house.

"Caleb," Rachel said, a smile lighting up her face, "I believe you've met my new guest, Lily."

I stood next to Rachel, a basket of eggs clutched in my arms, and glanced up at Caleb. Today, he looked like a cowboy right out of the movies. Tan Stetson hat, plain blue denim shirt, chaps over his jeans, cowboy boots thrust into the stirrups.

"Yes, we met yesterday," he said, dismounting and grinning pleasantly at me.

I smiled, glad to see my new acquaintance. "Thanks again for helping me with that tire."

He nodded, smiling back at me.

"Caleb and his family have been a big help to me over the years," Rachel said.

"I wanted those warm cookies." Caleb's smile widened. "You've always had them handy whenever I finished a job."

"That's the secret of getting good help. Since he was just a little guy, Caleb has helped me with the farm every time he could."

His golden retriever walked forward.

"And this is Molly," he said. "Molly, sit. Shake hands with Lily."

The dog sat and lifted her paw, which I took in my hand.

"Hello, Molly." I let her sniff my hand before I rubbed behind her ears.

I looked up at Caleb and shook my head. "I can't picture you as a *little* guy." He was taller than my dad, probably over six feet in height, tanned from the sun, looking thoroughly capable of any task that came his way. I remembered the ease with which he had changed my tire. His broad, muscular shoulders spoke of hard work.

Rachel laughed. "Well, I have pictures to prove it. I'll show you after we get those eggs put away." Turning to Caleb she said, "I'd like to invite our young people to come over here Sunday around two o'clock to get acquainted with Lily. Could you spread the word?"

"Sure. My pleasure." Caleb touched the rim of his hat, smiled, and mounted his horse. "See you later. Nice seeing you again, Lily. Welcome to Thechihila." He turned his horse back toward his own land.

I watched him go, fascinated by seeing my first real cowboy. He seemed different from the men I'd known on the west coast. More unconsciously self-assured. More mature.

"There goes a good neighbor." Rachel nodded approval. "Now let's get those eggs ready for market."

Rachel and I put the clean eggs into cardboard cartons, each holding a dozen, and set the boxes into a larger plastic container.

"I keep the eggs in here," Rachel said, carrying the container toward another refrigerator separate from the main one.

I opened the door, and Rachel placed the container inside next to two gallons of milk in big glass jars.

"Friends come by during the week to buy the eggs and milk, usually in the evening, and we have nice visits." Rachel shot me a peaceful smile. "I enjoy the company. Now let me fix you some breakfast."

I knew Rachel had already milked the cow before I was awake. She'd been too quiet to awaken me as I slept. With morning sickness these days, I appreciated the thoughtfulness, but I planned to pitch in as soon as I could in the days ahead.

"Rachel, you work so hard!"

"Farming is a way of life for me, Lily." She shrugged and smiled. "Sure, there's a lot of work, but there's a lot of satisfaction too."

"Let me help you as much as possible."

She eyed me for a moment. "Well, as long as you don't overdo things. That baby of yours will be work enough as it grows. How far along are you?"

"I've been carrying this baby for over two months, but I don't know exactly how long." I pressed my hands to my abdomen. "I haven't seen a doctor yet."

"Then let's make an appointment for you. We have a clinic staffed by a nurse. Jesse Webster. You'll like her. But we also have a doctor here once a week. We can call for an appointment."

"Okay." I brightened up thinking of my baby.

"What would you like for breakfast? Eggs? Bacon? Pancakes? Cereal?"

"Oh, I like all your suggestions. Um, a couple pancakes and an egg sound good. Let me help."

Together we made a good breakfast and sat down at the table to eat. But before we did, Rachel reached out and took my hand. "I'd like to pray before we eat."

I watched her as she lowered her eyes. Her face glowed as she spoke to God. There was something about the way she prayed which touched me. I could tell she loved God with all her heart. *I wished I had her surety, her confidence in God's presence.*

"Father in heaven, thank you for bringing Lily to me. Thank you for providing food for us each day. Bless the work of our hands as we serve you. Amen."

I felt the warmth of her love for God spill over to me with wonder. I put small servings on my plate, unsure of how much I could eat. Since Konnor's death, I hadn't had much of an appetite.

"Eat what you wish, Lily. There's more if you want it."

Later, after we'd washed the dishes together, Rachel made tea. We sipped the sweet liquid on the covered front porch while warm sunbeams lit up the lawn and birds chirped in the trees.

"Lily, tell me more about yourself." Rachel settled back into the porch bench and turned her clear blue eyes on my face.

By then, I relaxed completely with her. She accepted me. I could feel her love reaching out to my broken heart. Slowly, I told her more about Konnor, about our dreams, about our plans to get married. But I couldn't talk about the blood-stained marriage license. That still hurt too much. I told her about Konnor's new belief in Jesus—about the last words he said before he was taken from me. I also told her about my mother's reactions to this precious baby I carried.

Rachel listened, asking a question here and there, nodding in agreement at my love for this baby.

"There is no way I would ever give away my baby. This child is all I have left of Konnor. I was stunned and angry when Mom ordered me to abort my baby. How could she? All my life, she has dominated me, but I wasn't about to let her force me into an abortion. I had to get out of there because she has a way of wearing me down until I do what she demands. I don't understand her at all. So, I made up my mind to leave—to go far away from her. When she left the house that day, Dad suggested I come to you. He said I'd be safe here."

When I finished my indignant outburst, I gasped. I wasn't used to speaking up like that.

Rachel sighed. "You've been through a hard time lately, Lily. I'm glad you're here with me. I'll help you however I can."

"Thank you."

Rachel had brought the tea pot outside with us. Seeing my cup was empty, she poured more into my cup.

"Rachel?"

"Yes?"

"Dad said you went to high school together."

"We did."

"He never talks about this place. But when I needed help, he immediately thought of you." I'm sure she heard the question in my voice. I waited in silence for her explanation.

CHAPTER 3

"I told you my family lived in a small town without a high school, and I came here to live with Auntie June. I met Will my freshman year. We were in the same class. Your grandparents had a ranch just up the road, so I saw a lot of Will."

"Yes?"

"We were high school sweethearts. But then he went off to college and met Margaret." She shrugged. "It was a difficult time for me at first. I loved your father dearly. But life goes on. After he left, I went home to my family. Three years later, Auntie June passed away and left me this ranch and a comfortable inheritance. I came back and added onto what she had started. I've had a good life, Lily."

"I wondered why Dad thought of you right away." I wondered if I dared voice what I was thinking. I hesitated, then went ahead and asked. "He loved you too, didn't he?"

"Yes. For a while. But we were very young at the time—barely out of childhood."

"Tell me about him. He doesn't say much about himself."

"No, he wouldn't. He's always been quiet and thoughtful. He was very intelligent ... valedictorian of our graduating class. He wanted to go to college. When his parents died, his brother sold the ranch to make sure he could do just that. Your father met Margaret his first year at college. He came back here for a visit after he met Margaret and showed me a picture of her. She was very beautiful. I don't blame him for falling in love with her. Besides being beautiful and talented, she was outgoing. Captivating, in fact. She made him feel alive. I was just the girl he grew up with."

"I'm sorry, Rachel," I said, touching her hand.

"It's okay, Lily. That was all a very long time ago. I got over him and went on to make a good life for myself here in Lake Thechihila. This is a pleasant, lovely place to live—with good friends and a strong community of faith at church. I'm content."

"Are your parents still alive?

"Yes. But we aren't close. They live with my sister Jeanne down in Texas. I was closer to your grandmother than I was to them.

"Tell me about my grandparents and Uncle Jarod."

"Well, you look a lot like your grandma Betty. She was quiet and sweet, like you, with blonde hair and blue eyes. In fact, you look so much like her, you startled me at first. Your grandpa Bill was outgoing, helping everyone who needed a hand. Jarod? I only met him a few times. He was a sergeant in the Marines—tall, competent, and efficient. He had the same coloring as your dad, but they were not alike in personality. He was proud of Will's achievements and did all he could to make sure Will went to college. We heard he died in a helicopter crash on a rescue mission a couple years after Will left Thechihila."

"I wish I'd known them all."

"You would have loved them."

A truck pulled into the driveway.

"This is Gage Bower. He's here for eggs and milk." Rachel stood, setting her empty cup on the table next to her. "Come, Lily. Let me introduce you."

Rachel's confidences for the day had ended. I was grateful she had told me more about Dad, his family, and about his young love for Rachel. She must have made a deep impression on him, for she was the first person he thought of when I needed a safe place to go.

She stood and greeted the young man who climbed out of the truck.

"Gage, this is my friend, Lily. She's staying with me this year."

"Hi, Lily. Good to meet you." His cheerful eyes crinkled at the corners.

"Let me get the eggs and milk." Rachel turned back to the door.

"Let me help you," Gage insisted, following her into the house.

A few minutes later, after the milk and eggs were in his truck, Gage came back to talk with us. "Caleb said there's a get-together here on Sunday afternoon?"

"Yes." Rachel nodded. "I want our young people to meet Lily. Come over about two o'clock and have some cake, cookies, and ice cream. Bring Jesse with you."

"Will do. And thanks for the milk and eggs."

"Anytime."

As Gage backed out to the road, Rachel told me about him. "He's the drummer in our church worship band. He and Jesse Webster—our local nurse, you'll remember I told you about her—are an item now. Gage is the local Fish and Game warden, the only one in town. When there's a problem, he's the point man."

Rachel hesitated, looking down the road at the log church. "Would you come to church with me Sunday, Lily?"

"Yes. I'd like that very much. I want to learn more about God. Like Konnor."

"Good." Rachel nodded. "Now let's go pick some cherries out back."

We spent the rest of the afternoon picking berries, resting frequently at Rachel's insistence, and chattering together. My heart soon warmed toward this kind woman who had once loved my father. Like me, Rachel was hesitant to reveal her own thoughts. When she told me about her gardens and animals, her face lit up, though. She clearly loved her farm.

"These raspberry bushes were a gift from Caleb's mother, Dianne. She was thinning her patch and brought some plants down the hill to me. Caleb hauled them in his red wagon. He must have been about eight at the time."

I smiled, imagining the scene. "Did he help you plant them?"

Rachel laughed. "Yes. He would dig the holes, I would plop the berries into them, then he would carefully fill the holes and pat the dirt down. Afterward, I let him play in my sprinkler on the lawn to cool off."

I plopped a ripe raspberry into my mouth and savored its flavor.

"Your grandma Betty helped Auntie June and me plant that ash tree in the back yard. That's the tree with the feathery leaves. In another month or two, the berries will turn red, and the tree will stay beautiful through the fall and part of the winter. You'll see birds eating the berries later on. I like to watch them sometimes from the kitchen."

"Maybe I'll paint a picture of that tree when it has berries," I said.

"You could paint on some old barnwood squares and sell them this winter at the local fair if you wanted."

"What a good idea! When is your fair?"

"Early November. You have some time to get ready, if you want."

Being around Rachel was pleasant. I found myself drawn to this woman.

As we sat together in the living room that evening, with the sun dipping behind the mountains, Rachel asked, "Lily, I like to read a little from the Bible and pray at the end of each day. Would you like to do that with me?"

"Yes, I would like that."

I hope I can understand all those old words! They're a lot like Shakespeare's writing. But I do want to learn about God. Maybe Rachel can explain what the words mean.

Rachel picked up a book that didn't look at all like a Bible. I was used to seeing the old black style with gold print on the front.

"That's a Bible?" I was astonished.

"Yes. This translation is the New Living Translation, which uses modern language, so it's much easier to understand than the older Bibles that use ancient words."

"Oh!" I hadn't known there was a modern translation.

"Hm. I think you'd like Psalm 139, my favorite part of the Bible. King David, one of Israel's greatest leaders, wrote it. He's called a man after God's own heart."

Rachel began to read. I sat back and closed my eyes as the words rolled over me, comforting my heart. David described how God knows all about me and loves me. He watches over me every day with his hand on me. There is no place I could ever hide from him because he's there already. He will always guide me.

Then came the verses that pierced through the sorrow in my heart like a ray of light.

You made all the delicate, inner parts of my body and knit me together in my mother's womb. Thank you for making me so wonderfully complex! Your workmanship is marvelous—how well I know it. You watched me as I was being formed in utter seclusion, as I was woven together in the dark of the womb. You saw me before I was born. Every day of my life was recorded in your book. Every moment was laid out before a single day had passed. How precious are your thoughts about me, O God. They cannot be numbered.

A surge of emotion swept over me. I gasped and felt tears of wonder fill my eyes and wash down my face. No wonder Konnor had wanted me to know about this God. I touched my midsection, wanting my baby to learn about God too.

Suddenly, Rachel's arms were around me. "It's okay, honey. It's okay." She stroked my hair and held me close. "Oh, Lily. God loves you so much!"

I cried on her shoulder as she comforted me.

That night as I lay in bed, I whispered into the starlight, "God, thank you for loving me! Show me more about yourself and help me raise this baby inside me—the baby you are forming—the baby you love already. I want this baby to know and love you."

The fragrant scent of lilacs in bloom filled the room, wafted in on a soft breeze. I fell into a deep sleep, exhausted by emotion, yet at peace.

The warmth and comfort of Psalm 139 stayed with me and began to heal the sorrow in my heart from that moment forward. I peppered Rachel with questions about God, and she smiled as she told me about him. By Sunday, I was eager to go to church with her to learn even more. My hunger for God was strong. He had begun pouring healing into my heart, and the pain inside was growing less, even this early in my search.

Sunbeams danced through the giant cottonwood trees along the road Sunday morning as Rachel and I walked down to the church. Birds chirped and darted through the air, rounding up food for their babies. The morning breeze was filled with perfume from the many flowers in tubs and along the roadside, and the pungent scent of pine trees drifted across the fields in the morning sun.

I noticed several others were also walking to the church from their houses in town, and there was a well-worn path coming from that direction. Others from outlying ranches drove, and the church parking lot had a sprinkling of SUVs and pickups scattered around it.

I saw Gage with a girl on his arm, a girl with lovely blue-black hair and deep brown eyes. That must be Jesse. Caleb was already at church, standing up front with the band.

Rachel introduced me to everyone there. I wondered how I could ever remember them all. Everyone was friendly and welcoming.

Gage came over with Jesse, a big, satisfied smile on his face.

Jesse beamed too and held out her left hand. "Gage took me out to Thechihila Point for a picnic."

Rachel laughed. "How lovely!" She took Rachel's hand and admired the ring. "When's the wedding?"

"We're thinking the Saturday before Thanksgiving would work best. Things start to slow down at Ben and Tara's ranch about then, so it's a good time for them to come." Jesse turned to me. "Tara is my sister and Ben's her husband. They've already reserved a cabin by the lake for their family. Our summer visitors will leave Thechihila soon. Then, Gage and I will be able to look around for a house or a cabin to rent. My place is way too small to hold all Gage's things. We'll need a house with a garage."

"Well, blessings on you both." Rachel beamed.

The band started playing, breaking up our greeting time. Rachel led me to a seat on the right-hand side of the church next to a window revealing the fields between her house and the church. Such a peaceful scene.

I'd never been in a church service like this one. The music was modern and joyful, unlike the traditional music I'd expected. Caleb led, playing a guitar. There were three singers—including Caleb. A young woman with short, curly black hair sang alto, and a tall blonde woman sang tenor. Caleb sang melody in his strong, baritone voice. They blended well. Gage played the drums, another man was on the bass guitar, and another at the keyboard. With such a small town, I hadn't expected the church to have a band. It was a nice surprise.

Our family only went to church on Easter and Christmas. The music there was sung by a talented choir and was rather old-fashioned. But not here. I especially liked a song called "Blessed Be Your Name," which spoke of blessing God's name no matter what life is like, even in suffering.

I glanced at Rachel as we sang. The words spoke of God giving and taking away, yet our hearts would still bless his name, I saw tears pouring down Rachel's face, though she smiled.

I wonder what great sorrow Rachel has experienced. Her tears show grief, but her face shows peace and joy. I can't imagine how this blessing thing works, but she's obviously found strength and comfort. I want to learn how to find that same thing.

There were tears in my own eyes as I tentatively sang these new words and thoughts, remembering Konner. I didn't understand, but for some reason, the message in the song felt right.

Caleb led a song called *Great Is Thy Faithfulness,* his voice rising in praise to God. The band's instruments were silent. The congregation sang in harmony. It was beautiful and touching. I didn't know the song, but after the first verse, I sang along with the words on the screen. How satisfying it was to be singing with those who knew and loved God! I drank in the beauty of their song and worshipped God along with them.

Later, as Rachel and I ate lunch, I brought up Jesse and Gage. "Rachel, what did Jesse mean when she said Gage took her out to Thechihila Point? I assume that's where he proposed, right?"

Rachel smiled. "It's an old tradition here, Lily. The young men always ask their girlfriends to marry them at the point. The legend says anyone who pledges their love at Thechihila Point—a piece of land that juts out into the lake—will have a love that lasts forever."

"What a nice tradition. How long has this legend been around?"

"I'm not sure. Caleb knows the story of how it began. One of his ancestors started it. You should ask him."

"Um, I don't know him well enough to ask that."

Rachel laughed. "Okay. You can ask when you're more comfortable around him. Now let's get this kitchen cleaned up. The young people should start arriving in another hour, and I've baked a cake and need to frost it before they get here. We can combine your welcome party with our own little celebration for Gage and Jesse after everyone meets you."

Cody Duggen arrived first. He was the star quarterback at the local high school with only one more year to go until graduation. Cody lived and worked at home on his parents' ranch as well as working in the town grocery store. He was saving up for his own place. J. J. Morgan, who operated the marina store, arrived next. When Colleen, from the church worship team, entered the room, I noticed J. J. navigated to a seat where he could watch her but didn't speak with her most of the evening.

Hm. Something's going on there. I wonder if Colleen knows J. J. is interested in her?

"Let's go in the back yard where we'll have more room," Rachel said, carrying a large, rectangular, chocolate cake toward the back door, which she pushed open with her foot. "Lily, would you put a sign on the front door telling our visitors to come around back, please?"

I found a sheet of paper and obliged. Caleb arrived as I taped the sign on the front door.

"Hi, Lily. We're meeting out back?"

I whirled around. "Hi, Caleb. Yes. Rachel said we'd need more space."

He nodded. "Anything I can carry outside for you?"

"Sure." I led him to the kitchen and handed him a big plate of fresh veggies and dip and grabbed a bowl of chips to carry myself.

"I see you've been helping Rachel with the farm."

"Yes. I enjoy working with the animals."

"I'm glad you're here, Lily. I've noticed Rachel works too hard, especially this time of year. With you here to share the work, I know you will be a blessing to her."

"*She's* a blessing to *me!* I–I needed someone to help me too."

"Rachel is a special lady." He hesitated. "Lily, I've noticed how hard you've been working around the ranch. I want you to promise me you won't work too hard. Rachel will insist you rest now and then. Take those breaks and don't feel you must work as hard as she does. Okay?"

I felt my face grow hot. "She told you?"

"Yes." He looked straight into my eyes. "She wants to make sure you feel welcome and safe here. We all do. We're all going to be here for you and your baby. We'll help you with whatever you need. Let us be your family."

"Oh!" I didn't know what to say. His boldness and acceptance were something I wasn't used to. I certainly hadn't expected it from church people. Others had assured me Christians were stern and judgmental. But that was not what I had experienced so far. "Thank you, Caleb."

"You are most welcome." He nodded, still looking into my eyes. "I'm your nearest neighbor. Don't hesitate to call me if you ever need anything."

"Okay," I murmured. *This is different from California! I'm not used to people saying exactly what they think, like Caleb does. But I like his honesty. At least I know where I stand with him. He's on my side, and I do feel welcomed.*

Just then a car pulled up in front of the house along the road, much to my relief. This was getting too intense for me.

Joe and Misty Spaulding brought their toddler, Elijah, with them. They were the only married couple among the young people so far. I recognized Joe and Misty from the church band. Joe played keyboard. Misty was the one who sang alto.

After that, the names all blurred together with everyone talking and laughing. I would need a little time to learn about them all, although the group wasn't large. Gage, Jesse, and Colleen introduced themselves to me at once and made me feel welcome. J.J. managed the local marina. At seventeen, Cody was the youngest member of the group. Colleen taught fifth and sixth grades at the local school.

Misty babysat to bring in money, and her husband Joe was the only local electrician. Now if I could only remember all that!

I soon began to relax and feel at home among them, though they were strangers to me. I wasn't ready to talk about Konnor or my coming baby yet. But by their kindness and because of Caleb's assurance, I knew they would accept me when I did.

From the beginning, I noticed the way others responded to Caleb. He wasn't the center of attention, but I saw people often looked to him for comment or approval. I could tell they all looked up to him. Even little Elijah demanded Caleb's attention frequently, so he swooped the toddler up and carried him on his shoulders for a while, avoiding trees to protect the toddler's head and face.

Rachel had the men help her set up lawn chairs. Pots of nasturtiums, alyssum, geraniums, and day lilies lined the back of the cottage and filled some large, wooden barrels under the trees. Bees and a hummingbird buzzed around the bright blossoms. Birds chirped in the trees, hopping from branch to branch. A black and white cat sauntered across the lawn, zeroing in on Rachel, who scooped him up, while friends smiled and laughed, drawing me into their group.

I sat back in my chair and relaxed. My mind turned to Konnor.

My love, I will be okay now. These kind people have welcomed me into their circle. They know about our baby. We are accepted here. It is a good place. And yes, I will meet you again someday, for though I am still learning, I believe in your God. He is real, and he loves us.

Tears welled up in my eyes, and I quickly dashed them away. When I looked up, I saw Caleb had noticed. He nodded at me, raised his hand, and placed it over his heart. He understood. No words. No fuss. Just understanding and compassion sent silently my way.

Deep inside, I felt safe now. These would become my people, my family.

CHAPTER 4

Margaret Mains reacted badly to Lily's departure. She complained she could no longer hope to draw the Jantzens into her orbit. She scolded Will, who played dumb when she asked where Lily had gone, although he knew.

For a week she raged, throwing couch pillows around, slamming doors, and yelling at Will, who chose to sleep on the couch in his office to avoid her. His heart had grown cold. He didn't know if he could ever love Margaret again. Yes, she was beautiful. But hers was a brittle beauty built on self-centeredness and vanity. There was little true warmth in her.

Charming, calculating, and manipulative. Will could see through her now, but he was a realist. This was the woman he had chosen, even though he now saw her differently. He must find a way to make their relationship work somehow. Divorce? No. The habits of years and the dislike of change held him in check.

In the days ahead, Will devoted himself more and more to work. Wednesdays were his one joy. It was his time to talk with Lily. The second Wednesday after she left, he drove to a local park for privacy and called her at Rachel's house.

"Hi, Dad."

"Hi, Lily. How are you settling in there at Rachel's place?"

"Great! She's sweet and kind! I'm going to be okay here. Don't worry about me."

Will's voice relaxed. "I'm glad."

"The town is beautiful, and the people are very nice. Rachel invited the young people from church over to meet me on Sunday, and we had a party on the back lawn. Caleb, our neighbor, said Rachel told him about my baby and the situation. He said they are all going to help me. It's incredible! These people are really special."

"I'm glad to hear that, Lily." Will breathed a sigh of relief. His daughter would be happy there. People were surrounding her with kindness as he had hoped they would. He wandered deeper into the park, strolling beneath towering eucalyptus trees with the moon spilling patterns of light through their branches.

"Rachel has a small farm going here. She inherited it from her Auntie June."

"That would be June Monroe. Rachel stayed with her during high school. She had a nice little farm there."

"It's a pleasant place. Rachel has a dairy cow—she said it's a Jersey—some calves, chickens, an orchard, a big garden. I love it. I'm helping her with the chores, but she and Caleb have both told me not to work too hard. I'm not feeling tired at all, but later, as the baby grows, I may. I'm glad to have these new friends helping me."

Caleb. That's the second time she's mentioned him. I wonder what he's like. Is Caleb Rachel's age? Surely Rachel would have drawn suitors! What was he to Rachel?

Will felt a flash of jealousy and quickly stomped it out. *I blew it with her. I can't resent this man who's helping her.*

"You said someone named Caleb is helping there. Tell me about him."

"Um, he's a little older than me. Maybe in his late twenties or maybe even thirty. He's pleasant and very kind. He and his dad have helped Rachel since he was a little boy."

"I see." Will relaxed. This man Caleb was not old enough to be interested in Rachel. Why did that make him happy?

"Dad?"

"Yes?"

"I know about Rachel."

"You do?" Will felt a sudden panic race through him.

"Yes. She told me you were sweethearts in high school."

Will was silent for a moment. He wasn't sure what to say.

"Dad, I know you loved her, but then you met Mom and married her instead. It's okay. Rachel is a lovely, warm person. She said you were both very young, barely more than children. She said it was a long time ago. I like Rachel a lot. I'll be fine here."

His voice constrained, Will said, "It's good you can be with her now, honey. I'm glad everything is okay. Now tell me about Thechihila. What's happening there?"

Lily told him about her new friends from church. Finally, she told him what Konnor had said about God. "Dad, I have been reading Rachel's Bible. I want to know more about God. I have the strongest sense God is helping me now."

"Good, Lily. This should bring you some comfort. I don't understand much about God myself, but I'm glad for you."

"Rachel read some beautiful verses to me out of Psalm 139. The words encouraged me so much! They were not written in some ancient language, either. They were modern and easy to understand. I loved what she read."

She paused for a moment. "Dad, Rachel is the kindest, most loving person I've ever met. Thank you for sending me here."

"I thought you would be safe and happy with her."

"I am. And Dad?"

"What?"

"She looks just like you described her. I knew her at once."

"She hasn't gotten old, like me?"

"You aren't old, Dad! You're just a little bit seasoned. But no, Rachel doesn't look old at all. If I didn't know you went to high school together, I'd say she was about thirty. She still looks young."

After his conversation with Lily, Will took a walk in the moonlight to digest what she'd said.

Rachel handled the subject of our young love well. What a relief! That was the only thing worrying me about sending Lily to her. But it's okay now. Margaret has always resented Rachel. She flames up with jealousy whenever I mention her. I haven't spoken of Rachel for years because of Margaret. Yet, Rachel still haunts me. Her face when I told her I was marrying Margaret ... Quiet, peaceful Rachel, withdrawing into herself when she was hurt, her eyes filling with tears, but no words of reproach on her lips. I know Margaret would never have permitted me to send Lily there if she'd known my plans. But she doesn't need to know. It's best this way.

Lily's talk about God reminded him of his own family and how they used to go to church together when he was young. He'd been involved with the youth group in high school, but after his parents died, and after he'd met Margaret, he'd let that part of his life slip away. He wondered whether God would want him back. He hadn't paid much attention to God since then. Lily was comforted by reading Rachel's Bible. Maybe he should buy a modern version as well. Then, he could talk about it with her. He could probably comfort Lily by trying to understand what was important to her.

Will sighed. With his daughter back in Thechihila and a grandchild on the way, he wanted more than anything to be home in Montana again too. The family ranch belonged to someone else now, but just to be back in Lake Thechihila would be enough. He shook his head. *No, not yet. Wait for the baby to come first. Then, I'll have a good reason to return.*

Caleb rode home through the twilight after a long day working on his ranch, Molly trotting along at his side. He'd seen Lily walk into church with Rachel on Sunday. He'd also noticed Lily didn't know the songs at first but chimed in once she had the tune.

She must be musical, or she wouldn't have been able to do that. I wonder what she thought of our songs. Rachel said she wasn't sure whether Lily was a Christian or not. I think she's open to God, wherever she is spiritually. She's been through a tough time. I'm glad she's here where we can help her. She and Rachel have certainly become friends quickly. Good. Rachel is awesome with young people. Lily will thrive there.

He remembered the tears he'd seen on Lily's cheeks briefly the afternoon of the welcoming party, and how she'd dashed them away, pretending nothing was wrong. But he could see the pain in her eyes at that moment. His heart had gone out to her. Losing the man she loved must be rough on her.

Father in heaven, pour your healing touch on Lily. Help her to know you love her. Give me wisdom to know how I can share your love and kindness with her too.

Caleb sighed and dismounted. He led the horse into the barn and into its stall. Removing the saddle from his horse and placing it over a beam, he wiped the horse down and brushed it thoroughly before turning to walk toward his dark house, followed by his dog.

He stepped onto the covered front deck and looked out over the valley while Molly curled up in front of the door. Leaning against a support pole, Caleb gazed at the familiar scene. Lights gleamed in the houses below. Lemon yellow lined the horizon, blending gradually into the deep blue sky where Venus, the evening star, twinkled. The pleasant smell of warm pasture grass wafted up on the breeze. He never tired of this peaceful scene. The familiar sights and smells anchored him to this ranch and to this community. Still, he was lonely if he spent too much time away from his friends. He thought of the day his high school girlfriend had broken his heart and left Thechihila permanently.

I wish Michelle hadn't left. It was my fault we broke up. I should have understood she wanted more out of life than this little town. I heard she married a good man down in Colorado. Colleen said she has two children now, both boys. I guess it wouldn't have worked if we'd married and she'd had to stay here at the ranch. She would have been miserable. I just have to keep reminding myself God is in control, and it wasn't his will for us to marry. But I haven't found anyone else. Well, it is what it is. I will trust God's plan for my life.

He stepped into the house and flipped a switch. Warm, golden light filled the main room. The house was built of logs, large ones at the bottom and smaller ones as the walls rose higher. Doors and windows had been carved out where they were needed. His grandfather had built the home years ago. Large picture windows in the living room and dining room looked out over the town. A wood stove in the kitchen provided plenty of heat during the long winter. The fireplace on the wall opposite the front door had an insert, so the heat from the room would not be lost when he started a fire in it. The kitchen had a propane stove too. When there were power failures, his family had been able to fall back on using the wood stove for cooking, though they usually used the propane stove in the summer months.

An open loft rose over one side of the living room. The cozy loft with its own bathroom and large walk-in closet had always been his bedroom. The rising heat from the stove kept him warm in the winter, and a window showing the moon at night could be opened to let in cool breezes during warm summer nights. There were three other bedrooms on the entry level, but he rarely had company who stayed overnight. The house was meant for a family. He didn't have one.

Climbing the stairs alone to his bedroom, Caleb sent up a prayer for comfort. *God, you know my heart. You know my needs. You said it is not good for man to be alone. Show me what I am supposed to do.*

At breakfast the next morning, after we'd finished eggs, toast, and fruit, Rachel and I sat looking out over the front lawn as we sipped tea together. Hummingbirds fed from the petunias in hanging baskets which lined the outside beams of the porch. I watched a fat jackrabbit hop across the lawn in a leisurely fashion.

What a peaceful morning! I love this.

"Jesse said the doctor will be at the clinic today and asked if you'd like to come in around one o'clock."

"How thoughtful of her. Yes. I would like that. I do need to see a doctor and find out more about my baby. Thanks for setting things up for me, Rachel."

At a quarter to one, we parked outside the small clinic in town. A huge cottonwood tree separated the building from the street, shading the lawn beneath its leafy branches. Sunlight danced between shadows. A big blue pot of yellow Margarita daisies stood outside the clinic, a cheerful welcome for visitors.

Inside, the waiting room was homey, with magazines on a small table, comfortably padded chairs, and a bouquet of pink roses on the counter by the receptionist. I filled out some medical papers, guessing at how far along my baby was. Maybe ten weeks, I thought, not sure of when I'd conceived.

Jesse came out to take me into the exam room. "Hi, Lily. Ready to see your baby?"

"Yes!" I stood and followed her toward the exam room. At the door, I paused and looked back at Rachel.

"Don't worry, honey. I'll be here when you're finished," she said with a smile.

Doctor Fallon was a pleasant, middle-aged woman. Her hair, sprinkled with white, had once been blonde.

After the initial exam, she smiled and said, "We'll do an ultrasound and take a look at this baby now."

A couple minutes later, I saw my child for the first time and heard the heartbeat loud and clear over the Doppler ultrasound. Joy overwhelmed me. *My baby! Look at that face!* For the first time, my pregnancy felt real.

"Hm. I'd say your baby is about fifteen weeks along. Do you want to know the gender?"

"Yes, please!"

"You're having a boy." She smiled over at me. "A son is a precious gift. I know. I have two sons of my own."

Konnor! Konnor! We're having a son! Oh, I wish you could be here!

"After seeing him and calculating the days, I would say you are due around February 19. Perhaps he will come early and be your valentine," she said with a broad smile.

"I'd like that!"

Jesse handed me some of the ultrasound pictures, pictures I would cherish. "He's already a cutie. I look forward to seeing this little one." She smiled.

"I'll be here next month around this same time," the doctor informed me. "I'll see you then. Just make an appointment before you leave. In the meantime, Jesse can let me know if you have any problems or questions."

"Thank you, Doctor Fallon.

Back in the car, I handed the ultrasound pictures to Rachel. "The doctor said my baby is a boy."

Rachel took the ultrasound pictures with trembling hands, her eyes drinking in the pictures of this new life. "My dear, this is a lovely child. Look at how clear his face is!

"Yes," I said, nodding with delight. "These pictures are amazing! I didn't realize how real the baby would look."

Rachel handed the pictures back and started the car, her face glowing. "Let's frame these pictures. I have some frames in my art room."

"What a great idea!"

All the way home we discussed baby things, this experience bonding us even more.

I must tell Dad when he calls next week. He will love knowing he will have a grandson. I wish I could call him now. But Mom's probably home. I guess I'll have to wait.

Five days later, Dad called.

"Hi, Dad. I saw the doctor this week."

"How'd it go, honey?"

"Great! She did an ultrasound and I saw my baby. And Dad, I'm having a boy!"

"A boy? Oh, this ought to be fun. Congratulations, Lily!"

"Thanks, Dad. I never realized how early babies take shape until I saw my son's hands and feet and sweet little face on the ultrasound pictures! I'll send you an email of the pictures."

"I will treasure it." Dad's voice sounded warm and happy.

Smiling, I filled him in on other details of my life in Lake Thechihila. We didn't talk long since Dad never was much of a talker. But when I went to bed that night, I sent up a prayer for God to bring joy into his life.

Rachel and I sat at the kitchen table sipping lemon tea after breakfast, talking about our plans before the day's work began. I'd been in Thechihila for three weeks now.

Looking at the rows of cherry jam lining the kitchen counter, I felt a strong sense of satisfaction. "That is the best jam I've ever tasted, Rachel. Thanks for showing me how to make it."

"I enjoyed having you here helping me, honey. You have a knack for this sort of thing."

"Konnor used to say the same thing. I guess I'm a homebody."

"I noticed you haven't been spending any time on your artwork lately."

"No. But now that we've finished making jam, I'll spend today at the easel. That is, unless you have something else in mind?"

"You go ahead and paint. I know you're itching to do so."

I laughed. "How well you know me already!"

Rachel smiled. A big black and white cat wandered by the front door and stretched up to claw the screen. "Magpie has taken to you."

"Is that what you call the cat?"

"Yes. She has the coloring of a magpie—a bird you'll see a lot here."

"I like her. She's a nice friendly cat." I sat and thought about how she cuddled up to me whenever I sat in a comfortable chair. "Dad says cats think people are just warm furniture."

"Does he?"

"Yes. But I've noticed he likes to hold cats as much as I do."

"When he was young, he had a magpie cat which followed him around. Once Will got stuck up in a tree, and the cat ran down to the house and meowed until Betty came out to check on her. The cat ran part way up the hill, then stopped and meowed again. Sensing something was wrong, Betty followed the cat right back to Will."

"Amazing. I didn't know cats did things like that.'

"Most of them don't. But Wiley seemed to think Will was her kitten, I guess. She was very protective of him. Your grandma Betty had named the cat Riley, but Will couldn't say Riley yet. He was only two at the time. He called the cat Wiley. It stuck. Your grandma liked to tell the rescue story every now and then over the years."

I laughed. A cat that rescued a little boy sounded adorable. At that moment, I had an idea. I would write a short story about Wiley rescuing young Will and illustrate it. I stopped laughing and stared off into space. Dad would love it!

"Lily? What's up?"

"I was thinking that story would make a very good children's book. It would give me a direction to go in my illustration portfolio. Publishers like to see if the artist can illustrate the same characters in different scenes the same way. Of course, many artists are now moving to AI—artificial intelligence—to do their book illustrations. But I prefer actual painting to AI. More satisfying. But I can do both if I must."

"Are you going to write the story of your dad and Wiley?"

"Yes, I think I will, although I don't want to become a writer. Being an illustrator suits me better. Writers must tour to promote their books. With a baby, I won't be able to tour, but it would be nice to have a story of Dad for my baby." My mind was leaping from one scene to another already, planning the plot, choosing the colors.

"The story is a great idea, Lily." Rachel smiled. "I'd love to see what you come up with."

"It should be fun. Dad will enjoy it too."

Rachel smiled. "He certainly will."

For the next few days, I sketched, wrote, and tried out my ideas on Rachel, who was just as enthusiastic as I was. Once the sketches were finished, I began painting every chance I had between harvesting berries and vegetables, gathering eggs, and helping Rachel in the kitchen.

Working on the story and painting helped draw the sorrow out of my heart. The beautiful colors on the canvas brought rays of hope to replace my loss.

The joy of my coming child filled my thoughts much of the time too. I thought of Konnor and how pleased he would have been with our son and this new venture. I could almost hear his laughter and feel his arms around me at times. My grief drained away little by little, fading into acceptance. Anticipating my own little one helped me find closure as well. I imagined my baby playing with Magpie someday. Dreams of a bright future began replacing nightmares of sorrow as my heart began to heal.

CHAPTER 5

"Tell me where she went!" Dominic demanded, standing in Margaret's kitchen.

Margaret shook her head. "I don't know, Dominic. She didn't say. She just left. If Will knows where she is, he hasn't said."

"I'll talk to him. Where is he?"

"In his study."

Dominic strode to Will's office and knocked sharply on Will's study door.

Will opened the door. "Hello, Dominic. What can I do for you?"

"You can tell me where Lily went." He was determined.

Will shrugged. "I don't believe that's relevant to you anymore, Dominic. Lily has made her choice to leave. If she wants you to know where she is, she will contact you."

"You know where she is, don't you!"

"Dominic, let it go."

"Will, I love Lily. I want her back."

"I'm sorry." Will shook his head. "This is Lily's choice. I will respect it."

Dominic's face grew red, his steely eyes boring through Will.

But Lily's father didn't budge, nor did he seem at all impressed with Dominic's insistence.

"I'll find her, with or without your help." Dominic turned and stormed out of the house.

Will stepped into the hall, watching him leave.

Margaret came into the room and wrapped her arms around him, leaning her cheek against his chest. "Will, where is Lily?"

Will stood silent and stiff, unresponsive to Margaret's ploy.

She flung away from him. "I'm her *mother!* I have a right to know!"

"I don't believe you do. That final slap you delivered when she refused to abort her baby—*our grandchild*—caused her to leave. She doesn't want to be found. You need to respect her."

"She's too emotional! She's making bad choices!" Margaret's shrill voice grated on his ears.

"I don't agree." Will stared out the open door, not seeing the flowers or trees in the well-manicured yard. Instead, his mind saw a golden head with braids wrapped around it like a crown, and green eyes looking up at him as Rachel had once stood looking up into his face at Thechihila Point their last summer together. Adoring eyes. Peaceful acceptance. What a contrast to Margaret.

"Will, what can she do if she has a baby now—without anyone to look after her? She won't be able to pay for childcare while she works. She is too shy to compete with others in the art illustration world. She can't afford this baby! She can't make it on her own."

Will turned briefly, observing Margaret's angry face. "I think she can."

"But Will ... think!"

"I *have* thought about it." He walked back into his study and shut the door, locking it. Hearing the back door slam, he looked out the window. He watched Margaret fling herself into her car and rev the engine. He knew she wouldn't give up. But neither would he. Unmoved, he went back to his desk and sat looking at the enlarged picture of Lily on the opposite wall. Lily at age 4, shy smile, glowing eyes.

My little girl. No. I'll never tell Margaret where she is now.

"Can I come in?" Rachel stood at the open door of my painting room. It was early Thursday afternoon, the first week in October. I'd been at Lake Thechihila a month by then. I was standing by the easel with a brush in one hand, putting the final touches on a painting. I was glad to see her. "Of course. Come in."

She looked over my shoulder to see my progress. The painting showed Dad as a child holding a black and white cat next to his cheek, a cheerful smile on his young face. At least I imagined Dad must have looked like the boy in the painting. The familiar wave of dark-blonde hair above blue eyes and rosy cheeks could well have been Dad at that age.

"Lily, how beautiful!"

I smiled hesitantly. "I'm painting from memory. I have only seen a handful of photos of Dad from when he was a little boy, but he looked a lot like this. Fortunately, Magpie is right here. I can watch her movements and put them on paper."

"I see you're using acrylics."

"Yes. I want the more intense colors they provide. Watercolors are nice too, but acrylics have more depth." I'd been writing and painting in my spare time for three weeks and had sketched the basic story plus a couple of good illustrations. On a drying rack Caleb had built for me were three simple paintings of ash tree berries done on rustic barn wood. Walking over to the table, I picked up my accumulated growing file of artwork and handed it to Rachel. "I've been preparing a portfolio since Konnor and I graduated from SOC."

A knock at the front door interrupted us.

"I'll be right back." Rachel turned toward the door. A few moments later, I heard her returning with someone.

Startled, I turned.

"I wonder if you'd mind Caleb looking at your pictures?" Rachel asked hesitantly.

"Okay. If he's interested." I stepped back, allowing our neighbor to see my work.

Caleb stepped forward to study the paintings. After a moment, he looked up. "Lily, you are *very good* at this. I'm sure you will do well as an artist."

"Thank you." I felt my cheeks grow warm at his praise.

"Rachel tells me you're thinking of writing and illustrating a children's book?"

"Yes, but the story itself is not for publication. I don't want to become a writer too, because I'd have to travel to promote the book. I can't even consider that with a baby on the way. I'm only going to send copies of my illustrations to an art agent. I'll keep the story with the pictures for my baby." I looked into his face. He seemed genuinely interested.

"Tell me about it."

"Okay. This is a story about my dad and his cat when he was a little boy."

Caleb smiled, his eyes twinkling. "What did your dad and the cat do in this story?"

I looked back at the painting to help me focus. In a few short sentences, I gave him a brief sketch of the book."

He nodded. "You're doing great, Lily."

"Do you think so?" I searched his face.

"Absolutely."

Rachel handed him the file of my other illustrations.

Caleb looked at each painting. Then he looked at me, his eyes glowing. "These are really good, Lily!"

"Thank you, Caleb. I–I'm glad you like them." I hoped they would be good enough to help me land an illustration contract. I felt unsure, but if Caleb thought my work was good, maybe it was.

"I sure do. You just keep up the good work, Lily."

"Okay." I didn't know what else to say.

"I came over to ask if you sing." Caleb looked at me expectantly.

"Um, yes. I do."

"Well, would you be interested in filling in for Misty on the worship team this week? She's down with a cold."

"I–I don't know all the songs yet!"

"We'll teach you." Caleb smiled, studying my face. "Can you come over to the church tonight at seven for practice?"

"Yes, I will come." I felt a little dizzy. I reached for my paint stand to steady myself.

"Lily?" Caleb reached out his hand to my shoulder. "Are you okay?"

"Yes. I–I just haven't done any public singing since Konnor ... We used to sing together a lot."

His arm came around my shoulder in a gentle hug. "I'm sorry, Lily. I know how tough losing him has been for you."

I felt tears gathering in my eyes and leaned against him, his warmth drawing me in. "I'll be okay. I just wasn't prepared for the question." I smiled through the tears, brushing them away.

He squeezed my shoulder gently. "Lily. Are you sure you're okay with singing?"

I nodded. "Yes. I'll be there."

"Thank you. I'll look forward to hearing you."

Shaken, I went into the living room after Caleb left and sat down for a minute in one of the big, padded chairs covered in a faded rose-patterned design.

"Would you like some iced tea?" Rachel's anxious question reminded me of her presence.

"Yes, please. I'd like that."

She bustled into the kitchen. I heard ice cubes plopping into a glass, followed by the sound of the tea being poured. Coming back into the dining area, she sat the tea on a coaster she placed on the table next to me. "There you go."

Rachel sat in another armchair at an angle to mine. "Are you okay now?"

"Yes." I nodded. "I was just taken by surprise at his request. It brought flashbacks of Konnor and me singing together."

"Do you mind singing at church?"

I thought about it a moment. "No. I like the songs they sing. They're upbeat and help me feel closer to God, but I don't know many of them yet. I just need to get control of my emotions."

Rachel relaxed. "You'll do fine, honey. I've heard you singing in church and around the house. You have a lovely voice."

"Thank you." I sipped the tea and sat back in the chair, afraid to touch the arms and cushions in case there was paint on my hands or forearms.

"Do I have any paint on the back of my arms?" I asked, holding them up for Rachel to inspect. "I get kind of messy when I work."

Rachel smiled. "Your hands and arms are fine. But you do have a little paint on your cheek." She reached for a tissue and dipped it lightly in hot water from the tea kettle. "I'll get it for you." She walked over, knelt, and gently wiped my cheek, a whimsical smile crossing her face. "There. It's gone."

"Did I get any paint on Caleb's shirt?" I demanded.

"Not that I saw."

"Oh, good."

"I doubt he would have minded if you had." Rachel's eyes twinkled.

I chose to drink my tea and ignore the insinuation. "Well," I said a moment later, finishing the glass of cold liquid, "I'm going to get back to work now. Thanks for the tea."

Concentrating afterward was difficult. My mind kept flashing back to Caleb examining my work. I savored the praise he gave. Finally, I shook my head, sighed, put my brush to soak in the jam jar filled with water, and went for a long walk along the lake.

∞───c◈◈◡───∞

Seven o'clock came swiftly. "See you later, Rachel," I called, waving and stepping out the front door.

"Have fun!"

"Okay."

The church was a five-minute walk down the narrow road. I could see a couple of pickup trucks in the parking lot and glanced at my wristwatch. Right on time. Entering

73

the church, I paused, looking toward the stage. Caleb, his back to me, was tuning his guitar to the keyboard off to the side where J. J. tapped the appropriate notes to give him the right pitch. Colleen stood waiting by the music stands.

I walked to the stage and stood next to her.

"I'm glad you could fill in." She flashed me a smile. "Misty can barely croak between coughs."

"That's too bad. I hope she feels better soon."

"Here's the music." Colleen showed me their songs. "I don't know if you know all of them."

I looked at the sheet music, recognizing only one song. "I know this one, 'Blessed Be Your Name.'" I glanced at the composer's name so I could look it up online later. Matt Redman. "I don't know the other songs. But I'm sure I'll figure them out once I've heard the rest of you sing."

"Oh, good."

Caleb turned and smiled. "Glad you could come, Lily. You know everyone here, don't you?"

"I think so. That's J. J. on bass, and this is Colleen. She'll sing tenor. Gage is on the drums, and that's Joe at the keyboard, right?"

"Right. Now let's get started."

Though I didn't know the songs at first, I caught on quickly. Being part of a musical group again satisfied my heart, filling me with peace. But through the practice, Konnor's beautiful tenor voice echoed in my mind as I imagined him singing along with us. Gradually, though, I was able to lose myself in the songs of praise and worship. The melodies freed my soul of sorrow.

They sang a song called "Blessed Be Your Name," which filled my broken heart with wonder. How could I bless God with so much pain in my heart? Yet, the song drew me. The words to the song's chorus echoed in the church.

Something that had been tightly clutching my heart began to melt the frozen core of my sorrow.

After practice, Caleb put his guitar back on its stand and turned to me. "Thanks for helping out, Lily. You did a really nice job on those alto parts."

"I'm glad I could be here." I smiled, relaxed around these new friends for the first time. "I've never sung this type of music before. I like it a lot."

As the team headed for the exit, Caleb asked, "Can I walk you home, Lily? I'm on foot too."

"Okay. That would be nice."

I waited while he locked the church door. Gage climbed into his truck and took off while J. J. helped Colleen climb into his jeep, a satisfied smile on his face.

The evening sun hung low above the hills as the heat of the day began to fade. A wide variety of birds chirped in the trees and bushes. Daylilies bloomed around the church garden, while twin wooden barrels full of deep purple asters stood on either side of the parking lot entrance. It was a beautiful evening.

Caleb put a hand on my shoulder and pointed toward a wetland pond near the church. "There's a gray heron. See?"

"How elegant!" The scent of marshland, the hoot of an owl, the sound of crickets, and a gentle breeze filled the air around us.

The big bird flapped his wings and rose into the air. In stillness, it flew majestically toward the lake below.

I turned to look up at Caleb happily.

He smiled. "Beautiful here, isn't it?"

"Yes. And peaceful." I sighed. For the first time in months, I was happy. "Caleb?"

"What?"

"Rachel said you know the story behind the legend of Thechihila Point. She said I should ask you. What makes it special?"

Caleb chuckled softly. "It's a family legend, Lily. One of my ancestors, Colonel James McFarland, served in the Confederate Army during the Civil War. When Union troops captured him, they decided it was a lot cheaper to send their prisoners west than to try housing and feeding them. The Union command sent him to Montana with the promise he would not fight again in the war.

"Colonel James, as we refer to him, chose to settle here on this lake. A Sioux chief in the area had a beautiful daughter named Ta-sheena. Colonel James and Ta-sheena fell in love, and at Thechihila Point, they pledged their lives to each other. They were happily married for around fifty years before Colonel James passed away. Since then, it has been the custom of our family for the men to propose to their sweethearts on Thechihila Point. The legend is this— Whoever pledges their love on the point will stay in love forever."

"Ahhh. What a beautiful story, Caleb."

He nodded. "Yes. What started as our family's legend spread to the entire settlement, and now it has become a tradition to become engaged on Thechihila Point."

A rabbit leaped onto the road right at my feet. I shrieked and jumped away, cannoning into Caleb, whose arms caught me and kept me from falling.

"Oh!" I gasped, staring after the rabbit, still caught in Caleb's arms. I could feel heat rising in my cheeks.

He laughed.

I laughed too before he let me go. Chuckling, we walked up to the house together.

"Thanks for walking me home, Caleb."

His eyes twinkled as he backed away. "You are most welcome, Lily. Let's do it again sometime. I'll just have to protect you from all those fierce bunnies out there."

I laughed and went inside. Warmth flooded my body along with a little shiver of excitement.

Later, as I brushed my hair before going to bed, I thought of that warm, intimate moment on the road with Caleb. Should I have felt guilty for enjoying the moment with him? Was I being disloyal to Konnor's memory?

A verse in Psalm 30, which I had read that morning, popped into my head.

Weeping may last through the night, but joy comes with the morning.

I remembered how Konnor had held me one day when I was sad. He spoke gently into my ear. "Chose joy over sorrow, hope over pain, love after mourning, sun after rain."

Life goes on. Pain lessens with time. But I must choose to let it go. In that moment, I decided to choose joy over sorrow. Soon. Like an ocean wave slipping back from the beach into the sea, the pain of my beloved Konnor's death began to recede a little.

"Konnor," I whispered as tears rose in my eyes. "I'm not ready to let go of you. Not yet. I miss you too much. But someday I will choose joy. It won't be easy! But I will. I'm going to be okay, my love."

CHAPTER 6

Dominic Jantzen was used to having his own way. Rich and handsome, he drew many girls to his side. Lily was different. Everyone liked her. She was shy and sweet like a dove. Elusive, gentle. Easily controlled. Her singing and guitar music were magical, which would be a great addition to their family house parties. But she wouldn't respond to him at all after she'd left for college. She'd removed herself from his orbit. But he wasn't going to let her go. She was the one who got away. Her return home placed her where he could once again try to win her as his wife. She was perfect for the part. He had set about it with unusual patience, zeroing in on her when she was emotionally vulnerable.

His father wanted that too. Dad was on his side. But Lily's dad was against him. After fruitlessly trying to get the information from him, Dominic spoke with Margaret.

"I want Lily back. I've asked Will where she is, but he won't tell me. I'm sure he knows where she is." He paced back and forth across the shaded patio.

"He wouldn't tell me, either. But I agree. He probably knows where she is. My guess would be she's returned to Ashland, Oregon. She has lots of friends in the Southern Oregon University area."

"Do you have any names I could contact?"

"Yes. Check with Aaron Strong, Mary Mallory, or Fiona Scott. I don't know their numbers, but they shouldn't be too hard to find. There are a few others too."

"I'll drive up there and have a look around. Make a list of names for me."

"Okay." Margaret walked back into the house to find a piece of paper. There was a notepad next to the phone. Writing down every name she could remember, she handed the pad of paper to Dominic. "Good luck finding her."

"Thanks, Margaret."

"Let me know when you locate her."

"Sure." Dominic had no intention of complying right away, but he was willing to humor her.

Arriving in Ashland, he searched for Lily's friends. Autumn leaves colored the landscape in brilliant hues, but he didn't notice. He was focused on finding Lily. But none of her friends had heard a thing about her. They all knew Konnor had been killed in a car accident, but that was the last they'd heard. Lily had gone silent.

He talked to others on SOU's campus, trying to get a feel for Lily's likes, dislikes, and any mention she might have made of a place she liked. Someone said she liked Hawaii, where she and Konnor had visited last winter. Another said she liked the redwood forest down by Santa Cruz.

Two weeks later, Dominic returned to Santa Rosa, frustrated at this lack of progress, fuming because he couldn't find Lily. Maybe he'd have to hire a detective. He had the money to do it, but he'd like to find her himself. The challenge appealed to his controlling nature.

As he sat there looking down at the pad with its list of names, he ripped the top sheet off, folded it, and put it in his shirt pocket. He tossed the pad to the table and stared at it. Suddenly, he looked at the pad closely. There were deep indentations in the sheet of paper he hadn't noticed on the previous sheet. It was heavily marked, something like a man would leave when writing.

Will must have written something on this pad.

Excitement rising in him, he reached for a pencil and began to lightly shade the paper. A phone number appeared. It was area code 406. He pulled his phone from his pocket and looked the area code up on his server. Montana.

Dominic called Margaret. "I found a phone number with a Montana area code on the pad of paper you gave me."

Margaret gasped.

"Who does your husband know in Montana?"

"Rachel!" Margaret exclaimed.

"Rachel who?"

"Rachel Carson. She lives at Lake Thechihila."

"Do you think he'd send Lily there?"

"Yes. I don't know why I didn't think of her!"

"Oka-a-a-ay!" Dominic said with satisfaction. "Now we're getting somewhere!"

Will called Lily every Wednesday night, following her life journey with great interest. He bought a modern version of the Bible and read the story of Jesus, from Matthew's gospel to John's words. The new translation helped him understand better, and he could relate to Lily's spiritual journey. This was a new dimension to their relationship, something he treasured. He began to understand Jesus better too.

Lily emailed him a scan of her baby's ultrasound pictures.

Wow! I didn't know these ultrasounds were so detailed. Look at that boy—beautiful! I can hardly wait to see him. Lily says he's due in February. Driving in Montana in February is difficult with all the snow and ice. But I'll go up there as soon as the snow melts. It's been a long time since I've tried driving in the snow, and I don't have the right tires on my car for it. I'll need studded ones if I go in February. Where I'd find them here is anyone's guess. I'd probably have to special-order them.

Will made copies of the ultrasound pictures and put them in a file in his desk, then deleted them from his computer. Margaret didn't know he'd kept a file on Lily since she was a baby, a file with baby pictures, school photos, awards, and events in which she'd participated.

Lily said she was involved with a group of young people at church. That sounded helpful. Will sighed. He wished he had a similar group. Maybe he could check out local churches and try to find one. A friend at work was in a men's Bible study. He'd ask about it and see if he could go with him.

As autumn descended on Lake Thechihila, Caleb invited me to join him at a Bible study on Friday evenings. The work of summer and harvest had passed, and a harvest party was being planned for Halloween night. Now, there was time to start their regular study time again. The group of young people took turns meeting at each other's homes.

The week after the bunny incident, Caleb stopped by in his truck to pick me up around seven o'clock on Friday evening. I felt a little shy about this, but it sounded like fun.

"I can bring Rachel's Bible, which has modern words. Is that okay?" I asked anxiously.

Caleb smiled. "Sure. I brought an extra one along, just in case you didn't have one."

"Oh, thank you, Caleb. Konnor was studying his Bible the month before he died, and he'd decided he believed in Jesus. His Bible used ancient words I have a hard time understanding. So, I've been reading Rachel's Bible."

"Good." Caleb smiled and nodded. "I've found the Bible to be a source of great encouragement. What have you read?"

"Well, my favorite verses are ones Rachel read to me out of Psalm 139, about how much God loves me. I've memorized most of those verses."

Caleb nodded. "I like Psalm 139 a lot too. There was a time when I wondered if God cared about me. Then one day, I just opened my Bible without thinking of anything, and there it was. I believed God arranged it so he could let me know how much he loves me."

"Does he do things like that?"

"Sometimes. I never know when he will speak something very special from verses I read. I look forward to the adventure." He smiled. "Sounds like you've already started on that same adventure, Lily."

"Yes!" I sat back and savored the moment, thinking of the ways God had shown me his love lately.

Caleb pulled into the driveway at Joe and Misty's house. "Don't try to climb down from the truck on your own. I'll come around and help you."

A few steps, and he was at my door. I took his hand and stepped down, landing close to him. His aftershave and the clean scent of his body filled my senses. I suddenly felt my knees go weak for a moment and took his arm to steady myself.

"Lily? Are you okay?" He held me up until I was steady again.

"Yes. Just give me a minute. I feel a little dizzy." I'd never felt like this before, not even with Konnor. I took a deep breath, turned, and walked with him to the house, his hand around my waist to steady me just in case I felt dizzy again.

"I'm okay now," I said as we neared the light.

Still, he kept his arm around me until we reached the doorway.

Jesse and Gage were already there, talking with Joe and Misty about their wedding plans.

"We have a lot to do in a short time." Jesse said.

"Did you settle on a date yet?" Misty asked.

"Yes. We've chosen the Saturday before Thanksgiving at eleven o'clock in the morning. That will give us plenty of time for the wedding and reception while we still have daylight."

"Will the wedding be at the church? Or did you have another place in mind."

"The church is perfect. We can have the reception in the fellowship room, so everything will be in the same place."

"Could I get you some tea or a soft drink, Lily?"

"Tea would be nice, Caleb, thank you."

"Do you use sugar?"

"Yes. One teaspoon is plenty."

Caleb wound his way through the growing crowd, headed for the kitchen.

"Hi, Lily!" Misty saw me standing there in the shadows. "Welcome to our home."

"Thank you. I'm pleased to be here."

Most of the people coming to the study were here now.

Caleb came from the kitchen carrying a hot cup of tea. "Come sit over here." He lifted his chin toward a well-cushioned chair in the living room.

Joe, who was leading the study that evening, stepped into the living room. "Okay, if everyone will find a seat, we'll get started.

The evening passed too quickly for me. I had so much to learn about the Bible. We read about two great heroes of Israel, Caleb and Joshua. Their faith, bravery, and long friendship fascinated me.

The prayer time was my first opportunity to verbalize my prayer to God around others. I took a deep breath and tried to relax. "God, thank you for bringing me here to this place of safety where I can learn about you. Thank you for these friends who are helping me. Amen."

I paid close attention as each one in the group prayed. The things they shared helped me understand them more, and their prayers lifted me. Prayer satisfied my soul.

All too soon, Caleb asked if I was ready to leave. I nodded. He said a quick goodbye, ushering me out of the house, and helping me back up into the truck.

Forcing myself to breathe normally, I accepted his help, hoping he wouldn't notice my nervousness. But, Caleb was calm and pleasant.

"Well, what did you think?"

"I loved it! Were you named after the Caleb in the Bible?"

He laughed. "Yes. Living up to that name is a challenge for sure."

"I wish I had a Bible name."

"You *do* have a Bible name, Lily."

"What? Who's named Lily in the Bible?"

"Nobody, but Jesus once said, 'Look at the lilies of the field and how they grow. They don't work or make their clothing, yet Solomon in all his glory was not dressed as beautifully as they are.'"

"Oh! I guess that counts then. What a nice verse. Where is it?"

Caleb laughed. "Matthew chapter six."

Parking by the walkway to Rachel's house, he came around to help me down from the truck again. This time, I was prepared. No weak knees, no dizziness, just a warm, happy feeling as we walked to the door together.

"Thanks for taking me to the Bible study, Caleb. I enjoyed it a lot."

"Want to go next week?"

"Definitely."

"Okay. I'll pick you up at the same time. We'll be heading for the Duggen's ranch next time. Cody lives with his parents, and his folks will host us. And by the way, the worship team loved having you sing with them and wondered if you'd sing again."

"I–I'd be happy to sing. If you're sure?"

"I'm sure."

"Then I'd like to sing. I enjoyed it very much." I thought of something else. "Caleb?"

"Yes?"

"When I first drove into town, you waved at me. And whenever I drive anywhere with Rachel, people wave too. Does everyone here know me?"

He smiled. "No. It's just the Montana way. We wave at everyone just to be neighborly."

"How nice."

"See you later." He grinned at me and stepped back as I opened the door.

I watched him drive away before going inside. Rachel was already in bed, for she arose at four each morning. I turned out the lights and entered my bedroom. There in the stillness of night with the moon rising in the sky, I felt immensely blessed. I knew now God was watching over my baby and me. Peace filled my heart as I fell asleep. Sweet dreams about Caleb flitted through my mind. Then, I saw Konnor standing before me. He smiled and said, "Our son needs a father. It's okay, Lily."

I awoke in the night, tears in my eyes. "I can't think of Caleb. Not yet, my love. You are too much a part of me still." I could almost hear Konnor saying, "Everything will be okay, Lily." Once again, I fell asleep, knowing God was with me, leading me along a new path.

But in the dark of night while I slept, headlight beams lit the mountain roads between Santa Rosa and Lake Thechihila. Dominic Jantzen was headed north.

CHAPTER 7

Dominic was determined. He would find Lily and bring her back home. He'd looked up weather in Montana for October—already in the second week—and saw there wasn't much snow yet, but he'd have to leave soon, because snow could arrive in another week or so. He packed a suitcase and tossed it into his new SUV.

Lily needed someone to rescue her from herself. Help her snap out of this depression. He was confident he could do it, though his mother was not so sure. Her words echoed in his mind as he drove.

"Dominic, she has suffered a great loss," Juanita Jantzen said hesitantly, standing beside the four-wheel drive he'd bought for the trip north. "She has gone away to be alone, to grieve for her lost lover. She will not welcome you."

"Oh, Mom. She needs rescuing from herself. I love her. I won't lose her again. If I don't find her, she may find someone else. Last time we broke up, I made the mistake of letting her go, hoping she'd come back. But then she met this guy Konnor. I won't make the same mistake again."

Juanita shook her head silently. Her son was like his father—forceful, a strong leader. Why couldn't he see Lily was not cut out for him? She wouldn't fit into their family business, the entertaining they did, nor with their friends. She was too shy. Juanita understood Lily, as she was also shy. Learning to be the hostess of her successful husband's parties had taken supreme effort. What magic hold did Lily have on Dominic anyway? Was it just Dominic's bruised ego? She hoped not, for her son's sake.

Monty, Dominic's younger brother, spoke up. "Dom's right, Mom. The only way to win her back is to find her and shower her with romance. Lily's shy, but she's easily led."

"Thanks for the support, Monty." Dominic stuffed his suitcase in the back of his new Toyota Sequoia. *There should be room for Lily's things too*, he thought as he admired the SUV's interior.

"Look," he said, straightening up. "She's all alone in a new place. She'll be lonely. I think she will be happy to see me."

"Go slow, Dominic," his dad Brett cautioned. "She will resist you if you're too aggressive. She needs a gentle touch."

"Okay. I appreciate the advice." He shook his dad's hand and climbed into the car.

Now, almost to Lake Thechihila, he planned his approach. He'd be casual, kind, thoughtful … yes. That should work. Margaret had never been to Lake Thechihila, and didn't know how to direct him, but he had Rachel's address. He pulled the notebook from the seat beside him and looked at it again. 318 Lake Drive. He slowed down to look at the numbers on the mailboxes.

There it was. He grunted in satisfaction and turned into the driveway. He'd picked afternoon, thinking it would be a good time to arrive.

He parked by the house and walked up to the door, looking around with disdain at the plain, country setting. He rang the doorbell, but nobody answered. He rang again. And again. Still no answer. He walked around the house to see if Lily might be there.

A duck pond surrounded by reeds lay beyond the backyard fence. Closer, off to the left, he saw two women working among the autumn flowers surrounding the house, their blonde hair shining in the sun. That must be Lily and her father's friend, Rachel.

Confidently, he walked around the fence, striding toward the two women.

I straightened up, my hand on the small of my back.

"Oh, honey, you are tired!" Rachel said. "Let's go back to the house and ..."

I saw him. "Dominic! What are you doing here?"

"Why, Lily. What a way to greet me! I drove all this way just to make sure you're okay." He smiled at me.

"How did you find me?"

"Your mother helped me. She's very concerned about you, Lily."

Rachel moved closer to me. "Lily? Let's invite this young man in for some tea or coffee, and we'll talk things over."

"Okay. Dominic, would you like some coffee?" I asked, suppressing my anger and attempting to be polite. I knew he detested tea.

"I would love some."

Together, the three of us walked back to the house. Rachel and I took off our jackets and hung them on wooden pegs by the back door. I read Dominic's face with ease. The frown he directed toward Rachel indicated he wished she would go away and leave us alone.

"You must be Rachel," he said, forcing a smile.

"Yes, I'm Rachel."

"Nice place you have here," he said.

I could tell from his face he was not impressed.

Rachel motioned to a comfortable chair. "Do sit down and be comfortable while we wash up."

Washing my hands gave me time to steady my nerves. "Do you like your coffee sweet or plain?" Rachel asked.

"Black is fine."

In an awkward silence, Rachel added ground coffee beans and cold water to the coffee maker. A few moments later, she placed a cup of hot coffee in Dominic's hands and sat down on the couch with some tea. I didn't want anything to drink. I just wanted to get this conversation over. I sat in the rocking chair across from Dominic. He obviously hadn't planned to make his case in front of another person. How annoying this must be for him. I hid a smile.

He made small talk for a few minutes, asking about the farm. Rachel answered, but I remained quiet. Finally, he turned to me. "Lily, I've been worried about you. I've come to take you home where you belong."

"Dom, I like where I am. I'm not going to Santa Rosa with you." I looked him straight in the eye.

His face told me he wasn't convinced.

"But, Lily! Your mother is worried and wants you home!

"I'm happy here."

"Now look ..." he started, his face growing red.

I watched him force himself to be calm and polite. "I know you want to get away from the pain you've suffered, my love. Things have been difficult for you. Let me help you."

"Dominic, I am expecting Konnor's baby."

His mouth dropped open. His face paled. He glanced at my waist.

I wasn't showing yet. I watched his face grow determined as a betraying shade of red rose up his neck and spread across his cheeks.

"I see. Well, we can talk about that later. But right now, let's get you home where you can have proper care."

"No."

"Now, Lily—"

"Dominic, I have chosen to make a life here for my son and me. This is where I want to be. I like the peace and quiet. I like working on the farm. This is where we belong."

"No!" he declared, his eyes flashing. "You belong with your friends and family in Santa Rosa. Come on! What could you ever hope to achieve here?"

"Peace."

Dominic shook his head. *"Peace?* What about *love?"*

"I have all the love I need. Right here." I stood, walked toward the door, opened it, and waited.

Dominic carefully set the cup on a coaster and stood. I had once seen his humiliation when another girl had pushed him away. That same rigid expression turned his mouth into a straight line now as I waited for him to leave.

"Lily, I will be back tomorrow to talk with you about this. I can see you're not thinking clearly today."

"Don't bother to come back, Dom. I'm not going with you."

But Dominic wasn't going to take no for an answer. "I will be back tomorrow morning, and we'll talk about this some more. Just you and me next time." He turned to Rachel. "Thank you for the coffee, ma'am," he said politely. "I'll see you tomorrow."

He walked out the door, shut it with a bang, and returned to his SUV.

I watched Dominic pull out of the driveway with a screech of tires and head into town. My racing heart gradually slowed in the presence of Rachel's calmness.

I thought I'd escaped him. How could Mom have known where I was? Dad wouldn't have told her. Dominic isn't a safe person. He's violent—probably would have hit me if Rachel hadn't been here. He would surely hurt my baby if he could. He's so steamed now, he's probably swearing.

"I think he means it," Rachel said. She came up beside me and put her arm across my shoulder.

I lay my head on her shoulder and shuddered, my heart trembling at the encounter, tears welling up in my eyes.

"Yes, he does," I said, trying to pull myself together. "He's always gotten his own way in the past. I don't think he understands the word *no*. I had to leave for college to get away from him last time. Even then, he kept coming up to visit me until I started dating Konnor. When he found out I was dating, he blew up and almost hit me. Fortunately, Konnor showed up right about then."

"What do you want to do about this man?"

"I don't want to talk with him. Period." I straightened up.

"I think you should talk with Caleb about this situation. He might know what to do." Rachel looked worried. "I don't want this man hurting you."

I stood looking out the window, wondering if dragging Caleb into this situation was a good idea. Finally, I sighed. "Okay. I'll go up to his place and tell him what's happened."

Rachel visibly relaxed. "Good." She hurried into the kitchen and brought out a plate of cookies. "Here. Take some of these with you." She began putting cookies into a paper bag.

Cookies would provide a convenient excuse to talk with Caleb. "Good idea."

I accepted the cookies and headed out the back door toward Caleb's house. It was the first time I'd gone up there. Walking onto the covered deck toward Caleb's front door, I looked out over the valley. What a lovely view.

I knocked on the door, but he didn't answer. Maybe he was out. No, his truck was there. His horses were all in the corral. Curiously, I walked toward the building next to the house. Was it a storage shed for equipment?

"Caleb?" I called.

Molly trotted up to me.

"Hi, Molly," I said, patting her head. "Where's Caleb?"

She barked.

A moment later, the door opened. "Lily! Hi." He was wearing clear goggles which he quickly pulled up to rest on top of his head.

I held out the bag of cookies. "Rachel sent me up with these."

He accepted the bag and looked inside. "Thank you. These cookies smell great." He looked up. "Since you're here, do you want to see my latest project?"

"Okay."

He held the door open for me.

Down the center of the room stood two rows of plants growing under a light in raised troughs of what looked like water.

"Here," Caleb said, reaching for a shelf and handing me a pair of plastic goggles. He pulled his own over his eyes. "You'll need to wear these. They protect against UV rays."

I put on the goggles and followed him toward the plants. "What are you growing here?"

"Well, for starters, there's romaine lettuce." He brushed a section of plants with his hand. "In the winter, all the shipments to our store in town bring limp lettuce. If there's one thing I detest, it's limp salads. Nothing is fresh, and we don't get a good variety anyway. I decided to put some of my college classes to good use. I studied hydroponics, among other things. That's growing plants in water containing specific nutrients."

"Growing vegetables in water? This is fascinating, Caleb."

"Thanks. I set up my own little nursery. I grow lettuce, tomatoes, sugar snap peas, cucumbers, strawberries, and blueberries in here. The berries are still green, but they'll be ready soon. I use LED grow lights. We have to wear goggles because grow lights emit ultraviolet rays. When I'm working for any length of time, I usually turn the grow lights off and use the regular bulbs overhead. I'm just harvesting a few things now. See?"

He pointed to a basket on a small table nearby. I went over to see what he'd picked.

"Looks to me like you're making a salad—lettuce, tomatoes, and cucumbers."

"Yes. Would you like to take some back to Rachel?"

"Sure."

Caleb grinned and picked some for me. "Let's take these things inside and put them in a bag for you."

We walked down the bark-covered path toward the side door of the house and entered a big kitchen with a center island, where Caleb put the vegetables. Reaching into a drawer, he pulled out a plastic bag and put half the produce into it.

"There. No pesticides, no dirt, just organic vegetables. You can have fresh salad for dinner now." His smile touched something inside me, warming my heart and making me want to laugh.

"Thank you, Caleb. I think Rachel is making chicken soup for this evening. Salad will go good with it." I felt nervous about telling him what was up, but I braved it. "Caleb?"

"Yes?'

"Today someone came to see me at Rachel's house. A guy I dated in high school. Dominic Jantzen. He said my mom helped him find me. Dad promised he wouldn't tell Mom where I was, so I don't know how she knew. Anyway, Dominic's insisting I return home with him. I don't want to do that. I turned him away, but he said he's coming back tomorrow to talk with me alone. Rachel stayed with me during his visit today. He's wealthy and moves in high society. My mom wanted me to marry him. She started pushing me toward him just two months after Konner died. But I'm not interested."

"What's the problem, Lily?"

"Dominic can be abusive. I'm afraid of him."

"I see." Caleb watched my face as I spoke. "What do you want to do?"

"I want to stay here! I *love* being here with Rachel. She's—she's calm and comforting. And I'm learning about God now. I don't want to give that up. I like you and all my other friends here. This is where I want to live. I want to raise my baby here."

"You like it out here in the country?" Caleb's eyes opened wide.

"Yes. I've never known a place so peaceful, so beautiful. The doctor said my baby is a boy. This valley is just what I want for him."

Caleb smiled slowly, his eyes warm and accepting. "Lily, I'm glad you like it here. We're glad to have you. *I'm* glad you're here."

I looked up at him, my heart in my throat. He was close, just a step away. I put my hand out and touched his arm for a second. "Thank you, Caleb."

"So ... what would you like to do tomorrow when he comes back?"

"I don't know." I shivered. "He's very persistent. I just want him to go away. To stay away from me."

"Would you like me to come over and stick around while he's there?"

"Could you?"

"Of course." Caleb smiled, looking into my eyes. "I'll come over and help you and Rachel with the garden and the chores tomorrow. Okay?"

"Perfect!" I smiled up at him.

When he looked down at my lips, I caught my breath and move back a step.

No! Konnor, I cannot let go of you yet! You were my one true love!

I found myself breathless. Taking another step backward, I turned and looked around the kitchen. "This is a nice room. I like all the space and the island where people can work together fixing meals." I looked over my shoulder at him and saw he was smiling, a teasing look in his eyes.

"My mom liked it here too," he said. "She'd have friends up often, and they'd sit in here and talk for hours."

"Your mom sounds like a nice person. Where is she now?"

"She and Dad moved to Prescott, Arizona, to be near my sisters, Julie and Jan, and their families. Julie and Jan are twins. They're three years younger than I am. They both have kids, and my parents wanted to be nearby. I'm glad to stay here, but I miss having the family around."

What a fun childhood he must have had here in this big house, surrounded by his parents and sisters. I wish I'd had sisters and brothers. Growing up wouldn't have been so lonely.

I moved toward the front door. "Thank you for the veggies. We'll enjoy them tonight."

"Let me walk you home." He put his hand at the small of my back and steered me toward the front door. His nearness comforted me.

I looked around the living room, taking in the stairs ascending to the loft. A fireplace adorned the center wall, surrounded by a leather couch and recliner, a comfortable big chair with red throw pillows. Beneath the furniture was a big, round hooked rug in multiple colors covering the floor, making the room inviting. I could imagine a crowd gathering, the laughter, the simple togetherness of family.

At the front door, Caleb ushered me onto the deck.

"Your view is incredible," I said, stopping once more to gaze out over the valley and lake.

"You should see this view at night. The lights of the homes across the lake reflect on the water."

"I love it."

"How's your artwork coming?"

"I think I'll have enough good illustrations to send to an art agent soon. One of the things they look for is the ability to draw characters consistently the same. I didn't have that until I started on the set of pictures of my dad as a little boy plus Rachel's cat, Magpie. Thanks for asking."

"You are an incredibly good artist, Lily. I'm sure you'll find an agent."

"I appreciate your faith in me. But there are tons of good artists out there, Caleb. I'm just a small fish in a very big pond."

Caleb laughed. "You may be small, Lily, but if God wants you to be an illustrator, he will open the door for you. Have faith."

"I–I'm just learning about faith. It's new to me. Thanks for the encouragement."

Together we walked down the hill toward Rachel's house, enjoying the evening together, and entering through the back door.

Rachel came in from the front room where she had been knitting a blue jacket for the baby. "Caleb, did Lily tell you about our visitor?"

"Yes. And tomorrow, I'm going to be working here from eight o'clock on. I'll be here if you need me."

"Oh, thank you, Caleb. I'll have breakfast ready at eight. You're welcome to join us."

"Thanks. I'll enjoy eating someone else's cooking for a change."

"Look." I held out the bag with the vegetables in it. "Caleb is growing these in his shed. In *water.*"

"So that's what you've been up to," Rachel said. "How clever."

Caleb smiled. "I hope you like them. I'll be getting back to my work. See you in the morning."

I walked back out with him. As soon as the door closed behind us, I touched his arm. Caleb turned and looked down at me.

"Thank you for helping me, Caleb. I feel safer already, just knowing you'll be here."

"You're most welcome, Lily. I'm glad you asked for my help."

He smiled and turned to walk back up the hill.

I stayed near the door, watching him go.

He is a good man, and I feel drawn to him, but Konnor is still too dear to my heart. I cannot be fair to myself or any other man yet. Grief still comes to me at unexpected times, and Konnor haunts my dreams. Maybe when the grief is less, I will have room in my heart for Caleb. But I'm not there yet. Oh, Konnor! I miss you so! I will keep my face turned toward joy, but you are still the love of my life.

CHAPTER 8

Dominic walked swiftly away from the quaint hotel. He needed a walk along the lakeshore to work out his anger. Lily's lack of response frustrated him. Did Margaret know Lily was pregnant? She must have.

Why didn't Margaret tell me? Did she think I wouldn't want Lily if I knew she was pregnant with another man's child? Oh, it's an inconvenience. But I'm sure I can convince her she'd be better off without the baby. If I can't talk her into an abortion, I can talk her into giving it up for adoption. Either way, I still want her. She will make the perfect hostess for our family parties. She has impeccable manners. She's always been easily led ... until today. And she's beautiful. Hm. How can I win her over? Girls respond well when I bring flowers. Maybe I should find some flowers to soften her up. Do they even have any in that run-down store? I'll have to check.

He turned back toward the town, hurrying along the dirt pathway beneath the golden leaves of the cottonwood trees. He was too intent upon his mission to notice the scenery. Just a lake. He'd seen classier ones in Europe, lakes surrounded by walkways, shops, well-manicured landscapes. He didn't like the wild disorganization of this lake in the wilds of Montana.

Maybe I should take Lily to Europe for a honeymoon. Yes. Good idea. She seems to like lakes. Once we get rid of this pregnancy of hers, she will go back to being the compliant girl she used to be. Of course, there's Selina. I can't let Lily know about her. Lily would object for sure. But there's no way I'm giving her up. Selina's fascinating and exciting. But she's not wife material. I'm sure I can keep Selina a secret. Lily will never suspect. Dad's been keeping a mistress down in Napa for years, and Mom doesn't know.

He thought again about meeting his father, who had a beautiful woman on his arm, one day when he had taken Selina to lunch in Napa. His dad had been most uncomfortable. He'd explained to Dominic his lady friend was a business associate and had told him not to say anything to his mother. Yes, he would keep his father's secret. But had Dad guessed Selina was his own mistress? He grinned. Probably not. Dad had been too embarrassed to notice the beautiful girl waiting for Dom in the lobby.

Dominic's thoughts savored his last meeting with Selina, the feel of her in his arms, her deep brown eyes, and luscious, full lips. He sighed and shook his head. She'd never fit into his family or business world. Never be accepted by society. He needed to concentrate on Lily now.

He strode into the country store and looked around. The air smelled of fresh cookies. At the bakery, he picked up a variety box to enjoy while he waited to see Lily again. He wouldn't go up to Rachel's place until late morning. Making Lily wait for him would build her anticipation. His audacity pleased him.

A few bouquets of daisies, but no roses, stood by the cash register. Well, first thing in the morning, he'd have to drive back to the town he'd passed earlier. He paid for the cookies and headed back to his room at the hotel.

Remembering Selina, he took out his phone and spent the next hour sweetening her up. He pictured her in the luxury apartment he'd rented for her. She'd be lounging, maybe pouting because he hadn't been there in a week. He would want to see her as soon as he returned to Santa Rosa and had made sure Lily was back in her parents' home. He had no doubts he could convince Lily to return with him. In the meantime, there was Selina, lovely Selina.

Alone in his house that evening, Caleb stood on the deck, looking out over the valley. The evening mist was rising from the ground and lake. Warm lights beamed from houses below. The lone grey heron slowly drifted above the mist, its great wings moving up and down majestically. Subdued cricket songs filled the air. A bunny hopped across his lawn.

Caleb grinned, remembering Lily's reaction when a rabbit had darted across the road. She had turned to him, her arms clutching his shirt, frightened at the sudden movement. For a moment there, he'd caught his breath as he held her in his arms, his heart pounding at her nearness. Then he'd realized she was just startled and would have turned to anyone. It wasn't personal, so why should he feel let down?

But then this afternoon when she'd appealed to him for help, he'd realized maybe there was some small hint of growing attachment on her part. When her blue eyes had looked up into his face, crystal clear and beautiful, he'd wanted to draw her into his arms and kiss her. Her beauty reminded him of wildflowers in the fields. For a moment, he'd thought she would yield, for her eyes dilated, and she caught her breath. But then, she'd stepped back and changed the subject. Her cheeks had turned scarlet. Yes, she'd felt what he had felt. But she was not ready. Yet.

He'd marveled when she told him she wanted to stay in Lake Thechihila forever and raise her son here. He would have time to court her. Yes, there was hope of a future with Lily. His heart remembered his prayer, asking God for a mate. Had God brought Lily here for him? Maybe. She'd called on him to help guard her against Dominic, an old boyfriend. Well, he'd do it with pleasure.

Taking a deep breath, Caleb looked down at Rachel's house, the lights shining brightly from the kitchen.

Father, if this is your plan for me, show me how to proceed. Lily is still grieving. I can see it in her eyes. She's having a son. You know I've always wanted a son. If Lily is the one you have sent to me, I will gladly welcome her little boy as my own. Please show me what to do here. Lily is quiet. She's not going to tell me what she wants. So, guard my heart and grant me wisdom, Father. Thank you.

Roosters crowing at the crack of dawn dragged me out of a deep sleep. Snuggling under my warm comforter, I blinked and yawned. I felt my baby moving and put my hand where I could feel his little feet pushing outward. Smiling, I stretched along with him, imagining the day when I would hold him in my arms.

"Good morning, Sunshine," I whispered to my son.

Then I remembered. Dominic. He would come to my place of refuge to try to talk me out of staying here. Fear threatened to stifle my peace. But then, I remembered Caleb would be here. Caleb would protect me from Dom's manipulative ways.

God, let your peace guard my heart today. Help me to stand up to Dominic. Keep my baby and me safe. Thank you for Rachel and Caleb. Rachel is dear to me. I don't ever want to leave here. I'm learning so much about you, God! And Caleb ... I feel protected around him. He's becoming a good friend. I want to stay here always. Please watch over us today.

I heard Rachel in the kitchen. It would soon be time to gather eggs. Farm life goes on even when human crises threaten to disrupt everything.

Later, as Rachel and I prepared breakfast, I noticed the pucker between her brows.

"Is something wrong, Rachel?"

She smiled and looked up. "Hm. I must admit I'm a little concerned about your friend Dominic. He seems sincere about wanting to take you back to California."

"You don't know him like I do. All he wants is his own way. Well, he won't succeed in getting it this time. With you and Caleb here to help me, he'll have to give up."

"He seems determined."

"Yes. But I can be determined too."

A knock sounded on the kitchen door, and Caleb stepped inside.

"I could smell the bacon halfway up the hill."

Rachel laughed. "Come in, Caleb. You're right on time."

The three of us sat together, and Rachel reached out to hold both our hands before she prayed. "Lord, thank you for all your blessings. For food and friends, we bless your name. Keep us in the hollow of your hand as we face today's work and conversations. Amen."

"Amen," Caleb echoed.

Bacon, eggs, French toast, and blackberries made a filling breakfast to start the day. In the city, I'd had only toast and tea each morning. Rachel had changed that.

"Work on this farm requires lots of energy. Besides, you need to consider your baby's nutritional needs too, Lily," she had said the first morning I'd been with her. So, I was now eating healthier at breakfast.

"Caleb, tell me about your greenhouse," Rachel said

"Sure. Hydroponics is something I read about in college, and I wanted to try it out. I put special nutrients into the water to make sure the produce grows well and is nutritious. I like my vegetables fresh from the garden, and since we don't get them fresh during the winter months, I started growing my own back in February."

"But doesn't it take a lot of electricity to run a greenhouse?"

"Yes. That's why I built my own power plant."

"What? You have your own power plant?" I asked in surprise.

"A small one. You see, there's a cave up the hill behind my house with a year-round stream running inside. The stream never comes to the surface but flows swiftly inside the mountain. There's a place where it rushes down through a narrow cleft from a higher level to a lower one. I put a water-powered generator there and ran a line down to the greenhouse. I'm planning to hook the house up to the generator as well."

"What a good idea, Caleb." Rachel smiled across the table at him. "The vegetables you sent yesterday were delicious. Are you going to expand the greenhouse?"

"I'd like to, but we don't have enough workers in town for me to do that. Expansion will require someone working part of every day."

"I see. Well, I will ask God to send you someone to help."

"Thanks, Rachel."

I sat there silently, marveling at Caleb's inventive spirit. This man would go far.

After Rachel and I cleaned the kitchen, we joined Caleb by the creek where he was cutting back blackberry bushes, readying them for winter. Molly sat in the sun patiently watching him work, her tail thumping when she saw us.

"We'd best dig the rest of the carrots. There's a frost coming this week." Rachel handed me a pair of gloves. "Now, Lily, if you can't do this, you just sit back and watch."

"I'll be fine." I smiled, taking a trowel and heading for the far end of the carrot row.

We'd been working in the garden for a half hour before we heard Dominic's SUV pull up in the driveway. I kept working. The carrots needed to be pulled before frost.

Dominic came around the house and out to the garden carrying a bouquet of red roses. "Lily?"

I looked up and sighed. Might as well get this over. I pulled off my gloves and rose. Caleb, still working on the berry patch, straightened up, giving me a questioning look. I shook my head slightly and went forward to meet Dom.

"Hello, Dominic."

"May I speak with you alone, Lily?"

"There are some lawn chairs under the ash tree. Let's go over there."

"What's an ash tree?"

"That one." I pointed toward the tree covered with feathery, gold leaves which had already started to fall in the crisp, autumn air. Abundant red-orange berries, which the birds liked to eat, covered the branches. Leading the way, I indicated two chairs and sat in one which gave me a view of the garden.

Dominic pulled his chair closer to mine. "Lily, you are lovely. Like a rose." He handed me the bouquet of red roses. "You have always held my heart in your hands. Won't you please come back to Santa Rosa with me? Your mother has been frantic with worry."

I doubted that. The only thing she wanted was to see me married into the Jantzen family, so she could become part of high society there in wine country. But I said, "Dominic if she knows where I am, then she is no longer frantic. I'm safe. I'm happier here than I've been since Konnor died. I need to stay here."

Dominic sighed. "Lily, darling, I lost you once when you left for college. I don't want to lose you again."

His words didn't impress me. He'd always thought only of himself, never me. "I'm having Konnor's baby, Dominic. You will not love this baby. He isn't yours."

"Well, Lily ... No man is going to feel the same about another man's child." He shrugged. "It's not natural. Do you intend to remain single forever? What will you do when this baby is born? How will you support it?"

"I'm counting on God to help me succeed in art illustration work."

"*God?* When did you start believing that nonsense?"

"Belief in God is not nonsense, Dominic. He is real. I can trust him."

"Oh, Lily, Lily, Lily." He shook his head in exasperation. "There is no God. You know it. And art illustration work? Why, artists can rarely support themselves. You need to be practical."

"What do you consider practical?"

"Well, since you asked, I'd say the most practical thing would be for you to come back home to Santa Rosa, get a quick abortion, and marry me." He looked at me, a superior smile on his face.

"No."

"What do you mean, *no?*"

I looked him square in the eye. Fierce anger flooded my heart. "This baby is the only part of Konnor I have left. I am not going to kill him!"

"But Lily. It's just a blob of tissue—not a real baby yet."

"That's a lie! I've had an ultrasound. I have seen his face, his hands, his feet. He is most certainly *not a blob of tissue!*" I jumped up from my seat, furious at his suggestion. "Dominic, there is no way on earth I would ever, ever marry you! And there is no way I would ever harm my precious son!"

Dominic stood and took my shoulders. "Would you consider giving him up for adoption when he's born?"

"Never!" I jerked away from him.

Suddenly, Caleb was standing beside me.

"Lily tells me you want to take her back to California, and she does not want to go. Kindly take your hands off her."

Dominic's grip grew tighter.

"Ow! Let me go!"

Dominic's eyes burned fiercely into mine before he dropped his hands.

Caleb drew me away from Dominic. "She means what she said. You had better go now."

Dominic's face was red. He clenched his fist. "And who are *you?*"

I moved closer to Caleb, and he put his arm around my shoulders.

"I am Caleb, one of Lily's friends. There is a group of us who are helping her, and we will be here for her son too. She belongs here."

Molly came up and stood next to me, a growl rising in her throat.

"That's right, Dom, I have all the friends I need right here. I'm not going back with you. So, you need to leave."

"Okay, but I'll be back."

I stared into his face from the safety of Caleb's arm. "I am not changing my mind, Dominic. Not ever." I slid my arm around Caleb, drawing closer to him. "You have always tried to control and manipulate me. No more! I do not want to see you ever again. My decision is final."

"Lily, I love you and want to marry you. You can't support a baby in a tiny town like this!"

Caleb spoke up. "We will help Lily and her baby. She is part of our community now."

"You don't even know her! How can you care about her like I do?" Dominic's eyes flashed.

"God has brought Lily to us and has told us to help her. She belongs to Jesus now, and we are her family in Christ."

"*Christ?*" Dominic spat. "You believe in that myth too? You're all crazy!"

"Goodbye, Dom," I said firmly. "And please take your roses with you." I stepped forward, reached down, and picked up the roses, which had fallen to the ground. I handed them to Dominic, turned, and walked back to Caleb to stand in the shelter of his arm again.

Dominic pivoted on his heel and stormed away. A moment later, we heard his SUV rev loudly. He backed out of the driveway and tore off up the road. I stepped back and smiled up at Caleb. "Thank you."

His eyes held mine. "My pleasure, Lily."

I took a deep breath and went back to the garden, pulling on my gloves as I walked. I felt a little shaky because of the confrontation, but it was okay. I wasn't used to standing up to others with stronger wills. Facing Dominic had drained me. But because I had stood up to him, I doubted he'd return.

Kneeling again in the garden, I glanced at Rachel, who smiled as she worked. Wordlessly, we went back to the task we'd started. Caleb whistled as he cut the dead blackberry canes and tossed them onto the burn pile. Molly settled again on the lawn and put her chin on her paws. All was well. Very well indeed.

CHAPTER 9

Caleb stayed to help Rachel and me clear the garden and get everything ready for winter. With three of us working, the gardens and outbuildings were in great shape by late afternoon.

"Thank you for helping us, Caleb," Rachel said. "I hardly expected to accomplish this much in one day."

"Well, you needed a man to manage some of the heavy cutting and lifting. Besides, I didn't want to leave, just in case Dominic decided to have another go at Lily."

Rachel nodded. "I think your being here made a strong statement, Caleb. I doubt he'll be back, but one never knows. I appreciate your standing up for Lily. Now if you would like to come back for dinner, we'd love to have you."

"Sure. Let me go home and clean up first."

Later in the evening after Caleb had left, I called Dad, though he'd said I shouldn't call him.

"Lily? What's up?" he asked in alarm, knowing I wouldn't call unless it was necessary. "Are you okay?"

"Yes, Dad. I'm okay. But Dom showed up here today."

"What! How did he know ...?"

"Mom told him."

Dad was silent for a moment. "I cannot imagine how she knew. I've said nothing to her. What did Dom want?"

"He wants me to abort my baby and marry him!" I was still indignant.

Dad was furious. "I told him to leave you alone. If he comes back, maybe you should get a restraining order. That was harassment."

"Dad, I'm okay. Dominic came yesterday, and Rachel stayed in the room with me. He said he'd come back to talk with me again, this time alone, but I told him no. I told him I was pregnant, which seemed to shock him. Apparently, Mom didn't tell him. He came back anyway. By then, I'd asked Caleb to be here to stand with us just in case he returned. When Dominic did return, Caleb, Rachel, and I were getting the garden ready for winter. Dom tried to talk me into aborting my baby, and I got angry, Caleb came over and stood by me and told Dominic to leave me alone. Caleb said I had all the help I needed here with my new friends. It worked. I think. Anyway, Dom didn't come back."

"Sounds to me like you have some solid support there, honey."

"Oh, I do! Rachel and Caleb and my friends at church. Everyone has been so kind. I love it here. I don't want to leave. Ever."

"I'm happy to hear you are doing so well, Lily." He paused for a moment. "I'll come up there to see you soon after the baby's born. Just me. I'll leave Margaret here."

"I'd love to see you, Dad. You can show me where you grew up and tell me about when you were little."

I could hear the smile in his voice when he said, "I will be glad to show you around. Are there still cabins for rent along the lake?"

"Yes."

"Okay. I'll rent one when the snow is gone and come there for a week or so to see you and my new grandson."

"I'll look forward to it, Dad."

"Do you have a good winter coat?"

"I think so. I brought my coat from college."

"Good. You'll need it."

"Yes. I understand the weather gets quite cold here in the winter.

"Around January and early February, you'll probably have a few weeks of below zero weather, if the pattern holds."

"Oh. Well, I will probably be okay."

"Good. I'll see you in the spring."

"Love you, Dad."

"Love you too, Lily."

Will stayed in his study after his talk with Lily. Should he confront Margaret? No. She would just get emotional. He'd wait for her to bring up the subject. He hated those times when she lost her temper. Why couldn't she just stay calm and talk things through? He sighed.

Peace. That's all I want. Living with Margaret is like living on the edge of a volcano at times. Rachel was always a peacemaker. Very different from Margaret. Not as exciting, but over time, peace matters more than excitement to me. I hope Rachel will be okay with my visiting Lily and the baby. It's going to be rather emotional, but we'll get through it. We need to ... for Lily's sake. Lily says she still looks young. Good. I'm glad life has treated her well. I know she became involved with some church after I left. I'm beginning to understand what that means, since I've been going to the men's Bible study. I don't understand much, but the spiritual support has been great. I wish I'd reached out sooner.

During the night, snowflakes began to fall over Lake Thechihila, blanketing the hills, the gardens, and the houses. The summer tourists had left, and the town had settled into its winter phase. Once the lake froze over, ice fishermen would begin showing up, and the town would perk up again with the business they brought.

Friday, Caleb picked me up for Bible study, his truck equipped with studded tires to handle the ice and snow. When I opened the front door to join him outside, our breath sent puffs of steam into the freezing air.

Caleb put a hand under my arm. "Now don't slip, Lily. Walking on icy sidewalks and roads can be challenging."

Laughing up at him, I said, "How could I possibly slip with you holding me up?"

He laughed with me and helped me into his truck. A few minutes later, we pulled into an unfamiliar house along the lake.

"Who lives here?"

"Jesse and Gage just rented this place."

"Oh! Of course. Their wedding is in just a couple weeks."

"Yes. Their families are coming for the wedding and have rented a couple other houses for the week too. Most of the homeowners welcome winter renters, if only for a night or two. We don't get many in the winter, but there are always a few visitors. Ice fishermen often come for a few days at a time. Mostly they stay in the small cabins along the lake. But sometimes they come in groups and want larger places to stay. Occasionally, families come here for Christmas vacation." Caleb pointed across the lake. "Over on the other side is a good ski slope which draws people too. But it's too early for winter sports. Business will start picking up about a month from now."

Caleb came around to help me down from the truck. "Hold onto my shoulders, Lily."

I placed my hands on his shoulders, and he lifted me in his arms and carried me a few steps to the covered entryway before setting me down.

"I don't want you slipping," he said, his hand once again under my arm.

"Thank you, Caleb. I appreciate that." I looked into his eyes and smiled. I saw him catch his breath.

"Lily!" he whispered, his eyes wide, fixed on mine.

"Hey, there," Jesse called from the front door. "Come on in and see our future home."

"We're coming." I tore my gaze away from Caleb and turned toward the doorway, eager to see what she and Gage had done to the place.

A fire crackled merrily in the fireplace insert, warming the room nicely and filling the air with the homey smell of burning logs. Hot chocolate and cookies, juice, cake, and napkins covered an oak table in the open kitchen. Folding chairs, two fluffy couches, and a matching easy chair, a bouquet of chrysanthemums on a coffee table, and a nice, thick carpet made the room feel warm and cozy.

"We just threw a few things into the house this week," Jesse told them. "We're slowly moving all our things in. Everything should be ready in another week. Then we can concentrate on the wedding."

"Back home, people plan for *months* for weddings!"

Gage threw back his head and laughed. "Sometimes they do that here too. But other than ordering a cake and flowers, we aren't planning anything fancy. This is a country wedding. There will be a potluck after the ceremony."

"How nice." I nodded, appreciating the simplicity.

"Having a potluck reception takes off a lot of pressure," Jesse said.

"Where are you headed for your honeymoon?" Caleb said.

"All Gage will tell me is that I should bring summer clothes and a swimsuit."

Gage laughed, his eyes dancing.

Others began crowding into the room, and the volume increased with laughter and friendly conversations. Caleb leaned down and asked, "Would you like hot chocolate or apple juice?"

"Hot chocolate sounds perfect."

"Okay. Go find us a place to sit, and I'll bring some to you. Cake too?"

"Yes, please." I walked toward the couch and sat down.

A couple minutes later, Caleb placed a paper plate of cake in my hands and a cup of hot chocolate on the small stand to my right, returning to the kitchen for his own refreshments before joining me on the couch.

Sipping the hot chocolate, I listened to the pleasant flow of conversation around us, enjoying the warmth and hospitality.

Jesse came in and perched on the other side of Caleb. Leaning forward and looking at us both, she said, "I have a favor to ask you. Would you two would be willing to sing a song at our wedding?"

Suddenly, I was swept back into the deep waters of grief. Memories of singing with Konnor, my beloved. Memories of standing over his grave. Memories of the blood-stained marriage license. I felt the smile on my face stiffen as I struggled for calmness.

Caleb glanced quickly at me. He reached out and took my hand. "We'll talk it over and get back to you, Jess. Did you have a song in mind?"

"No, just a romantic wedding song you feel comfortable with."

"Okay. I'll let you know tomorrow."

"Great. Thanks!" Jesse smiled brightly and moved back toward her fiancé.

Gage's voice rose over the cacophony of voices. "Let's get started."

Caleb leaned toward me and whispered, "Are you okay, Lily?"

I leaned closer to him and whispered, "I'll be fine in a few minutes. I was just taken by surprise."

"All right."

After the Bible study as Caleb drove me back to Rachel's house, I sighed and looked out at the night. I needed to tell someone what had happened to Konnor.

"Caleb?"

"Yes?"

"When we get back to Rachel's, could you come inside for a little while? I want to tell you about Konnor."

"I'd be honored."

This time when he helped me down from the truck, I leaned against his chest, seeking comfort. His arms came around me, and he gently stroked my hair. "It's okay, Lily. It's okay."

I just stood there and cried.

"Let's get inside out of the cold, honey." With his arm around my waist, he led me to the front door and into the living room.

"Please sit on the couch and wait for me," I said softly, not wanting to wake Rachel.

Caleb removed his cowboy hat and heavy coat, putting them on the rack next to the door while I went into my room. I grabbed a box of tissues and the envelope with the marriage license in it. This wasn't going to be easy, but I had been carrying my grief alone for too long.

Returning to Caleb, I joined him on the couch. He put his arm around my shoulder and drew me close. I told him about Konnor and our band, about our singing together during college, about moving in together, and then about how Konnor had come to believe in Jesus. I told him about Konnor's wish to follow Jesus regarding our relationship, and about the day the police told me of Konnor's death and his last words for me.

Caleb listened as I described what happened. I appreciated his quietness.

"The police gave me Konnor's things from the car, because he told them to." I clutched the envelope tightly. "I didn't open this until after his funeral." I opened the envelope and drew out the blood-stained marriage license.

Caleb gasped. "Oh, Lily!" He took the license, which was shaking in my hands, looked at it for a long minute, then set it on the coffee table. Turning to face me, he held me close in his arms while I sobbed, his hand stroking my hair. "You have been through so much. I'm glad you told me."

Exhausted from crying after what seemed an eternity, I leaned back, my head on Caleb's shoulder. "The memory of our marriage license hit me hard all at once when Jesse asked us to sing at her wedding."

"Lily, I'll be fine singing alone. You don't need to do this."

"Thank you, Caleb. For everything." I relaxed in his arms. "You are so good to me."

"I'll always be here for you, Lily. Anytime you want to talk, I'll listen." He stayed for a few more minutes comforting me. Then he kissed my hair and stood up. "I'd better be going and let you get some sleep." The door opened, and he was gone into the night, speaking softly to me from the door as he left. "I'll see you tomorrow, Lily."

As Caleb drove up the hill to his house, he shook his head at the tragedy Lily had experienced.

She's all torn up. Yes, she's starting to heal, but her heart is still fragile. I hope my friendship will bring healing. Right now, she needs understanding. She needs to let her pain out. Lord, help me know how to be the kind of friend she needs.

CHAPTER 10

"Rachel?" We were sitting together at the table the next morning, finishing breakfast.

"Yes, dear?"

"We sometimes sing a song I don't understand. 'Blessed Be Your Name' is the title. Why should we bless the Lord when we've lost someone we love?"

Rachel set her cup down, thoughtfully considering my question. "That song is very meaningful to me. My favorite, in fact. The song comes from the Bible story in the Book of Job. Job was a godly man who was generous and kind with the great riches God had given him. One day the devil, Satan, told God, 'Job is only faithful to you because you have given him so much. If you let me take away his wealth, he will curse you!'

"God allowed Satan to take everything away from Job except his wife. But Job's response was, 'The Lord gave, and the Lord has taken away; *blessed be the name of the Lord*.'

"Eventually, God vindicated Job and restored his health, his fortune, and gave him and his wife ten more children.

"The song we sing was inspired by Job's words, by his unwavering trust in God."

"Oh!" I sat thinking about Rachel's words.

Rachel spoke after a long moment of silence. "Lily, years ago, I had a baby too."

"You did?" I was astonished.

"My parents were ashamed and wouldn't let me stay with them. My father said some bitter things to me, and my mother wouldn't speak to me at all. My father told me I was on my own and not to ask them for help.

"When the baby came, I loved her so much! She was the light of my life. But about two months after she was born, I was in a bad accident and unconscious for almost a month. The doctors didn't know whether I would ever recover. They told my parents I would need months of therapy learning to walk again, and I would need special care. They also said I would not be able to take care of a baby while recovering … if I did recover.

"When I finally woke up, I didn't remember much at first, but eventually my memory did return. I was frantic about my baby. My parents told me she was in emergency foster care, but I wouldn't be able to take care of her because of my injuries, and they were not willing to take care of both of us. They would help me recover, but they insisted the baby should be adopted into a family who could love her and give her a good life. They said if I really loved her, I would let her go.

"I didn't want to give her up, but I couldn't take care of her. So, I allowed my baby to be adopted by a good couple, for her sake. My heart has ached ever since for my child.

"When we sing *Blessed Be Your Name*, I give that pain to God and follow Job's example. You see, God has given me so many blessings. I met Jesus after giving up my little girl. He has been my strength and comfort. God has provided for all my needs. He has given me a town full of wonderful friends and a good church to support me spiritually. Yes, God has blessed me greatly. And though I wish I could have kept my child, I have trusted him to watch over her and keep her safe. And I know he has done that."

"You really do understand my feelings for my baby, don't you." My gaze had never left Rachel's face.

"Yes. When your father told me of your situation and asked if you could stay with me, I welcomed you with open arms. Having you here has been a such blessing." She wiped a tear from her cheek.

"Thank you for telling me." I took her hands in both of mine. Together, we sat in the kitchen, feeling a closeness I'd never experienced with my own mother. Rachel and I didn't need words. What warmth and acceptance she had shown me! Now I understood.

"Lily, you can stay with me as long as you like. My home is here for you and your little boy."

I squeezed her hands and smiled through tears of understanding. "Thank you, Rachel. I never want to leave this town. You and the people here have been so good to me."

Alone in my room that afternoon, I took my guitar from the closet. I hadn't played since Konnor's death, but now a strong need for music washed through my broken heart. I sat the case on my bed and lifted the guitar.

Rachel had driven into town to spend some time with an elderly widow and help her with some cleaning chores. The day was warmer than usual with sun shining in a clear blue sky. The snow outside sparkled in rainbow colors like glitter.

Sitting on the couch, I strummed for a few minutes, then picked out a tune. My fingers weren't as nimble as they had been. I needed to practice. The compositions of Bach were my favorite warm-up exercises. Quick, lively tunes soon emanated from the instrument beneath my fingers, and I lost myself in them for an hour. My fingertips were painful by then. I hadn't played the guitar for months, and the calluses had softened.

Needing to stretch, I set the guitar down by the couch and looked out the window. A familiar cowboy hat and winter jacket showed Caleb sitting with his back to the window on the bench outside. I opened the door.

"Caleb! Come inside before you freeze!"

Grinning at me, he stood and walked toward me. "It's warm out today. I heard you playing and didn't want to interrupt. You are incredible on that guitar!"

I felt my face growing warm. "Oh! Thank you. I–I didn't know you were listening." I held the door open. "Come in."

He entered, placed his hat and coat on the rack and pulled off his snow boots.

"Would you like something hot to drink?"

"Do you have coffee?"

"Sure. Come in and sit while I make some." I led the way toward the open kitchen and started the coffee brewing while Caleb pulled out a chair at the table.

"I didn't realize you played guitar. You are a professional! Would you play and sing something for me while the coffee brews?"

I brought the guitar into the kitchen, where he pulled out a chair for me. Pausing to think, my head bowed over the guitar. Quickly picking out the chords one note at a time, I began singing the old English ballad, "Scarborough Fair."

Caleb listened, his gaze meeting my eyes. When the last chords died away, he said softly, "God has given you a tremendous gift for music. Whenever you feel ready to sing in church, please let me know."

"I will. But right now, I think the coffee is ready." I went into the kitchen, feeling overwhelmed by emotion from playing the guitar after all this time, and especially that song. Remembering Konnor. Remembering how we used to sing "Scarborough Fair" on the SOU campus. Remembering his last words to me. And remembering Caleb's words just now ... Caleb, who had earned my trust and confidence.

Our eyes met and held as I handed him the coffee mug. In that moment, I knew God had brought Caleb into my life. I knew he realized it too. I wasn't ready to respond to him yet, as my heart was still grieving for Konnor. I could see Caleb's love for me written in his eyes.

"Lily, I'm not going to rush you," Caleb said, as though he could read my thoughts.

I caught my breath. "Okay. I–I want our relationship to go slowly—make sure this is going to last. I can't lose another love." I sat near him on the couch. At least, I was willing to acknowledge we had some sort of relationship.

Setting the coffee on a coaster, he reached out and took my hand in his, rubbing his thumb against my open palm. "I agree. Let's go slow. I was in love once too, but it didn't work out. My high school girlfriend, Michelle, left me for life in a big city. She was restless here in Lake Thechihila. It took me a long time to get over losing her. Let's build a solid, healthy relationship together, one step at a time. And Lily?"

"Yes?"

"I'm looking forward to being here for your son too."

Words could not express how much that touched my heart.

He pulled me close and held me near to his heart. "I will wait however long you need to be sure of me," he whispered.

Gage and Jesse's wedding was like no wedding I'd ever seen. There was nothing formal about it—just two hearts joined together in front of friends and family.

Caleb sang Leon Patillo's "Flesh of My Flesh." I listened, entranced by the melody and words he sang. The song echoed Adam's reaction when he first saw Eve, whom God had created from one of his ribs. Adam had said, "This one is bone from my bone, and flesh from my flesh."

When I'd first read those words in Genesis chapter two, I'd been impressed by how romantic they were. For some reason, I'd never thought of the Bible as being romantic. But the more I read, the more I treasured those beautiful words from history—preserved for us. Now Caleb's melodious voice celebrated the first romance, and I was caught up in the song.

The ceremony was followed by a potluck put together by the community. Afterward, they pushed the tables back and had some line dancing and a few waltzes in the fellowship room at church, using recorded music. We didn't have a local band, except for the worship team. Recorded music worked just as well.

Caleb claimed every waltz with me. I could see people glancing our way and smiling, acknowledging we were a couple. I was okay with that.

Between dances, Caleb and I greeted our friends. "We should say hello to Jesse's family," he said, nodding to a couple close to the bride and groom.

"Hi, Ben and Tara," Caleb reached out his hand to Ben, a tall man with wavy, dark hair and a nice smile. "Ben, Tara, this is Lily Mains. She's staying with Rachel. Lily, Tara is Jesse's sister and Ben is her husband."

"Glad to meet you." I nodded and smiled.

"They have a ranch called Ruby Hollow near Elliston." He turned to Tara. "Are your kids here?"

"Yes," Tara said, nodding to the group of children playing games on the other side of the room. "Marc and Holly are over there."

Ben pointed them out to us. "Marc is four and Holly's six. Liam came too. He's Tara and Jesse's younger brother. He graduates from high school this summer." He lifted his chin to indicate Liam, a tall, dark-haired young man talking with Gage.

"Lily, I talked with Ben about buying logs from him to build a small guest cabin on my ranch," Caleb said.

"I've cut and peeled enough for a house or two," Ben said. "I've dried them in my kiln and stored them. Where do you plan to build?"

"In the pasture down by the road, near Rachel's place. I'd like to keep it on ground that's fairly level. I've already cleared the land and brought electricity to the site, excavated a septic tank, and sunk a well."

Ben nodded. "Shouldn't take long to put up the house, according to the plan you sent me. Do you want me to be here to help?"

"If you could, I'd appreciate it. You're more experienced than I am with log homes."

"Okay. I'll be there. Are you thinking of raising the house in June?"

"Yes."

The crowd shifted again when another dance was announced, and we moved into it together.

Later that evening, after the reception was over and we'd helped clean up, Caleb walked me home in the moonlight, past snowdrifts lining the plowed road.

"What's this about building another log house?" I asked.

"A small one I plan to rent to visitors. There are several cabins by the lake, but none of them are log. I can provide a unique vacation home for visitors, one that will provide a Montana atmosphere, and bring in a nice income too."

"Hm. I like that idea. Do you plan to advertise outside Montana?"

"Yes. I'm going to hire Ben to help set up a website when the cabin is ready. He's in advertising, so he'll know what to do. I'm not well-versed in that sort of thing. Ranching alone doesn't bring in enough income for a family these days. Rental property will help."

We walked in companionable silence, holding hands as we approached Rachel's door.

The baby suddenly kicked. "Oh!" I gasped, putting my other hand over the place he'd kicked.

"What is it?" Caleb asked.

"The baby is moving around, and his little foot just kicked me," I said, smiling.

Caleb laughed. "When is he due?"

"February 19 or about."

"Have you picked out a name?"

"Yes."

"What did you choose?"

"I'm not telling."

Caleb's throaty laugh made me smile. I loved that laugh.

"Let's get you inside." Caleb opened the door for me. "Good night, Lily." He leaned down to speak to my baby. "Good night, little guy."

"Lily?" Rachel said as we sat at the breakfast table the next morning.

"Yes?"

"I've noticed your coat is a little tight now. Would you like to use one of mine? I have one from years ago that would probably fit well."

"Do you? That would be nice. I am feeling a little squished in this one."

Rachel brought me a lovely blue coat with white fur around the hood.

"I wore this coat many years ago when I was expecting my own baby. Since we are about the same size, I thought it might fit you too."

"How beautiful!" I stood and reached for the coat, which fit perfectly, reaching to my knees. "Thank you, Rachel," I said, giving her a hug. "You are so good to me!"

She smiled, a little teary-eyed. "You are most welcome, Lily. I'm glad I could help."

Later, as I stood in my bedroom looking into the mirror, I marveled at how beautiful the coat was, and wondered how Rachel had felt when she had worn it. I wondered what had happened to her precious baby. She must have been devastated to have to give up her baby. Her pain from that loss showed in her eyes.

God in heaven, please comfort Rachel. Let me be a blessing to her. She is dear to my heart.

CHAPTER 11

Late autumn sunlight filtered through the window in my art room as I scanned my illustrations and sent them via Dropbox to an art agent. I'd talked with her on the phone, and she'd asked to see one or two paper copies of my work as well. It was a long shot, but her agency sounded like it was a good fit for me.

Since the weather was good, I decided to walk down the winding road into town to mail the samples at the small post office in the back of the general store. Snow covered the ground, but the road had been plowed, and the sun had dried the snow from the pavement. The sky was a heavenly blue. The air was scented with the faint aroma of wood smoke. A perfect day.

I heard clicking on the pavement behind me and turned. Molly, Caleb's golden retriever, galloped up to me.

"Hi, Molly," I said, patting her head and rubbing her around the ears. "What are you doing here without your master?"

The dog barked.

Caleb rounded the corner behind me and chuckled. "Her master is right here."

"Oh! Hi, Caleb. I'm walking into town to mail something. Are you headed that way too?"

"Yes. I need a few things at the store. May I join you?"

"Of course." I smiled up into his ruggedly handsome face.

"Let me guess—you're sending art samples somewhere. Right?"

"How clever of you. Yes. I found an agent who's interested. She asked for some samples, so I made some copies to send."

Caleb nodded his approval. "Good. I'm glad to see you pursuing this. I'm expecting great things of you."

"Thank you. I appreciate your vote of confidence." My heart warmed to his praise.

"Well, you're very good at art." He shrugged. "I like the way your characters show warmth. They're appealing. Let me know what comes of this."

"Okay. I painted some small pictures of Rachel's ash tree covered with berries—and one or two of just the leaves and berries. I used old barnwood, so the pictures would be different. Rachel said there's a craft sale soon. I'm going to see if I can sell them."

"We'll have some out-of-town people coming to the sale. It wouldn't surprise me a bit if you sell them all. That sort of thing is popular."

We walked along in a comfortable silence for a few minutes, Molly walking ahead.

"Have you thought of publishing on Amazon?"

"Yes, but it would take money to advertise, money I don't have yet. Maybe someday I will try it. But for now, I just need to earn a living, and illustrating books will bring in a fair amount of money. Not a lot at first, but if I can get established in the field, I hope the work will be enough to support me and my baby."

Caleb nodded. "I don't know much about illustration work, but I do know children's books are always in demand—a healthy market. My sisters Julie and Jan are always buying picture books for their kids."

"Yes, children's books are always popular, but there's a lot of competition."

"Of course. But always remember the Lord will open the doors he wants you to enter. If he wants you to do art illustrations, he will make a way as long as you keep trying."

"Thank you for telling me, Caleb. I never thought of it that way before. I'm just learning how God works. The idea of God being intimately involved in my life is new to me. Thank you for telling me." I smiled up at him and saw the love written on his face.

Maybe someday, I would be ready to think about love again. But for now, I missed Konnor too much. Good friendship was all I could offer Caleb.

The holidays descended on our small town. Thanksgiving at Rachel's saw ten people sitting around the table—some were from church, some were friends from town who had no family nearby.

During the preceding week, Rachel and I had baked and frozen cookies, then pulled them out of the freezer Thanksgiving morning. The night before, we had baked four fruit pies—two apple and two pumpkin. We had planned and created hors d'oeuvres to go with the meal, and I confess I couldn't resist snacking on them as we worked. Rachel laughed and made more. On Thanksgiving Day, she slow-baked a large turkey, filling the house with its delicious aroma.

Late that afternoon, Caleb arrived first, followed closely by J. J., Colleen, and Nate Smith, whose families lived far away. Nate worked in Fish and Game with Gage, taking the shifts and days Gage didn't work. Manuel Gonzales and his wife, Rosa, who owned and operated the local Mexican restaurant, plus their children, Diego, Julisa, and Carlos completed our guest list. A merry group.

As the food circulated around the table, Rachel said, "Manuel, please share with my other friends about why you immigrated to the United States."

Manuel nodded. "Okay." He looked around at us and began, "You are most fortunate to live here. Our home was in Nuevo Victorio. All towns where we live are controlled by cartels. But an enemy cartel was moving in, trying to take over. Where we live in Mexico, if a man does not join a cartel, his life is in danger. He is considered disloyal, and the cartel of his town do not protect him. I do not want to join, because I am *un Cristiano*. I am seen as disloyal by some. But there are other Cristianos who do not join too. We risk much for our faith in Jesus.

"One day when we are working in our *iglesia*—our church—we hear machine gun fire and explosions very loud. We are working outside, but when that happen, we go inside where it was safe. Adobe walls are thick. They stop bullets.

"The battle go on all day. We know it is a cartel battle, like many others. The big booms are grenades they launch. Then more *federales* come in and began hunting down cartel in our town. We stay in the church until the battle is over, and the federales leave. You must understand, many federales belong to the cartels. Four federales are killed that day—one of them is from enemy cartel *familia*—and three are hurt. Seven members of cartels die, including Miguel, Rosa's brother.

"That evening, Rosa and I talk it over and decide to immigrate to the United States."

"Do battles like that happen a lot?" Caleb asked.

"Yes. Our town was at war with the enemy cartel. Rosa and I travel north to Juarez, where we stay with *mi familia* while we apply to come here. It take two years, but we are accepted."

Rosa spoke softly, "Now we have our own restaurant, *La Cocina del Lago!* It means the Kitchen of the Lake. It is wonderful what we can do here in America. And it is safe for our children."

"Do you ever visit your family in Mexico?" J. J. asked.

Manuel shook his head sadly. "No. The cost is too much. And it is not safe. But we have email with them."

"Well, we're glad you're here," Rachel said. "Your restaurant is the best one I've visited, even in the city."

Manuel's teeth flashed in a wide smile. "Thank you, Senorita Rachel!"

"I certainly enjoy your food too," Caleb said, and we all agreed. I'd been to La Cocina del Lago once with Rachel. The food was excellent.

Sitting next to Rosa, I asked her about her town in Mexico, Nuevo Victorio. She smiled shyly but opened up and told us a little about her life in Mexico.

"My town, it is warm and sunny in summer. There are flowers in *las ventanas*—the windows—and we have gardens with flowers. This I remember most when thinking of Nuevo Victorio. It is always in sunshine in my heart. But winter is cold in the mountains. We must wear warm clothes when there is snow. All cost lots of money. But there are always tortillas and *frijoles*—beans. In summer, we have garden. We grow jalapeños, tomatoes, beans and *maiz*—that is corn.

"I meet Manuel when we visit Juarez, where my grandfather and grandmother live. He is in church when we go. He is older than me. Five years. He sing beautiful! He see me and talk to me many times. One day, when we visit Juarez, he say he love me. He ask if I love him too. I say yes." Rosa's eyes shown and her face lit up. "We marry when I am seventeen years. We go to Nuevo Victorio to live with mi familia while I have babies. It is easier to have Mama close when babies are small."

Rosa's eyes held a sad, far-away look, as though she saw a life she had loved and lost.

"My father, he make the pottery, and my mother, she weave the ponchos. My brother Raul own shop in town where they sell the pottery and the ponchos they make. Manuel work in store too. But it is difficult to earn enough for living in such a small town, especially when always there is danger from the cartels.

"Then my brother Miguel is shot in the big battle. One does not know who they can trust among the federales. The cartels have people in the federales."

J. J.'s eyebrows rose. "Some of the federales in the battle were members of the cartels?"

"Yes. Many federales are also part of cartels. One who die that day was of enemy cartel family. He is come to town to arrest the leader of our town's cartel. This cause the battle where Miguel is killed. The enemy always kill all the brothers and fathers of our men who die in battle so there can be no *vengaza*—how you say? Vengeance? My father and brother Raul go quickly to other place to hide after the battle. That is when we decide to move here. It is not safe for our children in Mexico. Diego is four and Julisa is three then. Carlos is born after we move to United States. To protect our children, we leave Mexico."

I shook my head. "I am sorry for your loss, Rosa. It is hard to lose someone you love."

Rosa touched my arm. "Yes, you understand. I know this. *Gracias, mi amiga.*"

My parents had taken me to Acapulco and Cancun when I was a child, but they were nothing like the town where Rosa and Manuel had once lived.

Rachel started a question around the table, asking everyone to tell a story of how God had blessed them in the past year. "Diego, let's start with you. What has God done for you this year?"

Diego, who was now nearly nine years old, answered in a shy voice. "God helped me learn to speak English in the school here. I am happy for this."

"Julisa, what has God done for you this year?"

Julisa, who was seven years old and not at all shy, said, "I am happy God has given me so many friends in this town. They have helped me learn to speak English, and they do not let others make fun of me." She lifted her chin.

"How about you, Carlos?" Rachel asked, smiling at the four-year-old sitting next to Caleb.

"I'm happy for Jesus. He lives in my heart now, 'cause I axed him to." He looked down at his shirt, patted it, and shook his head. "I don't know how he fits in there."

We all laughed.

"Good job, Carlos!" Caleb said, rubbing the top of his head.

Rachel spoke. "Okay, J. J., your turn now."

J. J., who managed the marina with its bait shop by the lake, said, "Last June, I was working on the docks alone loading my boat, when I slipped and hit my head on the edge of the dock and fell into the lake. I was stunned and couldn't move. I thought I would drown. I prayed God would send someone to help me. I was about to give up when a boat pulled alongside, and a man dove into the water. He hauled me to the surface and towed me to the shore. He saved my life. He was a fisherman I'd never met before, and I haven't seen him since. He never even told me his name. I know God sent him."

Colleen, sitting next to J. J., said, "There is a girl in my class at school who was struggling with her work. One day, I noticed she kept sitting closer and closer to the whiteboard. I contacted her parents and asked them to take her to an eye doctor, but they didn't have the money for it. I couldn't say anything about the need for fear of embarrassing the parents, and I didn't have money myself after buying the supplies for my classroom. I asked God to help. He did. Someone gave a gift to the school for student needs, and the school provided the money for the child's eye exam. She needed glasses. The money paid for those too. Now, the girl is doing much better in school. I am thankful for God's blessing in this."

Nate shared an incident. "One day in September, I saw smoke up on the mountains across the lake. It was nearing the end of my shift, so I left a note for Gage, and I hiked up there to check if it was a wildfire or someone camping. I'd almost reached the fire when I saw dust rising from a fresh slide of earth and rocks across the trail, and a man buried up to his chest in the debris. His hands were bloody from trying to dig his way out. He shouted that his son was with him and told me to find him first. He pointed where I should look. I was sure the son was lost, for I couldn't see anything showing across the slide. But I began searching as best I could, praying the whole time.

"I saw some tree branches caught in the dirt, and suddenly, the branches moved. I rushed over there, pulled on my gloves, and started digging with my hands as fast as I could. The boy had been sheltered by a small tree and had been able to breathe, but he was completely buried, though the tree opened a way for air to get to him. I was able to get him out, then helped his dad. The boy was miraculously uninjured.

"I radioed the sheriff to send a helicopter to airlift the dad out. The dad had a broken leg, which I splinted while we waited. I walked up the hill to the camp and put the fire out before leaving with the son, whom I took to the hospital to be with his dad. I'm sure the Lord protected the boy and his father. The Lord performed two miracles—the man and boy lived through that landslide, and I saw their campfire smoke at the right time."

Caleb, who sat between Rachel and me, smiled to himself and then said, "I'm grateful for how the Lord has provided all I need this year, in ways I could never have expected."

Everyone there understood and smiled at the two of us.

My face grew warm, and I reached my hand out to Caleb's under the table. Without looking at me, he took my hand in his and gave it a little squeeze.

"Your turn, Lily," Rachel said, her eyes twinkling.

I always struggle when speaking in a group, but with Caleb holding my hand, I felt braver. "As you all know, I lost my fiancé, Konnor, in June. He had just discovered Jesus before he died, and he told me he would see me again if I believed. When I first came to Lake Thechihila,

I was searching for God. Here among you, I have learned much about him and have come to believe in Jesus too. This is my greatest blessing. Even though I lost Konnor, he pointed me to Jesus and showed me the way. Rachel has taught me more, as you have as well." I looked around the table at my new friends. "I–I have learned about the love of Jesus through listening to you and watching you love one another. Thank you all for your love and support."

Rachel nodded and smiled. Looking around at us, she said, "My greatest blessing this year has been Lily. Having her here in my home fills me with joy."

Teary-eyed, I smiled at Rachel. Caleb put his arm around my shoulders and gave me a quick squeeze. "Me too."

I didn't know how I'd manage to eat dessert after that meal, but a small slice of pumpkin pie topped with a dollop of whipped cream went down smoothly.

"Ladies, that was a delicious meal. Thank you," Caleb said. "I'm stuffed to the gills."

His words echoed around the table.

"Let me help you in the kitchen," Rosa said, standing and reaching for empty plates.

"I'll help too." Manuel gathered more plates.

Everyone pitched in, clearing the table in record time. With Manuel and Rosa helping Rachel, there was no more room in the kitchen. Rachel waved the rest of us out. "There are games on the side table for those who want to play."

"I need to walk off this meal," Caleb said. "Lily, do you feel like walking with me?"

"Sure. Let me get my coat." I snuggled into the warmth of Rachel's blue coat as we walked outside into the snowy world.

"That coat looks great on you. It matches your eyes," Caleb said approvingly.

"Rachel gave it to me. She said she wore this many years ago." I didn't share Rachel's secret, which she had shared in confidence.

Caleb reached out his gloved hand and took mine. "Are you up for a walk to the lake?"

"Yes. It looks like a fairyland with the snow covering everything. The trees and fences look lacey."

"The lake will soon be frozen enough to attract ice fishermen. They take tents and camp stoves out on the lake and drill holes in the ice. Once in a while, someone drives a truck onto the lake when it's not frozen well, and the truck goes through the ice, and they have to haul it out."

"Oh, my. Sounds dangerous."

"Always. But the driver usually gets out in time. A person can freeze in that water within minutes."

"I can imagine."

When we reached the lakeshore, we turned and walked along a well-trod pathway beneath snow-covered cottonwood trees, their bare limbs reaching upward to the sky. Everything was white and gray, except for the blue sky overhead, where the setting sun turned a few clouds pink.

"It's beautiful!" I exclaimed. "In Santa Rosa, the sunsets were never like this. They were gold and orange."

"Tell me about your family, Lily."

"Well, my dad is kind of quiet. He's tall, like you. He doesn't say a lot, but when he does, it's worth hearing. I've always thought he was wise. And he's kind. I love him very much. He has always protected me. He's the one who told me to come here to Rachel. You see, he grew up here at Lake Thechihila, and he and Rachel were high school sweethearts from what I have gathered.

"When he left for college, he met my mom. She's beautiful and sophisticated. I can see why he would have been drawn to her, but I don't think they've been happy together for a long time now. Dad escapes into his study after dinner and rarely spends time with her. I–I can't say I blame him. She's very demanding."

"I see." Caleb waited for me to continue.

"She didn't want me to keep my baby. She demanded I have an abortion. But I wouldn't do such a thing. Not ever! This baby is all I have left of Konnor. She ordered me to marry Dominic. When I said no, she—she slapped me."

Caleb stopped. His eyes widened. "She did?"

"Yes. She's used to getting her own way, and I've never been able to stand up to her. When she slapped me, Dad came in and told her to stop. She stormed out. I told Dad I didn't want to lose my baby, and I didn't know how to resist Mom. So, he sent me here to Rachel's place. I've been happy here, and Rachel wants me to stay. She is such a comfort, and I would love to stay with her as long as she will have me."

Caleb put his arms around me and held me close. "You have gone through such deep pain, Lily. I'm glad you are here now. Maybe Rachel's love ... and mine ... can bring healing to your heart."

I nodded against his jacket. "I'm glad for your love, Caleb. I'm healing more each day. Don't give up on me, please."

"I won't, my love. I won't."

CHAPTER 12

The day after Thanksgiving, everyone in town began putting up Christmas decorations. Streetlights along the lake were festooned with lights and tinsel. Children built snow creatures in their front yards, competing with each other in originality. One house had an entire snow family in front, all wearing scarves and hats, plus a snow dog. Another home displayed a giant teddy bear with a bow around his neck. In front of the marina, J. J. built a snow whale.

Rachel and I walked up and down the street before we shopped, admiring all the activity and the resulting art. Shouts, greetings, and laughter filled the air. I sighed with contentment. This would be *my* town. *My* home. My son would grow up here among these people. What a different world from the one I'd left.

We headed into the small general store. An old man leaned against the counter, talking loudly to the cashier. "And what I always say is, swat one fly, and ten will come to his funeral. What's the point, I say."

"You have something there, Harry," the cashier said. "But you stock up on this fly ribbon I'm ordering, and you'll catch 'em all, even the ones coming to the funeral."

"Well, you order me some of that there fly ribbon early, and then, you call me. Everybody will be wanting it come July, and I don't want to miss out."

Two young girls bundled up in coats and scarves were examining the toy exhibit at the window.

"'Tis the season to be shopping, fa-la-la-la-laaaa, la-la-la-laaaa," one girl sang.

The other girl giggled and picked up a doll.

I smiled and exchanged glances with Rachel, who laughed. Shopping in Lake Thechihila's general store was always amusing.

"We need to go Christmas shopping over in Bozeman soon," Rachel said later as we put our groceries into the car. "When would you like to go?"

"Sometime this week would be good," I said hesitantly, knowing the work required at home with all the animals.

"Okay. I'll ask Caleb to help with milking the cow. He's good at pitching in when needed."

Two days later, we drove into Bozeman to shop. At the mall, we split up and went our separate ways, planning to meet in an hour in the food court. Choosing gifts was always difficult for me, and never more so than now. I didn't know what to get for Rachel. Dad and Mom were easy. Mom always preferred fancy sweets for Christmas, and Dad liked books. I found one for him about Montana history and bought Mom a box of decorated taffy. In the kitchen store, I found a china teapot with roses painted on the side, plus two matching cups. Remembering Rachel's chipped teapot, I chose this new one for her, plus the matching cups.

But what would Caleb like? From store to store I wandered, examining the gifts on display. Finally, I saw a small plaque, which said what I was beginning to feel. Should I be so bold? I hesitated a moment and then lifted it off the shelf. Yes. This was the gift. I took it to the counter where the clerk boxed and wrapped it for me.

My phone vibrated. "Lily, did you get everything you wanted?"

"Yes, Rachel. I'm just finishing now."

"Good. I'm done too. Meet me at the food court."

"Okay." I was very ready for lunch.

Munching on pizza, we talked about some of the things we'd found for Christmas.

"We should look at some of the baby clothes and equipment too, if you're feeling up to it," Rachel suggested.

"Yes, I'd like to do that today, if we have time. Dad sent some money so I could buy some things for the baby."

After lunch, we prowled through the baby sections of local stores. I found several newborn outfits, a large box of disposable diapers, and a few soft blankets. I noticed a bassinet and gravitated toward it.

"You know," Rachel said in a subdued voice. "I saved my baby's bassinet. It's in the attic at home if you want to use it."

I looked up. "Oh, that would be lovely, Rachel. Thank you!"

"I'm glad you can use it, though you'll need a crib as he gets bigger."

"Yes. But the bassinet will do for the first couple months. And it will be extra special because your baby slept there."

Rachel's arm came around my shoulder. "I'm glad you can use it, my dear."

Our shopping done, we headed home, arriving well after dark. Caleb had put the milk into the refrigerator.

Exhausted, we headed for bed, content with our shopping expedition.

As I lay there in the moonlight, I thought of my last Christmas with Konnor. In my dreams, he was still with me. Lately, though, I'd been unable to reach him. He stood at a distance and smiled. Then Caleb's voice would call to me, drawing me away. Letting go of Konnor and turning toward Caleb was not easy. I often awoke in tears during the night. But this night was different. In my dreams, Caleb held me close to his heart, and my sorrow turned into peace.

But was the feeling of safety enough upon which to build a relationship? I had my doubts. I must be fair to Caleb.

"Hi, Dad." It was Wednesday—time for his weekly call.

"Hi, honey. How's it going?"

"Very well. I'm happy and have some great friends here."

"And Caleb?"

"Well ... I like him a lot. He's become a very good friend."

"Uh-huh."

I could hear the smile in his voice.

"Dad, Caleb is interested in me, and I like him a lot. He makes me feel safe. But is that enough to build a marriage on?"

"Do you love him?"

"I don't know! Konnor is still very much a part of me. But ..."

"Lily, you can't think just about feelings. Your son is going to need a father. Do you think Caleb would be a good father?"

"Oh, yes! He's great with kids, and he's calm and steady. You'd like him, Dad."

"Well then, give him a chance, honey."

"I–I'm trying to. I just have a hard time letting Konnor's memory go."

"You don't need to let Konnor's memory go, Lily. You just have to keep making new memories with Caleb and not live in the past. You need to ask yourself what Konnor would have wanted for you and your—his—baby."

I sighed. "I think he would want me to get married and be happy. It's just that I still miss him."

"I know. His memory will never fade away, but you'll miss him with less ache as the years pass."

"I'm working through this, Dad. I'm praying about it. God will show me what to do."

"Yes, he will."

"You are such a comfort, Dad."

Will grabbed his jacket and headed out for a walk in the crisp, damp air of Santa Rosa.

Lily has found someone who loves her. Caleb. He sounds like a good man, from all the things she's said about him. But Margaret will never approve. I just won't tell her. She'll find out once Lily makes up her mind.

I wish I could be there with Lily. There must be a fair amount of snow at Lake Thechihila by now, and driving would be complicated since I don't have snow tires. But I can't get away to visit right now.

I wonder how Rachel feels about Caleb. Well, I'll just have to trust she's keeping a close watch on this growing romance. She has a good head on her shoulders. She won't let our girl make a mistake.

"Lily, would you like to sing a Christmas song next week during church?" Caleb had stopped by for a minute on Monday evening.

"What did you have in mind?"

"Well, after listening to you sing and play your guitar, and seeing how you like old English ballads, I thought you might like to sing 'What Child Is This?'"

"I'm not familiar with it. How does it go?"

"The tune is the same as 'Greensleeves,' which you sang to me once."

"I remember. That's a lovely tune."

"Here are the words," Caleb opened a book of Christmas songs to the right page.

"What Child is this who laid to rest on Mary's lap is sleeping ..." I read through the rest of the words silently. "Oh, Caleb ... it's beautiful! Yes, I'll sing it."

"Good." Caleb looked satisfied. "It's time others hear you sing on your own—without the team. Can you still manage the guitar?"

I laughed and looked down at my baby bump. "Yes, I think so. But in another month, I may not be able to hold a guitar comfortably."

"This is good timing."

"Yes."

The following Sunday, I stood before the church and sang the lovely song, identifying with Mary as she looked over her newborn son. Soon, I would have a son too. Plucking the strings of the guitar, singing the words about the Christ child sleeping on his mother's lap, greeted by angels and shepherds carried me away to ancient days. My own child, moving inside my body, made it all seem very real to me.

As verse followed verse, I lost myself in the pictures the song painted in my mind, pictures of that night so long ago, the night our Savior was born, and the adulation he received from angels, shepherds, and later from wisemen.

As the last note faded away, I looked up to see my friends' faces. They too had felt the scene painted by the lovely song.

Caleb led in prayer, praising God for the gift of Jesus. Then he led us in singing a cappella the chorus of the old hymn "O Come, All Ye Faithful." The sounds of voices raised in harmony echoed and settled into silence. I felt the presence of the Holy Spirit among us in that moment in a unity I'd never experienced with others.

Christmas day dawned amid snowflakes drifting gently to earth. Standing at my bedroom window, I reveled in the peaceful scene spread out before me. The town below lay nestled in snowbanks next to the lake, reminding me of a snow globe.

Delicious smells came from the kitchen. Rachel was preparing breakfast.

Pulling on my warmest sweater and slacks, and shoving my feet into wooly slippers, I ran a brush through my hair and went to the kitchen to help.

"Merry Christmas, Lily. Did you sleep well?"

"Merry Christmas. Yes, very well. I dreamed of Christmas cookies and hot apple cider." I gave her a quick hug and kissed her cheek.

Rachel laughed. "Maybe we can do something about that later today. I've invited the young people to stop by later for a snack. I have the sugar cookie dough ready in the fridge. We can get started after we've fed the chickens and gathered the eggs."

"You spoil us all, Rachel, but don't ever stop! We all love you. Especially me."

Rachel smiled, her face aglow. "And I love you right back, honey. This is going to be a wonderful, happy Christmas."

After breakfast, Rachel and I exchanged presents.

"How lovely!" she said as she lifted the china teapot from its box and held it up. "Oh, I will enjoy using this. I have never had such a nice teapot before. Now, open your present, my dear."

I carefully removed the red and white striped paper and matching ribbon which enclosed the box. Lifting the lid, I found a beautiful, soft pink sweater. It was a perfect fit. At the back of the neck, a label read, "Made by Rachel."

"Rachel! This is incredible! You made this for me?"

She laughed. "Yes. But I had to do it at night in my room so you wouldn't see it."

We hugged each other, pleased to share this special Christmas moment.

"Here's a present for you from my dad." I pulled the present from under the tree where I'd placed it the night before.

Rachel's cheeks glowed as she reached for it. Opening the card attached to the gift, she smiled at the few words Dad had written, and set it aside. She carefully removed the bow and wrapping.

"Oh! It's an original copy of my favorite book from high school." She lifted a copy of L. M. Montgomery's *Rilla of Ingleside,* caressing the cover with wonder. "Imagine him remembering this!"

I leaned over to look at it. "I read that book when I was in high school too, but it was a paperback edition. It's a good story." I was pleased Dad had chosen such a thoughtful gift for Rachel.

His present to me was a blue and white beret with a blue tassel on top.

"It will look lovely with that blue coat." Rachel nodded approval.

Satisfied with our gifts, we went back into the kitchen to enjoy some hot chocolate. The scent of the Christmas tree, the aroma of warm sugar cookies fresh from the oven that morning, and the smell of wood burning in the stove gave the room a pleasant, homey atmosphere.

Later in the day, the young people from church came by. Cookies, steaming spiced apple cider, cheese and crackers lined the kitchen counter.

Misty was beaming. "I'm expecting another baby come July."

"How fun! Have you told Elijah yet?"

"Yes. I told him Baby is in my tummy, and he looked puzzled. He said, 'How can a baby be in your tummy?' I told him that's where babies grow. He doesn't understand now, but he will in a few months when the baby is bigger."

"I'm happy for you, Misty." I smiled, pleased to know there would be another baby for mine to grow up with.

"Congratulations, Misty. It will be nice to have new babies in the church nursery," Rachel said. "I heard Rosa is having another baby too. Hers is due in June."

"What's this?" Caleb said, joining our conversation. "Misty, Joe tells me you're expecting?"

The others crowded around offering congratulations, laughing, and slapping Joe on the back.

Caleb leaned down. "I have something for you, Lily. Can you come up to my place after this?"

"Okay. I have something for you too."

Later, as the crowd began dispersing, I slipped into my room, pulled on my coat and new beret, and slipped my gift for Caleb into one of the big pockets.

"I'm going up to Caleb's house for a little bit," I told Rachel before joining him at the back door.

"See you later, honey."

Once outside, Caleb took my hand in his and led me up the well-worn pathway to his house. The snow was slick in places. When I slipped, he steadied me and put his arm around my waist as we climbed the hill.

We paused on the deck to look out over the valley, a practice I was coming to love. At this distance, the town lights twinkled.

"Caleb, I love this view."

"Me too."

We stood close together, my head resting against his shoulder. "It's like a fairy land below. I'm glad Dad sent me here."

"Yes. Having you here is a gift, Lily."

"Speaking of gifts ..."

Caleb chuckled and opened the front door, ushering me inside.

I took off my coat in the warm living room and hung it on a peg by the door. I pulled off my boots, as Caleb did, and pulled my gift from my coat pocket.

I sat on the couch, placing my gift for Caleb on the seat next to me.

Caleb picked up one of the presents from under the Christmas tree. "Mom and Dad and the girls sent me some gifts too."

"You haven't opened them yet."

"No. I thought you might like to see what they sent. Besides, opening gifts alone is no fun." He handed me a shoebox-shaped gift. "I hope you will like this."

Carefully, I removed the paper and ribbons. Inside the box was a lovely pair of deer skin and lambswool boot moccasins that laced up the front. "They are beautiful! Thank you." I slid my feet into the wooly moccasins, and Caleb knelt before me to lace them up. "These look very Montanan. I love them!"

Caleb grinned up at me, then joined me on the couch. "Those should keep your feet nice and warm."

"I'm sure they will." I held my feet out in front of me, admiring their design. "Now it's your turn." I handed him the package I'd brought.

Caleb unwrapped and looked at the plaque I'd chosen. In a choked voice, he read, "My friend, my heart, my home."

I leaned my head against his shoulder. "You are that to me, Caleb. You have been so good to me! I know I'm safe when I'm with you."

His arms engulfed me as he gently leaned over and placed a lingering kiss on my lips. When he started to move away, I reached up and drew him back, desire sweeping over me. "Caleb!" I breathed.

His lips met mine again, this time with passion.

I melted into his arms for a long moment, then drew back, breathless and a little frightened of my feelings.

Caleb laughed softly in his deep, throaty laugh. "I love you, Lily."

I sat back, holding onto his hand tightly, his other arm around my shoulders. "Caleb, I–I'm sure of this much—you are dear to my heart. I just want to be sure I can be the woman you need. The past has not yet faded entirely from my heart. I'm still grieving over Konnor, and I need to be fair to you. I–I want your touch! I am powerfully drawn to you, so much that … Caleb, please help me keep our love pure. I want to honor Jesus with my life."

"Yes, Lily. I will guard this love we have and keep it pure," he whispered against my hair.

The fire crackled in the fireplace as we sat close together in silence. Finally, Caleb sighed. "I guess I'd better open those other gifts too."

"Yes."

CHAPTER 13

Rachel brought her bassinet wrapped in plastic from the attic the next day. Inside the bassinet were sheets for the tiny mattress, also wrapped in plastic, and yellowed with age.

"I will have to make new sheets for the mattress, but that shouldn't take long," Rachel said as she unwrapped the bassinet. "This should work well until your baby starts to roll over. Then we'd better have a crib ready. But we can find a crib later."

"Thank you, Rachel." My hands touched the bassinet she had used for her own baby once. "I feel you are treating me far too generously, but I am grateful for all you are doing for me."

Rachel hugged me. "It is a pleasure to see you using what I have saved, honey."

"I'm not sure of all the things I will need for my baby. Did we get enough when we were shopping?"

"Enough for a start. We'll buy more things before February. What you have is good for now."

When Caleb came over later that afternoon, I showed him the bassinet and the small pile of clothing and blankets stacked on the end table next to the couch. "Rachel said this is enough to start with. But I really do not know what I will need!" I shrugged helplessly. "I should probably ask Misty. She'll know."

Caleb fingered the bassinet. "Nice bassinet."

"Yes, it is. Rachel gave it to me. She once … Oh!" I stopped and looked up apprehensively. Rachel's secret was not mine to share.

"What is it, Lily?"

"Um, I probably shouldn't have said anything."

Caleb cocked his head and didn't ask any more questions, respecting my choice not to share. "Okay. Want to show me what else you bought?"

"Sure." Reaching over the end of the couch, I lifted a big shopping bag onto the couch. "I bought the baby some adorable little clothes to keep him warm, and some other things I'm sure he'll need." I laid the baby clothes on the bassinet one at a time. There were ten one-piece pajamas, two packets of tee shirts, and five small receiving blankets. "And I bought a big box of newborn disposable diapers." I pointed across the room to the big box.

Caleb smiled, looking at each item. "I can already imagine him wearing those pajamas."

I laughed and touched my baby bump, where my son was kicking me again. "I think he approves too. He's bouncing around in here."

Caleb knelt in front of me and watched how the baby's movements rippled my knit top.

"Here. Feel him." I reached for his hand and placed it over my baby's moving feet.

"Hm. He must be a football player." Caleb grinned and looked up at me.

Our eyes locked as he leaned forward, his hand still on my baby, and kissed me gently. Leaning back, he looked down and said, "Okay, Champ, I already have a football waiting for you."

I laughed. "You're going to be a great dad, Caleb."

His eyes gleaming, he looked up again. "I intend to be." He searched my face. "If you will let me."

I caught my breath and just looked into his eyes.

Rachel came into the house through the kitchen. "Is Caleb there?"

"Yes," he called, still looking into my eyes.

"Don't leave here without taking some cookies. I made a batch this afternoon."

"Thanks, Rachel. I will be sure to take some home with me."

"Is Lily going to practice with you this afternoon?"

"Yes. I'm taking her in a few minutes."

"Okay."

The tension broken, I quickly put the baby clothes back into the shopping bag. Caleb stood and held out his hand, helping me to my feet.

"Are you ready to go?"

"Yes." I grabbed my coat, and he helped me into it, zipping it up to my chin and kissing me lightly.

Colleen and Misty were already at the church when we arrived. J. J. was examining some songs while Joe warmed up at the keyboard and Gage sat down behind the drums.

"Lily, we'd like to have a baby shower for you at church next week, if that's okay with you?"

"Oh, Colleen! How nice. Yes. I would love that. Rachel and I found a few things at the stores in Bozeman, but she assures me I will need much more."

"Good. Then we'll have a luncheon and a baby shower in the fellowship room." She smiled broadly, turned, and headed across the stage toward J. J.

"Thank you, Colleen!" I turned to Caleb in amazement. "A baby shower!"

He laughed. "You'll be well-supplied with every little thing you could never have imagined."

"I feel so—so *accepted* here. You all are the kindest people I've ever met."

"Yes, we are rather special." He grinned.

Sunday after church, Colleen and Misty whisked me away from Caleb.

Rachel followed us downstairs, calling over her shoulder, "I'll take her home with me after this, Caleb."

The fellowship room was decorated with blue balloons and white and yellow ribbons. There were neatly cut sandwiches, punch, and a cake with matching writing on top that said, "We love you, Lily & Son!"

I was overcome with emotion. Tears filled my eyes. What precious friends God had given me!

Caleb was right. There were so many gifts, things I could not have imagined I'd need plus clothes. After the shower, Misty brought out a large paper bag full of other baby clothes.

"We pass these baby clothes around among the moms as they are needed and add to them when we have extras. They're yours now, Lily. When you're done, pass them along to the next mama. I think Rosa's baby is due in June. By then, you'll probably be finished with half the outfits here."

"Oh, my!" I took the bag. It was stuffed to the brim. "Thank you, Misty!"

My heart burst with gratitude at the sharing natures of my new friends. God had brought me through grief and heartache to this place where his people would help me more than I could have ever expected.

Another storm brought a foot of snow the first week in January of 2020. Power lines, weighed down with the burden, snapped in a couple places, leaving us without electricity.

Rachel was prepared for the outage. She naturally kept a flashlight in each room. Now, she brought her battery-operated lanterns into the main room, placing them where we could use them as needed. She lit scented candles in glass jars and set them on the kitchen table and on the counter to guide us when the room was dark.

Caleb used his snowblower to clear the path from his house to ours, cleared a path from Rachel's back door to the barn and chicken coop, and cleared our front walkway. Afterward, he plowed his own driveway and ours. He was busy most of the morning.

"Come join us for lunch," Rachel called to him as he finished.

"Okay." Caleb parked his truck with its great snow shovel and came inside, stomping snow from his boots before entering, then removing them once he was inside.

My own feet were toasty in the moccasins he'd given me for Christmas.

"I can't stay long," he said, joining us at the table where Rachel had laid out lunch. "Something is wrong with the electric connection between the cave and my greenhouse. I've stoked the wood stove in the shed, but I need to go up to the cave to find out what's wrong up there. If it's not the generator, I'll have to look for the problem after this snow melts a little."

"Sounds like a lot of work," Rachel said. "Are you taking anyone with you?"

"No. I'll go alone. It shouldn't take long to check the generator and the connections in the cave."

"Well, come back here when you're finished, so we'll know you're okay," I said anxiously.

He grinned. "Okay, Lily. I will return to you as soon as I can." Donning his coat and boots and pulling a woolen cap over his head, Caleb left to check on his generator.

After he left, I opened my guitar case and began working on fingering exercises to take my mind off Caleb's task.

Caleb worked his way up the mountain through deepening snow. He'd stopped at his house to strap on snowshoes, the only way to traverse the fresh snow with relative ease. Arriving at the cave, he removed his snowshoes, leaning them against the rock wall next to the shovel and pick he kept there on the off chance he'd need to do some work in the cave's tunnel. He turned on his large flashlight and walked back to the underground creek where a flume was supposed to direct the racing water toward the hydroelectric generator.

"There's the problem," he said to himself. A fair-sized rock had fallen from the wall of the cave, landing at the top edge of the flume. This diverted the water away from the generator. Climbing to the top of the fall area, he pushed the rock off to the side. The water returned to its rapid flow toward the generator.

Good. Things should be okay now.

Caleb climbed back down and headed back toward the cave entrance.

Suddenly, the ground began to shake. A great roar sounded.

I was in the middle of practicing a run on my guitar when I felt the house tremble and heard an ever-increasing sound like a jet engine. Dropping my guitar on the couch, I hurried to the back door. On the mountain above, an avalanche raced into the gap above the cave where Caleb worked, covering the high field around it.

"Caleb!" I screamed.

Rachel was right behind me. She gripped my shoulders. "Oh, God! Please, please keep him safe!"

The lights were on in the shed where Caleb's plants grew.

"He may already be back," Rachel said. She reached for her phone and pressed Caleb's number.

There was no answer.

"I'm going up there to check and see if he's back."

"I'm coming with you!"

"No, Lily. You're too far along in your pregnancy to climb the mountain now. I'll call you when I've checked the shed and house."

Releasing my shoulders, Rachel hurriedly donned her snow gear and slipped her phone into her pocket.

I waited helplessly at the back door, watching Rachel hurry up the path Caleb had plowed. Five minutes later, she called.

"He's not here Lily. He's on the mountain or in that cave of his. I'm calling Pastor and asking him to tell the men from church to come help find him."

"I'll call our group. Can Pastor call the other men?"

"Yes. I'll have him send Beth over to pray with us and help with food. We'll need to feed those who will be helping with the rescue."

I called Gage first.

"Hi, Lily. What's going on over there? I heard something loud ..."

"An avalanche, Gabe. Caleb went up to work on his generator in the cave, and the snow has completely covered the entrance. I don't know whether Caleb was inside or if he was on his way back. Can you come help find him? If he's in the cave, you'll have to dig him out."

"I'll be right there!"

"Good. I'm calling J. J., Mark, Nate, Cody, and Joe too."

Rachel walked in the back door as I finished the call. She wrapped me in her arms.

"Lily, we are going to pray and trust God. He knows where Caleb is."

Standing there in the kitchen, we poured out our hearts to God. I hadn't experienced the power of prayer yet. Though I tried to relax and trust God, the next three hours were pure torture for me.

Beth, Pastor's wife, helped us prepare hot soup. Jesse and Colleen came to help, bringing bread, meat, thermoses, and blankets. An hour and a half later, they began carrying sandwiches and soup up to the men, who devoured the food and went back to moving snow.

Rachel and the other women came back carrying the empty thermoses.

"They've divided into three teams. One team is working toward the cave mouth, the other two teams are clearing the snow on either side of the entrance. They'll find him," Rachel assured me, her arm around my shoulders as we stood looking up at the rescue effort.

Dear God, please keep Caleb safe! Help the men find him!

I prayed continually while the men worked to clear a path into the cave. Looking up into the fading light, I saw more men climb up to help. It seemed like all the men in town were there.

Jesse, Colleen, Beth, Rachel, and I prayed for safety for Caleb and the other men. The ground where the avalanche fell was unstable, with rocks and trees swept down with the snow.

I kept returning to the window, watching the lights bobbing in the snow above.

Will he be okay? Oh, God! Bring Caleb back to me! I cannot lose another love! Yes, I do love him! Please, please bring him safely back to me!

Inside the cave, Caleb dug away at the fallen debris. How deep was the avalanche? How far would he have to dig to escape? As he worked steadily forward and up, chipping away at the immense wall of snow, he worried it might collapse inward and bury him alive.

Would Lily and Rachel know he was still in the cave? After fixing the generator, he knew the lights would go back on in his shed and they would probably think he was there.

Father God, don't let Lily worry! Help her to trust you through this. Help me to dig my way through this avalanche. I need your help, Father.

Methodically, he pulled debris and snow away from the entrance and piled it off to one side. Sometimes he'd have to roll a boulder from the wall of snow or dig around a tree pulled down with the avalanche. Snow would collapse into the tunnel from time to time, and he'd have to move it back into the cave. A few tree branches helped brace the snow tunnel which lengthened as he carefully dug his way outward. His watch indicated he'd been digging for three hours. Pausing again for breath, giving his arms a rest, he heard what sounded like shovels beyond the tunnel he had dug. Help was coming! He began digging in the direction of the noise.

A few minutes later, a shovel broke through the snow above his tunnel.

"Caleb? Are you there?"

"Yes! I'm just below you, Mark, and a little to the left."

The hole above widened quickly. Hands came downward and he grasped them.

⁓——⁓⁓⁓——⁓

While standing at the window, I heard a shout from the mountain. They must have found him!

Oh, Caleb! Please, please be okay!

Rachel's phone rang. It was Pastor. "We have him. He's fine."

"Oh, thank God!"

"Is he okay?" I asked Rachel.

"Yes, indeed."

Ten minutes later, Caleb came into the kitchen, a crowd of smiling, tired men around him.

I walked straight into his arms, weeping tears of joy and relief.

"I'm okay, honey." He stroked my hair and held me close, only loosening his grip on me when the men tromped back outside toward their cars and trucks.

"Thanks, you all!" he called and waved, one arm still around my shoulders.

"Anytime, Caleb."

"See you later."

"We're expecting invitations to the wedding, you know," Gage grinned and waved.

Caleb laughed and looked down at me, a mischievous smile on his face.

Rachel tactfully went out to the barn to milk the cow, two hours later than usual, leaving us alone in the house. We heard the cow mooing when she opened the back door.

"I love you, Caleb," I whispered against his shoulder. "When you were buried in the avalanche, I knew for sure. I could not bear to lose you."

"I thought of you the whole time I was digging out of the snow. I didn't want you to worry, my love." He kissed my hair.

Lifting my lips to him, I reveled in his deepening kiss and stroked his cheek, rough with stubble after a long day of work.

He lifted his lips for a moment. "Lily, will you please, please marry me?"

"Yes, Caleb. Yes!"

The next morning, Caleb came down to Rachel's house after breakfast.

"Would you come for a drive with me, Lily?"

"Okay. Where are we going?"

"You'll see. You'll need to dress warm and wear boots."

Five minutes later, he lifted me into his truck. My baby was due in about a month, and the extra weight made climbing into the truck impossible.

Closing my door, Caleb went around to the driver's side and climbed in beside me. He let out the brakes, and a moment later, we were driving toward Lake Thechihila. The frozen lake stretched out before us. Snowbanks sparkled in the morning sunlight. Cottonwood trees stood laced with snow. Fir and pine trees sloped toward the ground under its weight. Houses surrounded by high drifts emitted ribbons of wood smoke from their chimneys.

We drove slowly through town and beyond. Finally, Caleb pulled into a snowy parking area which had been cleared earlier. He came around to my door to help me down. Lifting his hands up to lift me down, he said, "Lily, this is Thechihila Point."

"Oh!" I gasped, looking around with interest.

"Will you come with me?"

"Yes." I reached out and put my hands on his shoulders as he lifted me from the truck. I felt my cheeks growing warm. Feeling just a little dizzy from excitement, I leaned against the front of his jacket and held onto him.

He laughed gently. "Come along then."

Hand in hand, we walked through the snow to where the land met the frozen lake.

Caleb lifted my hand to his lips and kissed my fingers. "Lily, in this place where my ancestors have always pledged their love, I pledge my love to you today. I will love and protect you, pray for you, and keep you safe for the rest of my life. I will love your son ... he will be my son too. Lily, my love, I don't want to erase Konnor from your memory. He will always be a part of you. When you see your baby ...

as he grows ... you will be reminded of Konnor, but I hope my love for you will bring you comfort."

"Caleb, the love I have for you is different from what Konnor and I had because *you* are different. Konnor and I fell in love easily and without much thought. Our lives were exciting, built around musical performances and shared college experiences. But with you, I feel safe and protected. I don't know how to explain it ... I–I'm more secure. And excited too. I've needed assurance of safety because of losing Konnor and because of my baby. But I have come to love you because of your strength, your thoughtfulness, and peace. My love is different this time, but it's good. You completely satisfy my heart, Caleb. I love you so much!"

Looking up into his face, I said, "I read some beautiful words in the book of Ruth in the Bible. I feel this way about you. Wherever you go, I will go. Wherever you live, I will live. Your people will be my people, and your God will be my God."

His arms came around me, and I rested my head against his jacket, listening to his heartbeat. We stood there together in the snow beneath the lacey cottonwoods, finally at peace, knowing our love was forever.

"I have something for you," Caleb said, pulling back a little and reaching into his pocket. Opening a small, blue velvet box, he showed me the ring—a solitary diamond twinkled in the sunlight.

"Oh, Caleb! It's beautiful!"

He slipped it onto my finger. "I asked Rachel to find out your ring size last week. The ring has been burning a hole in my pocket."

I laughed. Of course, he would have asked Rachel.

Caleb drew me close to his heart. "Lily.'

"Yes, Caleb?"

"Would you be willing to marry me in a quiet ceremony at church as soon as we can get a marriage license?"

"Oh!"

"I want to give you and the baby my name. I can do that if we're married when he's born."

I thought about it a moment. It would mean Caleb's name, not Konnor's, listed as my baby's father. Was I ready for that?

"Would you mind if I choose Konnor as my baby's middle name?"

"Good idea, Lily. Having Konnor as a middle name will be a reminder that he has a daddy in heaven with Jesus too."

"Thank you, Caleb. And yes, I will marry you in a small ceremony. I've never liked the idea of having a big, complicated wedding anyway. Small and intimate works for me."

"Good. Then there's just one other thing I need to do this morning."

CHAPTER 14

"I need to speak with your father, Lily. It's customary, you know."

"Okay." I pulled out my phone.

"Good morning, Dad."

"Lily! Is everything all right?"

"Yes, Dad. Everything is fine. Are you in a place where you can talk?"

"I'm in my office. I'm alone in the house, so, yes. I can talk."

"Good. Then I'd like to introduce you to Caleb Maxwell. We're standing at Thechihila Point together. I'm putting him on my phone now."

"Hello, Mr. Mains. This is Caleb."

"Ah. You're the man I've been hearing about! What can I do for you?"

"Well, sir, I'd like your permission to marry Lily."

I could hear Dad laugh.

"So, you've made it to Thechihila Point. I am not at all surprised, Caleb. Yes, you may marry Lily. She'd be most upset at me if I said no."

"Good!"

"When are you planning to get married?"

"We would like to get married in about two weeks. We need a few days to get the marriage license, and we'd like to have a simple ceremony with the pastor and his wife, Rachel, and a few friends. If my parents can come, we'll have them here too. We'd like you to be here."

"Wow! That's quick. But yes, I'll be there. Lily's mother is in Cancun with some friends for the next three weeks, so she can't come. I assume Lily is fine with that."

"Let me ask her."

Caleb put the phone on mute and told me the situation.

"That's fine. I'm not ready to see her yet anyway."

Caleb unmuted the phone. "Mr. Mains, Lily is okay with that."

"Call me Will."

"Okay. Once we figure out the date, I'll call you. If you fly into Bozeman, I can meet you there. The roads are bad right now, but my truck has good tires."

"Good. I'll be glad to meet you, Caleb."

"Yes, sir."

"Would you put Lily back on the line?"

Caleb grinned and handed the phone back to me.

"Thanks, Dad."

"I'm happy for you, honey." He chuckled. "Thechihila Point was a nice touch."

"I thought you'd appreciate that."

"I'm glad you've found someone to take care of you and my grandson. I'll be at your wedding in two weeks."

"I'm looking forward to seeing you, Dad."

"Are there still cabins on the lake for rent?"

"Yes."

"Okay. Then I'll plan to stay there. Let me know if there's anything you need me to bring along."

"I think I have everything I need."

"Good. See you soon, Lily. Love you."

"Love you too. Bye, Dad."

Rachel was working in the kitchen putting eggs into the empty containers when we returned to the house.

"Good morning. Have a nice walk?"

"Yes," Caleb said, his face glowing. "We went to the point."

"I thought so." Rachel smiled, her eyes twinkling.

"Rachel, we want a small wedding with just a few people, including you. Dad will be here for the wedding too. We don't have his flight information yet, but Caleb will pick him up when he arrives. He plans to staying in a cabin by the lake. But Mom's in Mexico. Will you help me plan this wedding?"

"Of course, Lily. I would like nothing better. And let me say how happy I am for you and Caleb. But I'm very happy for my own self too. Having you here as a neighbor is going to be a pleasure."

I hugged her. "You are so good to me, Rachel."

She laughed with pure joy. I had never seen her as happy as she was that day.

"Rachel, I want to look nice for Caleb, but I do not want to wear white. I'd look like an egg!"

"Yes, white would be overwhelming at this point. What color do you want for your dress?"

"I like pastel colors. Pink, blue, green. I guess I like blue best."

"Come to my room and see what I have in my cloth collection." Rachel turned and walked upstairs. "I might have something you'd like me to make for you."

"Make?"

"Yes. You said we have two weeks. I sew a lot most winters, and a simple dress won't take long." She opened a cupboard and pulled out a big plastic tub. Setting it on the bed, she sorted through the fabric inside. "Here's a nice piece of blue." She pulled it out and did a quick measure. "There are about five yards here. We'll have plenty if you like it. It's rayon and polyester, so it won't wrinkle."

I fingered the soft, blue fabric. Walking to the mirror, I held it up to my face.

"Yes. This is perfect!"

Rachel was rummaging through another box in the cupboard. "Ah. Here it is." She held up a pattern. "It's high-waisted with a little gather at the front and long, fitted sleeves with a point at the end of them. What do you think?"

"It looks like something from Romeo and Juliet. I love it!"

"Good. Then I should measure you and get started right away."

For the next few days, Rachel cut and pinned and sewed while Caleb and I made the arrangements for our small wedding.

We decided to hold the ceremony on Saturday, January 19. Caleb called his parents, and I called my dad. Pastor Kyle Peters would officiate over the wedding, and Beth would help with the details.

Wednesday evening, we told our Bible study friends, who were not at all surprised to hear we were getting married.

"We don't want anything fancy," Caleb told them. "We don't have much time, and having our closest friends and family there is all we need. Please come."

Gage laughed. "I knew you'd be getting married when I saw Lily's face after we rescued you, but I didn't know it would be this soon."

I noticed Colleen, Misty, and Jesse huddled together after Bible study, smiling and giggling, and I wondered what they were up to, but Caleb took my hand and pulled me toward the door before I could ask.

"Time to go, honey." He grinned at his friends and waved. "See you all later." He led me out to the truck and helped me into it.

"Caleb," I protested. "Why did we have to leave so soon?"

He laughed. "Couldn't you see they wanted to talk about us? They probably started plotting the moment the door closed."

"Oh." I glanced back at the house. "I wonder what they are up to?"

"Whatever it is, we'll find out when they're ready—and not before." Caleb grinned. "Now, Lily, let's go spend some quality time together up at my place."

∞———c⊱⊰ᴐ———∞

Will stepped off the plane in Bozeman and looked around, wondering how he would recognize Caleb.

"Will?"

He spotted a tall young man dressed in snow gear coming toward him.

"Caleb?"

"Yes, sir." Caleb held out his hand. "Welcome back to Montana."

"Thank you. It's been a long time since I've visited Montana. I'd forgotten how cold it can be." Will gave a little shiver and shook his head.

Caleb grinned. "Then let's go have some coffee before heading back."

"Good idea."

"Do you have a suitcase coming?"

"Yes."

The two men headed for baggage claim.

"Lily tells me you've rigged an electric generator in the cave above your house."

Will listened as Caleb described his projects while they picked up luggage and drove to a coffee shop.

"I'm glad you were able to come to the wedding on such short notice," Caleb said.

"I wouldn't have missed it."

"Lily's looking forward to seeing you." Caleb laughed. "I've never seen her so lit up with excitement. She's bubbling over with things she wants to tell you—to show you."

Will laughed. "She hasn't been like that since she was a little girl."

As the two men talked, Will found himself relating to Caleb and his dreams. *This man is perfect for Lily. I can see how much he loves her. He has some good ideas to improve his land too. He's going to do well. I'm glad for my girl.*

Caleb's parents and sisters arrived on Thursday, filling his home with laughter and excitement. I loved meeting them. Jan and Julie, his twin sisters, were full of questions and laughter. Their faces looked alike, but their hairstyles were different, which helped me tell them apart. Both were moderately tall and had straight red hair and gray eyes. Caleb's dad, Russ, had wavy red hair. His mom, Diane, was quieter than the twins, but she smiled and listened to everything, tossing in an occasional comment or question. Caleb had inherited her light brown hair and green eyes and had his father's height and build.

Caleb's family was noisy, cheerful, and warm. In no time at all, we were chattering about how Caleb and I had met, about the wedding, about the twins' children and spouses.

"Travis wanted to come, but he couldn't get away from work on such short notice," Jan said. "He teaches the local grade school where our kids go."

"Yeah, Seth wanted to come too, but he couldn't get off work on such short notice. Our boys are four and six now, old enough for me to leave them with Seth for a few days. I hope." Julie crossed her fingers.

"I told Travis to ask his mom to look after our kids. She's usually happy to take them. They'll be fine," Jan said. "We'll be back here this summer to see you. This is going to be a blast!"

"When is your baby due?" Diane asked with interest.

"Around February 19."

"You're having a boy?"

"Yes." Caleb smiled, wrapping his arms around me from behind. "Isn't that great?"

"Caleb has always wanted a son. I'm glad he will be here from the beginning for your little boy. We can hardly wait to see him."

"Yes!" Jan and Julie echoed together.

I smiled at Diane's genuine warmth. Whatever strain there might have been over my baby, she swept it away with a smile and a welcome.

Caleb took his dad to his shed to show him the hydroponic garden and explain how everything worked while we put dinner together. Then, they tromped up the mountain to the cave so Caleb could show Ross his small power generating arrangement and tell him about the avalanche.

Rachel and my dad arrived just before the meal. Together, we had the best family time I'd ever experienced. Russ, Caleb, and Dad hit it off right away, just as the women of the family did.

Friday, the men gathered fir boughs and holly from the mountain behind the house. We women combined the branches into two giant bouquets decorated with colorful ribbons and Christmas tree balls. When we were finished, we tramped down to the church together and placed them on the sanctuary stage, one on each side.

"How festive!" Diane said.

"It's perfect!" I agreed, loving the fir scent filling the log room and reveling in the bright colors. "But I'm not sure what I'll do for a bouquet. The fir is sticky with resin."

"Don't worry, honey, I have that covered," Rachel said. "I asked the store to order white roses, blue bell flowers, and baby's breath. They came in this afternoon. I put them in the fridge. Tonight, we'll arrange your bouquet together."

Caleb slipped his arm around my waist and looked around at our united family. "Thank you all for coming and for helping. We couldn't have done all this without you. The room looks great!"

Later, when Rachel and I were alone in her open kitchen, I watched as she skillfully snipped stems, wrapped them with floral tape, and put my wedding bouquet together. The roses filled the room with their delicate scent. She made boutonnieres for Caleb, his best man, Dad, and Pastor Kyle too. For Colleen, she put together a small bouquet of white roses with blue ribbon. When it was finished, she placed the bouquets and boutonniere into plastic bags and set them in the extra refrigerator, propping the bouquet up between milk jars and eggs.

I smiled at that. How many brides kept their bouquets between milk jars and eggs? "Thank you, Rachel. You are a precious friend to me."

Her eyes misting a little, Rachel hugged me close. "And you are like a daughter to me, Lily. I'm glad you are settling down here in Lake Thechihila with Caleb. It will be a blessing to see you often." She released me, holding me by the shoulders. "Now, Lily my girl, you need to get some sleep ... if you can. Tomorrow will be here before you know it."

Our wedding day dawned with clear, blue skies, and relatively warm at thirty-four degrees. Warm for January in Montana, that is.

Rachel and I had breakfast together, enjoying this special time alone.

"I'll miss having you here, Lily."

"I'll be just up the hill, Rachel. You can come up whenever you want."

She sighed. "Thank you. But having you here every morning has been such a pleasure. These are memories I will always treasure, my dear."

"Me too."

"Is Colleen going to be your maid of honor?"

"Yes. When Caleb announced our wedding at Bible study, I asked her, and he asked Gage to be his best man. And Rachel, since my mom won't be coming, would you mind sitting on the front row with Dad? Or would you be uncomfortable with that? I don't want Dad to be alone."

"Lily, I would be honored."

"Good. Then it's settled." I smiled and hugged her.

The wedding was to be at eleven o'clock that morning. At ten o'clock, Rachel dressed in a floor-length, dark blue dress that emphasized her blue eyes, then helped me into the soft blue wedding dress she had made. She brought out a lovely crown of white rosebuds for my hair, fastening it securely. The bouquet she had made awaited in the refrigerator.

"Now let me take a few pictures of you, honey," she said, reaching for the camera she'd placed on an end table.

A few minutes later, we heard a knock at the door. My dad.

"Lily, you're beautiful," Dad said, taking my hands.

"Thanks, Dad."

He gazed at Rachel for a long moment. "You are as lovely as ever, Rachel. Thank you for taking such good care of Lily."

Rachel blushed. "Having her here has been a pleasure, Will."

I knew they hadn't been alone to talk yet, and there was an awkwardness between them. Once the wedding was over, though, I hoped they would be able to spend some time together to talk things over.

"Well, Lily, my girl, may we escort you to the church?" Dad asked.

"Yes."

"Let's take my car," Rachel offered. "I saw Caleb drop you off, so you'll need transportation."

"Sounds good to me."

Together, the three of us rode over to the church. I expected to see only a handful of cars, but the parking area was full, with people laughing, waving, and heading inside, each family carrying food of some kind.

"What?" I gasped at the crowd.

Rachel laughed. "I know you and Caleb only planned on a small wedding, Lily, but this town is not going to let the two of you get married without them."

I laughed too. "Well, I guess we're having a bigger wedding than we expected."

Dad nodded. "You're a good sport, Lily." He climbed out of the back seat and opened my door. "Now keep those skirts out of the snow."

Taking his arm and following Rachel, we entered the church and hurried down a side hallway to a classroom to wait for the ceremony to begin.

"I'll let you know when we're ready," Rachel said, exiting and leaving us alone.

"I like your Caleb, honey. He's a good man." Dad nodded his approval.

"He is. I'm glad the two of you had some time to talk and get to know one another."

"I'm sure he will take good care of you and my grandson. God has blessed you, Lily."

"I'm glad you believe in Jesus too, Dad."

"Yes. I've been attending a men's Bible study with my friend, Sam. The men in the group have helped me understand what Jesus did for us, and I have chosen to follow him."

"Oh, Dad, I'm so happy!" I hugged him as closely as I could.

Dad smiled. "Me too."

Rachel came to the door. "It's time."

Together, we walked out into the foyer. Soft music floated through the air as J. J. escorted Rachel to the front row. Caleb, handsome in a gray suit and white shirt, with the blue and white boutonniere pinned to his front pocket, stepped out onto the stage with Pastor Kyle and Gage.

Colleen, dressed in a long, pink gown, waited at the back with us.

Joe began playing "Jesu, Joy of Man's Desiring," and Colleen stepped out into the aisle.

"Are you ready?" Dad asked, looking into my eyes as the music paused, then stepped up in volume.

"Yes."

Holding my dad's arm, I walked forward toward Caleb, my gaze fixed on his face.

As we reached the front and paused, Pastor Kyle asked, "Who gives this woman?"

Dad spoke. "Her mother and I."

I gave a fleeting thought to Mom and remembered Dad loved her, so it was natural for him to include her in the wedding. I was still glad she was not there. The slap she gave me was still sharp in my memory. The thought evaporated in a moment, for Caleb stood before me, his eyes on my face. I forgot all else but my beloved.

Caleb stepped down. Dad placed my hand on Caleb's arm and turned to sit on the front row next to Rachel as Caleb led me back up the two steps to where Pastor Lyle stood.

My entire focus turned to Caleb, and all else faded from my mind. I handed my bouquet to Colleen and Caleb took both my hands in his.

CHAPTER 15

The only Christian wedding I had ever attended was Gage and Jesse's. All my other friends had written their own vows, and there was a marked absence of God in them. But when I heard the traditional vows Gage and Jesse said, I decided those words were just what I wanted. Caleb preferred them too. Time stood still while we said the timeless words to each other.

Pastor spoke first, talking briefly about the sacredness of marriage. Then, he asked Caleb, "Do you, Caleb Russell Maxwell, take this woman to be your wife? Do you promise to love, honor, cherish, and protect her, forsaking all others and holding only to her from this day forward, for better, for worse, for richer, for poorer, in sickness and health, until death do you part?"'

Looking deep into my eyes, Caleb said, "I do."

My heart beat with deep emotion. This man was pledging his love and his life to me!

Turning to me, Pastor asked, "Do you, Lily Annette Mains, take this man to be your husband? Do you promise to love, honor, cherish, and protect him, forsaking all others and holding only to him from this day forward, for better, for worse, for richer, for poorer, in sickness and health, until death do you part?"

"I do," I said, losing myself in Caleb's gaze.

Reaching into his pocket, Caleb pulled out my wedding ring and placed it on my finger. "With this ring, I thee wed and pledge my heart's devotion."

My heart was full of joy, I could barely breathe at first as we stood there gazing at each other—so much in love.

Colleen handed me Caleb's ring. Taking his left hand in mine, I slid the ring onto his finger, my hands trembling slightly. "With this ring, I thee wed and pledge my heart's devotion."

Pastor said, "Then by the power vested in me, I now pronounce you man and wife." He turned to Caleb. "You may kiss the bride."

I was in Caleb's arms, our lips meeting for the first time as man and wife. As we stood together, full of joy, Gage and Colleen sang "When I Say I Do," by Matthew West. I barely heard the words. Caleb sang the song to me later, and I loved the words. I would never forget them. In that moment, I was totally caught up in Caleb. No one else existed.

After the song, Pastor said to the congregation, "I present to you Mr. and Mrs. Caleb Maxwell," and we turned to face our guests. They rose, clapped, and a few whistled their approval.

I laughed and looked up at Caleb, who was also laughing, his eyes glowing with joy.

The music began, and we walked down the aisle, greeting friends as we walked toward the back of the room.

Total exhaustion took over by the time our unexpected, but welcome, reception ended. We left the church amid showers of birdseed and shouts of congratulations. Dad and Rachel stood together waving as we left the church—two people, star-crossed in love years ago, offering us their love and approval.

I had never experienced such total acceptance and love as I felt that day from our friends at Lake Thechihila.

PART TWO

CHAPTER 16

"Well done, Rachel," Will said as they waved goodbye to Caleb and Lily. "You've helped our Lily find her way back to happiness and love."

"I'm glad you sent her to me, Will. I have enjoyed every moment of our time together. She's a precious young woman with a generous heart. I am not the only one who has helped Lily, however. Caleb played a huge role in lifting her heart out of her grief over Konnor. There's also a group of young people who have reached out to her."

"Rachel?" Colleen walked toward them with her arms full of tablecloths from the reception.

"Yes?"

"You've done enough now. Why don't you let the rest of us finish here?"

"Oh, thank you very much, Colleen. I appreciate that."

Colleen smiled and moved toward her car with the linens.

"Would you like to come up to my place for a cup of coffee or tea?" Rachel turned to Will, clasping her hands together.

"Yes. Thank you. We've been so busy the last couple of days, we haven't had a chance to talk."

A few minutes later, they sat at Rachel's kitchen table, the tea kettle warming on the stove.

"How have you been, Rachel?"

"I've done okay. I like this farm. Auntie June left it to me along with some finances to keep me going until I could get things producing again. She was sick for a couple years before she passed, and the farm suffered. I liked the challenge of putting things right after she passed."

"You know, you don't look much older than the last time I saw you." Will searched her eyes.

"The Lord has been good to me. I found his peace, and his joy has strengthened my heart. He has given me some very good friends here, and I was doing okay. But then you sent Lily to me, and ..." She shrugged and smiled. "Oh, Will, she has been such a blessing to me!"

"I'm glad. She loves you very much, and I know she doesn't give her love without just cause."

"How's Margaret?" Rachel asked awkwardly, the ghost of her rival rising between her and Will.

"She's fine." Will sipped his coffee and stared out the window. "This past year has been difficult for her. She wanted Lily to marry a rich man. Dominic Jantzen. His parents own a big wine company in Santa Rosa. But Lily wouldn't have anything to do with him, and I'm glad. He was not right for our girl. He's something of a bully."

"We sent him packing." Rachel nodded with satisfaction. "Caleb is just what she needs. He's kind and thoughtful, but he's also strong. He has some creative business ideas he's developing, which will not only help him but will also help this town. He's a good man, Will."

He set his coffee down and reached for Rachel's hand. "Rachel, I wish ..." His voice trailed off.

"It's okay, Will."

He sighed. A troubled note came into his voice. "Rachel, have you heard about the virus they've been talking about on the news lately?"

"What virus?"

"They think this one came from a lab leak in Wuhan, China. They're calling it COVID 19. Some people think it might be something they were developing for biological warfare. There was some suggestion this was to develop vaccines, but I don't know what to believe. All I know is it's deadly, and it's spreading from China to other countries now. The government is starting to take measures to guard against it. But I don't know how they can succeed. Viruses spread quickly."

"Oh. No, I hadn't heard. My mind has been on this wedding."

"Well, it's coming our way. Please be careful, Rachel."

"I will. But remember this—the Lord is always in control, in life and in death. This world is not our home. We who believe in Jesus only live here until we enter God's presence and our eternal home."

"Yes. I've been learning about that at the men's Bible study I attend. I just want to make sure you and Lily are safe."

"I understand." Rachel patted his hand. "You be careful too, Will. You'll be out there in California with lots of people. We'll be here in a small community with lots of fresh air and sunshine. We're probably safer here than you will be in Santa Rosa."

"I hope so."

Fairmont Hot Springs Resort had been the perfect place for a honeymoon, particularly since my body had not yet adjusted to the freezing temperatures of Montana. The warm water was relaxing, and the atmosphere was romantic.

"I wish we could stay here forever," I said with a sigh as we drove away from the resort.

"We can come back here again."

"I'd love that."

Back at Lake Thechihila that evening, I felt a strong sense of homecoming as we drove up the driveway to the log house. Our home. That thought filled me with joy. Smoke drifted into the sky from the chimney. Rachel had volunteered to keep the fire going after Caleb's parents and sisters left. At the house, Caleb helped me down from the truck. Together, we walked onto the deck, looking out over the sleepy town nestled in the snow.

Standing there, bundled up against the cold, I breathed a prayer of thanks to God for these people who had welcomed me. Suddenly, Caleb swept me off my feet. I squealed with surprise and wrapped my arms around his neck.

Laughing, Caleb carried me through the open front door. "Welcome home, my love," he murmured in his deep, lover's voice, placing a soft kiss on my lips before setting me down.

I laughed, joy filling my heart almost to bursting point. After a long moment in Caleb's arms, I stepped back and looked around. Caleb's family and Rachel had prepared a lovely homecoming for us. The evergreen decorations from the wedding, now sitting in large buckets of water, filled the house with the smell of the forest. Food was prepared and in the refrigerator for our first evening together at home. The wedding presents were piled in the center of the living room, awaiting our attention.

On our bed, a sachet packet of lavender lay on the pillows. An intricate, hand-made quilt covered the silky sheets. The window looked out over a star-studded sky where the moon would soon rise.

No one could ask for a more romantic homecoming.

Those early weeks of our marriage seemed to fly as we settled into our home, laughed, and loved together.

Early on Valentine's Day, I awoke to labor pains. I must have slept through the early contractions, for these were intense. Thankful that Jesse had explained what I could expect, I lay there and timed them for a while then sat up and reached for my robe. Another contraction hit, so I lay back down.

"Caleb?"

"What is it, honey?" he murmured sleepily and reached his arm out to draw me close.

"I'm having contractions."

He sat up, his eyes alert.

"How far apart are they?"

"About every four minutes. They last about thirty seconds."

"Okay. I'll call Jesse and let her know."

He sat up in bed and reached for his phone. "Jesse, this is Caleb. Lily is in labor."

"How far apart are her contractions?"

"Four minutes."

"Okay. I've already put my things together. Let me have a bite of breakfast, and I'll be up there in about thirty minutes. Lily shouldn't eat anything. You can give her crushed ice in small spoonful."

"Right. I'll see you in a bit."

Caleb called Rachel next. "The baby's on his way. I'm not sure what to do. Could you come and help us?"

"I'll be right there." She reached our house a full twenty minutes before Jesse. It was a relief to have her.

For the next few hours, Caleb held my hand while Jesse coaxed me in proper breathing techniques during the contractions.

My son arrived at eleven o'clock that morning, and through exhaustion, I heard him cry for the first time. What a beautiful sound!

Jesse wrapped him in a soft blanket and laid him on my chest. His head was covered with wet, black curls, just like Konnor's.

Oh, Konnor, we have a son! He looks like you! And he will have a daddy here to help him grow up to be a good man who loves God.

I looked into my baby's wide-open eyes and said, "Hello, Joshua."

"Joshua?" Caleb asked.

"Yes. Caleb and Joshua were heroes together in the Bible. Now you will be my heroes in this life, my own Caleb and Joshua."

Caleb laughed softly and lifted one of Joshua's tiny hands in his own and murmured, "Hello, son. Your mama has set a great task before us. I'm up to it if you are."

Jesse piped up. "What's his middle name?"

"Konnor. His name is Joshua Konnor."

"Joshua Konnor Maxwell," Caleb added with satisfaction.

"Go ahead. You can hold him." I lifted Joshua up toward Caleb, who gently slipped his arm around our son. For this child also belonged to Caleb, who had stepped into my life and had drawn me out of my sorrow and had led me into a new joy.

I watched the expression of amazement and tenderness on Caleb's face as he studied Joshua. When he finally looked up at me, his face was full of delight.

Turning to Rachel, Caleb said simply, "It's your turn now, Rachel."

Her face beamed as she took Joshua in her arms. "Oh, you are beautiful!" As she leaned down and kissed his forehead, I saw a tear slide down her cheek. I knew she was remembering the baby she had surrendered years before. Now, maybe she would not ache so much for her lost child. I was determined to make sure she spent plenty of time with him in the future.

Will's phone rang while he was at work on Friday. "Hello?"

"Dad, it's me. You are now a grandpa!"

"Great! What did you name him?"

"Joshua Konnor Maxwell."

"I like that." After a brief hesitation, he continued, "Caleb strikes me as a man who wouldn't object to your naming the baby after another man. The combination sounds masculine and strong. What does he look like?"

"He has Konnor's black curls. Lots of them. And I think his eyes will be blue, though it's hard to tell right now. He's twenty-inches long and weighs seven pounds ten ounces."

"How are you doing?"

"I'm good. Jesse came over to help deliver the baby, and Rachel assisted her. Caleb held my hand and kept me focused. He's excited about the baby."

Will laughed. "I'm glad you are all okay. I'll be out there as soon as the snow melts enough for me to drive without snow tires."

After Lily's call, Will left work early and headed home. Margaret knew the baby was due, and he had told her about Lily's marriage to Caleb. She was furious but resigned to the fact Lily had married a rancher in Montana. Maybe she would be pleased to hear about their grandson. At least, Will hoped she would be happy. She had been impatient with him since she learned Lily was staying with Rachel.

Margaret had always resented Rachel, the girl he had loved before he'd met her. He wished he could help his wife find happiness, but that was something she would have to discover on her own. He sent up a prayer for her as he drove home.

Margaret was reading a fashion magazine in the living room when he arrived at the house.

"Will! You're home early. Is everything okay?"

"Yes. I just heard from Lily. The baby has come." Will smiled. "It's a boy, like they were expecting. He arrived this morning around eleven o'clock. He's healthy, and Lily is doing well."

"What did they name him?"

"Joshua Konnor Maxwell."

"I see." Margaret shrugged and turned away. "Well, you have your grandson now."

"Margaret?" he pleaded.

"Don't try to pull me into your drama, Will. I've had it with Lily. She was your idea, not mine."

Margaret walked out of the room, calling over her shoulder, "I'm going to lunch with Delores. I'll be back in time to fix your dinner."

"Don't bother." He went back into his office where he looked at his favorite picture of Lily. She was worth it.

Margaret never did want her, but Lily had taken over his heart from the first day he had held her.

Will slipped to his knees beside his chair and bowed his head.

How can I make peace with Margaret now? Is the distance between us too wide? Or can I find a way to bridge the gap? Father in heaven, I need your help. Margaret needs you, though she doesn't know it. You are the only one who can fix this. I hand it over to you, Lord.

Beyond the walls of his house, a menace began spreading across the land like low-lying tule fog, a menace which would change his city, his country, and the entire world.

CHAPTER 17

I sat in the rocking chair nursing Joshua while Caleb listened to the news, the radio dial turned down low so the baby would sleep. President Trump was addressing the nation.

The date was March 11, 2020.

Our hearts trembled at the message.

COVID 19, a deadly plague, was spreading around the world. The virus, for which we had no defense, came from China and was spreading rapidly across the United States and around the world. With symptoms much like influenza, this new virus was killing people. We would need to take measures as a nation to protect ourselves. Those who were most vulnerable were older people in their sixties and older, but it was a danger to everyone. All travel was suspended between Europe and the United States. Anti-viral therapies were being made available across the country. School closures were being considered. Social distancing was recommended. Financial relief would be available as needs arose. If we started feeling ill, we were to stay home and not spread the virus.

Caleb and I looked at each other, not sure what to think.

"Will our parents be safe?" I asked.

"I think so. They aren't exactly elderly. Yours are in their early forties. Mine are fifty. They all seem in good shape and in good health. Still, we can't know how this is going to play out. I've heard this virus was designed as a biological weapon, which scares me because we don't know what to expect. But know this, my love, God is still in control. He holds our lives in his hands. We can trust him no matter what."

On March 15, the governor of Montana ordered all public schools in the state to close from March 16 through March 27, and he ordered nursing homes to suspend home visits for clients, except for end-of-life situations. On March 24, he extended the closures and added more places to be closed. All social gatherings were limited to ten people, which meant churches must close. He ordered social distancing of at least six feet between people. Food and drug stores remained open, but restaurants were not. People in our town isolated themselves behind closed doors as news about increasing danger and death from the virus spread.

Late one afternoon, as Caleb and I stood looking out the front window at the snowy scene below, Caleb said, "Lily, I'm not sure what to do, but shutting down the church is against what Paul the Apostle told us to do." He reached for his Bible and read from Hebrews 10:25. "And let us not neglect our meeting together, as some people do, but encourage one another, especially now that the day of his return is drawing near."

Caleb sighed, his head bowed. "I'm sure of one thing. We need to get in touch with Pastor Kyle and our Bible study group leaders to discuss this."

"I agree."

Caleb reached for his phone. "Pastor, Caleb here. I think we need to have a meeting of all our group and church ministry leaders about how to handle this shutdown. The governor said it will be for only a few weeks, but I don't think a shutdown will be that short a time. If there's a serious viral outbreak, the situation will get a lot worse. We need to plan what we should do for the long haul. Could we have a meeting at church tomorrow evening?"

"Yes. I agree. I think we need to talk about this. Does six-thirty tomorrow evening sound okay with you?"

"Sure. I'll be there."

"Good. If you can, bring Lily too. I'll call the other leaders."

Rachel volunteered to stay with Joshua while Caleb and I went down to the church the next evening to discuss the problem.

"Thank you, Rachel. I know Joshua will be happy with you. I've mixed some formula in case he gets hungry. He's growing fast, and he seems to want to eat constantly."

"I'll enjoy every minute with this little guy," Rachel said, lifting Joshua up to her face and kissing his chubby cheeks.

Joshua reached out his hands to her, waving his arms and kicking his feet out.

I smiled. "I don't know how long the meeting will last."

"Don't worry. We'll be fine."

Caleb took my hand and pulled me toward the door. "See you, Rachel. Thanks for coming over to help."

There were five other couples who led Bible study groups or oversaw ministries at church. In addition to Pastor Kyle and Beth, Bob and Sandra Newton, Adrien and Naomi Carpenter, Cole and Mandi Roberts, and Dave and Jolene Matthews were there. Though I was not a leader, Caleb was. Pastor Kyle had insisted we always meet as couples, so we could evaluate our efforts from multiple viewpoints. I didn't know the older group leaders well yet, but I had met them and spoken with them occasionally at church.

Pastor Kyle Peters and his wife Beth oversaw the groups. After opening in a prayer for wisdom, he introduced the problem we faced.

"Our government has ordered our churches to close. We have been told this is just for a short time, but it seems unlikely the virus will go away any time soon. We must decide how to address this problem. How will we stay together as a church if we're scattered? I believe we need to stay connected. What are your thoughts?"

Jolene Matthews agreed. "People will want to stay in contact with each other. We're all going to need encouragement during this time. I don't see how we can encourage each other if we're scattered." Jolene and her husband, Dave, led the senior adult Bible study group.

Dave nodded. "Our group is the most vulnerable to this virus, so we must find a way to stay in touch, which doesn't expose us to illness."

"We could film the Sunday morning message and put it on YouTube." Caleb suggested.

"One problem," Dave said. "Some in our group are not familiar with computers. I know of at least two people who don't even have them and don't intend to buy them, either."

Pastor Kyle scribbled the problem onto his notebook. "Okay. Some of them don't have cell phones, but they do have landlines. And they do read newsletters. Maybe we can help them with home visits. I can provide your group with written copies of my sermons, and I could have CDs made."

Adrien Carpenter, who led the high schoolers and junior high, spoke up. "Naomi and I can have groups meet in our home. We have nine high schoolers and eight middle schoolers. We'll divide them up until summer, then start meeting together outside when it's warm. I'm sure fresh air will help keep the contagion down."

Beth, who was sitting next to me, said, "I'll keep in close phone contact with the mothers with babies and small children. I'll make sure everyone knows we're here for them."

"Thank you, Beth," I said softly, leaning toward her.

"Glad to help, Lily," she said with a smile.

Mandi Roberts spoke up. "We have about fifteen grade-school children in our department, scattered all over town. I agree with Adrien. Once summer arrives, we can do outdoor activities. But for now, Cole and I can keep in touch with them via texts, email, and Zoom, and we can have small parties, dividing them into age groups when we can. I'll prepare a Sunday lesson for them and email it to them. Once we get Zoom set up, we can meet online."

Caleb looked around at the assembled group. "I will talk it over with our group. There are eleven of us. I think we can continue meeting in each other's homes, since we aren't likely to be as affected by COVID as the older people are. I'll see how the group feels.

Bob Newton spoke up. "I think our group will want to meet regardless of COVID. Some of us are over fifty. They'll have to make their own choice about that. But for the most part, I think we will continue meeting too."

"I agree," his wife Sandra said.

"That brings us back to the question of how we are going to do our Sunday morning service. Posting on YouTube is good." Pastor Kyle grimaced. "But I'm not very savvy about filming or posting online. I'll be glad to provide content, but someone with knowledge about this will need to film and post the sermons."

"I'm glad to help," Adrien volunteered. "I'll film and post your sermons on YouTube until we're through this epidemic."

"Thanks, Adrien." Pastor Kyle smiled. "Any other questions or suggestions?" He looked around, but nobody had anything to add. "Okay, then let's close with prayer. I'd like one from each group to pray, then I'll finish."

I listened as each group leader lifted the problem up to God, and Pastor Kyle closed, quoting a verse from Psalm 91 in his prayer.

"As King David wrote, 'Those who live in the shelter of the Most High will find rest in the shadow of the Almighty.' Our Father, we ask you to protect us during these times of plague. Our hope and confidence is in you alone. We ask for your protection in Jesus's name, amen."

Caleb and I walked home in the darkness, lit by the silvery moon above.

"Are you afraid, Lily?"

"I'm a little nervous, but I trust God to help us get through this."

"We're likely to come down with COVID at some point."

"Yes. And that concerns me. I'm new at learning to let go of anxiety and leaning on Jesus."

Caleb put his arm around me and held me close to his side as we walked. "I think you will do just fine, honey."

"As long as I have Jesus ... and you."

At the house, we recounted the meeting to Rachel, who calmly rocked the sleeping Joshua. She nodded.

"Sounds like you have come up with some good ideas. I don't think this is going to be easy, but I'm sure God will be with us all." She looked up at me. "Your dad mentioned this coming plague when he was here for your wedding. He'd heard bits and pieces on the news about it. I've had some time to consider it since, and I truly am not afraid. God is with us in all things. Our lives belong to him to do with as he pleases. I'm content with that."

Her calm acceptance soothed my spirit. "What a blessing you are to me, Rachel."

She smiled peacefully and stood with Joshua cradled in her arms. "Would you like me to put Joshua in his bassinet?"

"Yes, please."

After she had laid our baby down to sleep, Rachel said, "I'm going home now. Morning will come quickly. Good night, my dears."

"Would you like me to drive you home?" Caleb asked.

"No thanks. I'll enjoy the walk."

"Well, I'm going to watch you until that kitchen light comes on," Caleb insisted stubbornly. "It's dark and slippery out on that slope."

"As you wish." Rachel smiled indulgently. "See you tomorrow."

As she left, I took out my phone. "I should call Dad."

"Okay. I'll be here if you need me. Afterward, I'm calling my folks too."

Our Bible study group met at Rachel's place on Wednesday evening. Before we began, Caleb talked about the shutdown order and how we might want to deal with it.

"The president said the risk from COVID 19 to our age group is very low. Those at greatest risk are the older people. Dave and Jolene think their group may want to isolate or limit their social lives until this problem passes, but the rest of us thought our groups could continue meeting in homes. None of our groups are large, except for the youth. They're going to divide into two groups to meet. What do you all want to do? Shall we continue meeting? Or should we shut down?"

"Doesn't the Bible say we're supposed to keep meeting together?" Misty asked.

"Yes. So, we need to decide how that will look for our group," Caleb said.

"Continue meeting in person," Gage said.

"I agree." Joe nodded.

The others nodded their heads and murmured agreement.

"If I may make a suggestion," Rachel spoke up. "My house is large enough for all of you, and my driveway holds all your vehicles. I would like to offer my home as a meeting place. I would be glad to help with Elijah and Joshua if they're fussy. That would free you up to fellowship and study the Bible together. Plus, I'm not in town, where people might resent our meetings and report us to the authorities."

"Thank you, Rachel. That would be great." Caleb looked around to see what the others thought and saw smiles and nods. "Okay. Then let's do it. But I'd like to ask us to think about each other before we get together each week. If anyone has a cold, please remain at home until you are well. COVID is supposed to start like a cold, so let's avoid spreading any germs. Agreed?"

Again, we nodded our approval.

Caleb looked around at our group. "We will probably all get COVID at some point. When we do, we will pray for one another and if there are needs, like meals, we can organize and find ways to provide help without exposing ourselves to the virus. Beth Peters will call the group leaders if we need to help anyone outside our own group. But I hope you will call Lily or me if any of you fall ill."

Jesse spoke up. "As the town nurse, I'm going to be exposed to COVID a lot. I will probably be among the first to catch it. Please, please pray for me, and for Gage too."

"Let's do that now," Caleb said.

Everyone gathered around Jesse and Gage and placed their hands on their heads or shoulders. One by one, we prayed for their safety and physical health, asking God to shield them from sickness.

"We're facing a world-wide plague, a pandemic," Caleb said. "I believe we should face it with confidence in God, faith in his healing power, and we should trust our lives to his care. Does that mean none will die? I do not know. But I believe we need to trust God for the outcomes as we pray for healing. Our lives belong to him, and we can trust him to do what is best for all who believe in him, for all who put their hope in him. We must always ask for healing, as Jesus said. Then we leave our hands open, ready to receive his will, trusting him in all things.

"It is not wrong to go to doctors. Luke was a physician, and he wrote of Jesus's miracles. But our first response toward illness should be to go immediately to the Father with our requests, in Jesus's name. Then, recognizing God has given us doctors and medicine, we can go to a medical professional when needed. God works through miracles as well as through doctors. He is above all."

My heart pondered these thoughts as we went our separate ways that night. Rachel's words about blessing the Lord, no matter what, came back to me. In joy and in grief, I knew Jesus would always be with me. He would give me the courage to ask and to receive by faith.

CHAPTER 18

The next day while Caleb was feeding the cattle in the pasture below, and Joshua was down for a nap, I checked my email. There was something from the art agent I'd contacted. I opened it eagerly, hoping against hope for good news.

The agent had a client who wanted me to illustrate her book! I danced around the room and laughed aloud.

He had enclosed the manuscript for me to consider. Reading it through, I thought of many ways to illustrate the story. The agent wanted me to do a pencil sketch of the illustrations I would use for the book, with a suggested layout to show to the author for her approval.

Wanting to run it by Caleb first, I printed it out to share with him. When he returned home for lunch, I showed him the offer.

"Lily, that looks great!"

"Yes. Children's books have always remained more stable than adult books, and the pay is the equivalent of six month's full-time wages."

"I'm happy for you, honey. This is a great opportunity for you."

"Thanks for the support, Caleb. You know, I'm going to need your help with Joshua when I paint."

"Okay. I'm glad to help. The first thing we'll need is to set up your painting room. Where would you like it to be?"

"It needs a northern exposure, so I'd say the room next to ours would be best. That back window faces north."

"Okay. I'll help you set things up this afternoon. Do you have all the equipment you'll need?"

"Most of it. I've never had a drafting table, but to get the right perspective on my art, it would be helpful."

"Then let's check online and see if we can order one."

By the end of the day, my painting room was organized well enough for me to begin my initial work. Soon, I was fully set up.

As I began my illustration sketches, I thought back to what Mom had said about my not being confident enough to succeed on my own. Not true. I just needed to work in a field where I could use the skills God had given me. Peace and thankfulness flooded my heart as I tuned out Mom's negative predictions. Yes, she had seen me when I was at my lowest. I truly was not ready to succeed at that time. I could understand how she saw things. But God had brought me into a place where I had all the love and support that I need to achieve my goals as an illustrator.

God, you are the one who changed my life. You gave me this community where people love and support me. You brought me to Rachel and Caleb and blessed me. Knowing you have forgiven me of my own sins, I know I must forgive Mom of her sins against me. Jesus said we must do that. It isn't easy, but I can forgive her of undermining me now, for you have built me up and given me the desires of my heart. I need to be generous toward her. Lord, help me to forgive,

Will and Margaret sat separately in their living room in Santa Rosa watching the nightly news together. The death toll from COVID was growing. California was mostly shut down, except for the big box stores, banks, and other essential businesses.

"Margaret, maybe you should think about giving up your card games on Wednesday mornings."

"What? Give up my only social activity? No! These are my friends. There are only a few of us. Besides, we're still young enough not to be in danger from COVID."

"I'm not so sure. I'm hearing reports some young people have been dying of COVID lately. The doctors don't know how to treat this virus. I'd feel better if you didn't endanger yourself, Margaret."

"Well, thank you for caring," Margaret said, still irritated. "But I think I know what I'm doing."

Will swallowed a sigh. "I just want to keep you safe, my dear."

Margaret softened a little. "I know, Will. You are good to me."

"If you have time this evening, I'd like to share with you some things I've been learning."

"What kind of things?"

"Oh, it's a study I've been doing."

"Hm. Well, okay."

Will turned off the news and held out a hand to Margaret. "Come along, my dear."

Leading her to the couch, he sat down next to her and put his arm around her shoulder, something he hadn't done in a long time.

"Margaret, I've been attending a men's Bible study at noon on Thursdays."

"A *Bible study?*"

"Yes. I'd like to tell you what I've learned."

"Well ... okay."

"I've been reading about Jesus. I've come to the place where I believe in him and want to follow him."

"Really!"

He ignored her snide remark. "Yes. Really. I like the things Jesus taught. I like what he demonstrated about loving and helping others. I like what he taught about letting God change my heart, not trying so hard in my own strength to be a good person, but letting God do the work in me. I have found peace in what I've been reading, Margaret."

"Peace?" Margaret turned her head away and frowned. "Isn't your job secure enough to give you peace?"

"Oh, my job is secure. The shutdowns haven't affected banks. But the peace Jesus put in my heart is not about my work, but about my soul, the invisible part of me that lives forever."

"What do you mean by something of you lives forever?"

"The soul of humankind lives forever, Margaret. There's something inside me which knows this to be true." Will looked at Margaret, who was glancing at him now. "Look inside yourself, my dear. Don't you feel you're going to live forever?"

After a moment, Margaret said, "Well, maybe. But I know we all die, Will. What's this about living forever?"

"Our souls live on after this lifetime. I know people say we all go to heaven when we die. But that's not true."

"Of course not. We cease to exist. This life is all there is."

"No, that is where too many people are wrong. There is a forever place with God in heaven. But not everyone goes there. Only those who have given their lives to Jesus."

"Oh, come on, Will! You don't really believe that do you?"

"I do. Our world has taught us not to believe in God. But God has found me, and he has opened my eyes to truth. His truth."

"I see." Margaret looked away.

"I'm not asking you to believe this, Margaret. I'm just asking you to listen with an open mind. Can you do that?"

Margaret paused for a long moment. "Okay. I'll listen. But don't expect me to change my mind!"

"That's fair enough." Will reached over and took her hand. "I care about you, Margaret. I know we've grown apart over the past few years. But I'd like to fix that. If you will listen to what I'm learning, it will help put our hearts back together."

She looked up, studying Will's face. "I would like that, Will. I've missed what we had together. I'll listen if you think it will help"

"Thank you, my dear."

Manuel and Rosa Gonzales sat together at an empty table in La Cocina del Lago surrounded by growing darkness, holding the notice the governor had just issued. They spoke together in Spanish, their heart language.

"The governor said we must shut La Cocina down because of the COVID?" Rosa asked.

"Yes, my heart, he did." Manuel sighed. "I don't know how we can keep the business or pay our rent if we cannot work."

Rosa gripped his hands in hers. "We will just trust the Lord for this, as we have always trusted him. He will show us what to do."

Manuel bowed his head. "Father God, you brought us here to this place. You blessed us with this business. You see what we face. We give back to you all the blessings you have given to us and trust you with our lives in this new country. We thank you for bringing us here. We know you are with us as we pray. We trust you and you alone. In the name of Jesus Christ, amen."

Silently they sat together in the empty room, looking around at all the work they had done.

"At least we still have food," Manuel said. "The meat must be eaten while we still have electricity and this building. But the flour, the rice, and the beans, they will keep."

"We will be fine, my love. God is with us in this as he is in all things." Rosa lifted her head high. "I know he will take care of us. We are his children."

J. J. walked out on the snow-covered ground in front of the marina. The docks had been drawn in and stacked on land before the lake froze over. Now the ice was breaking up as spring descended on their town. He rubbed his chin and looked around.

I can live off fish for a while, but I don't know how I'll pay my mortgage and stay in the house with my livelihood taken away. Lord, show me what to do. I know you're in charge of my life—it belongs to you. I'm okay walking one day at a time by faith. But if there is something I can do to provide for myself, please show me. I don't know how long this lockdown will last, but I know you will outlast all things. I trust you. There will be a lot of people applying for unemployment. I'm not sure I want to do that. I want to work. Please guide me, Lord.

Laura Sanders, who had worked in La Cocina del Lago before the COVID shutdown, stared out the window of her small cabin. Her toddler, coughing and sneezing from a cold, whimpered and held onto her legs. Reaching down, she scooped up the little girl and rocked back and forth, soothing her.

"Hush sweetheart, don't cry."

What can I do? Of course, I can apply for unemployment again. But will I have enough for rent? Just when things were going so well. I don't know what to do. My parents won't help. I can't ask Pete for help. He's hit me one too many times. And I can't let him hit Mesa. If he does, I'll ... I'll ... Well, it's best if Pete doesn't find out where we live. I don't care if he makes good wages. No price is worth his abuse. I'll just have to figure this out myself. Oh, I wish I knew what to do.

"Mommy sing," Mesa demanded fretfully.

Laura began singing "Itsy Bitsy Spider" while Mesa's eyes drooped and soon closed.

Alone in her now-empty house, Rachel sighed while she skimmed the cream off a gallon of milk. Tonight, the young people would come to her home for their weekly Bible study. She planned to make pumpkin pie, topped with whipped cream. She missed having Lily in her home but having her just up the hill in the Maxwell log home was certainly nice. Lily often came down to visit, sometimes bringing Joshua along. She looked forward to seeing Caleb, Lily, and Joshua tonight, a delight she had never expected in her many years at Lake Thechihila. Life was good, but she missed Lily's cheerful voice around the house.

The homes around Lake Thechihila faced uncertain times. Thankfully, the grocery store and gas station remained open. Jesse still worked at the doctor's office, keeping medical care available for us. Doctor Fallon still came once a week for more detailed care. Tourist shops and schools were closed. The town struggled under the weight of unemployment. No one knew what to expect as COVID crept over the land like fingers of fog drifting through the forests.

Caleb's phone rang one morning as we were finishing breakfast. "Lily, J. J. asked me to help him put the dock sections back in place. The lake is thawing around the edges, and we think people will still bring their boats out to fish and recreate as things warm up. At least, we're hoping they will."

"Okay. Tell J. J. hello for me."

"Will do."

Caleb kissed me and tickled Joshua under the chin. Joshua waved his hands up and down and made babbling sounds. Caleb laughed. "He's gonna be talking soon. I can hardly wait to find out what's on his mind."

"Oh, I think I know. He wants to be held and he wants to eat ... just like any other man."

"Ha!"

"I'm right. You'll see."

"Then he's a kid after my own heart." Caleb grinned, pulled on his fishing boots, and headed for the door. "I'll be back for supper so you can feed me. After that, you can hold me too."

I laughed and followed him onto the deck. "I look forward to that."

J. J. was already set to go with the forklift when Caleb reached the docking area. After the two men wrangled the bulky sections of the dock into the water and secured them, J. J. said, "Caleb, can you come in for a cup of coffee?"

"Sure. Sounds good."

J. J. fiddled with the coffee maker adding a fresh filter and grounds, making small talk at first. "How are things going for you these days? Has the shutdown affected you yet?"

"No." Caleb shook his head. "Not so far. But I plan to build a small log house down by the road in June, and I've heard building supplies are getting scarce. I've tried to get conduit for plumbing, but someone beats me to it every time a load comes into the hardware store in Bozeman."

"Hm. Shipping problems. Yes, I can see that."

"Ben Farley from the Elliston area will bring the timber here the first week in June, and once the spring rains stop, I'll start construction."

"Will you need any hired hands for that?"

Caleb nodded. "Yes. You interested?"

"Yes. I don't know if I'll be able to stay in town unless things change in a hurry. The government ordered me to shut the marina—it's not essential according to them."

J. J. handed Caleb fresh cup of coffee.

"Thanks." Caleb sipped the hot liquid carefully. "Okay. I'd be glad to have you on the crew. But I don't know how long the job will last."

"I'll take what I can get. Thank you. One day at a time is all God gives us anyway. Some people are going on unemployment, but I want to work. I'd go crazy not having something to do."

Caleb nodded. "I hear you."

"Thanks for helping with the dock."

"No problem."

CHAPTER 19

Later that evening, Caleb held me in his arms as we lounged on the couch, watching the fire crackle in the fireplace. He told me about J. J.'s dilemma. "Of course, I can use his help for putting up the walls of the new cabin, but that won't happen until the middle of June. He needs more work."

"What about parttime work? Could he help you move cattle?"

"Sure. But that's only two or three days a month."

I thought of Caleb's pet project. "Can we afford to hire him to work in the greenhouse?"

"That's a thought. In fact, we may need to grow a lot more fresh fruits and vegetables to sell locally if shipping gets any worse."

"Today Rachel said fresh fruit and veggies go fast, and sometimes she can't find any at the store in town. With the shutdown, we may have trouble getting food in Lake Thechihila."

"Well, we can help Rachel with that right now. We have plenty to share with her, but we don't have enough for many more people."

"If you grow more, would that be enough income for J. J.?"

"Maybe. But not at first. I'd have to build the stacks in the shed upward. We could put quite a lot of plants in that room if we did. J. J. could help with that if he wants. I can't afford to pay him unless I sell a steer or two. I could do that, even though they aren't quite big enough yet."

"Hm. I like that idea."

"I'll mention it and see if he'd be interested in working parttime." Caleb nuzzled my hair. "But let's think about other things for a while."

I chuckled. "Yes. Let's do."

And that was the end of any serious talk for the evening.

Later, as I lay in bed next to my sleeping husband, watching the moon move across the night sky, I thought of the problems facing our small town. Federal money had been sent to Montana to bolster unemployment, but so far it had not reached our people. Was J. J. the only one struggling to make ends meet? Probably not.

"Father in heaven," I whispered. "You know our needs, and you are faithful. Thank you for providing extra money for our family through my artwork. But now some of our friends are struggling. Show us how we can help our neighbors during this time of crisis. And please keep us safe from the plague crossing our country. In Jesus's name, amen."

Peace descended on my heart, and I fell asleep with my arms wrapped around Caleb.

One morning in April, Margaret awoke feeling very ill. She moaned and coughed.

Will's eyes flew open, and he sat up in bed. "Margaret? Are you okay?"

"No."

"What can I get for you?"

She coughed and gasped. "Hot tea and some cold medicine would be nice."

Will slipped out of bed and hurried to the bathroom where he found the medicines. Filling a glass of water, he took it to Margaret. "Here. Take this."

Margaret struggled to sit up. Will placed his arm behind her, lifting her into a sitting position. She moaned and rested her head on Will's shoulder, reaching for the water and the medicine.

Will felt her forehead. She was too warm. She seemed to have a fever. Was this COVID? Or was it just a cold? "I'll make you some tea and toast, then bring you some clothes. When you've finished eating and dressing, I'm taking you to the hospital, Margaret."

She nodded weakly. "Okay, Will."

An hour and a half later, the hospital admitted Margaret.

"She has COVID," the emergency room doctor told Will. "You will not be able to visit her, and you must quarantine for two weeks."

"I must see her," Will insisted.

"No. Hospital rules. We don't want this to spread, and we don't want you to be sick. She has her phone. If you want to speak with her, you'll have to call her."

"But ..."

"I'm sorry, Mr. Mains. But we're not messing around with COVID. Please go home and quarantine."

Reluctantly, Will left the hospital. In the parking lot, he called Margaret. "My dear, the doctor said I cannot visit you because you have COVID. But I will be here for you whenever you are feeling well enough to talk."

"I–I–I'm afraid, Will!" she wailed, then went into a coughing spasm.

"Margaret, put your trust in Jesus. You said you believed in him just last week. He will take care of you. He is faithful!"

"Okay, Will. But you must pray for me."

"I'm already doing that, sweetheart."

True to her prediction, Jesse was the first member of the young adult Bible study group to contract COVID. She was sick for three days. Gabe was the next victim. But because they were young and healthy, COVID did not hit them as severely as it hit the older population.

Members of their Bible study brought them food and left it outside their door. When they needed supplies, the group took turns buying them in the local grocery store. All through town, people were afraid as COVID spread through the population. Two older people across the lake from us died, but funerals were not permitted. Families buried their dead alone, except for their pastor or priest.

One by one, the citizens of Lake Thechihila came down with COVID. Rachel was also among the first to suffer.

"I'm milking Daisy for you," Caleb declared when Rachel called with the news. "I'll make sure all the animals are fed too."

"Tell her I'll gather the eggs and feed the chickens," Lily offered.

"No!" Rachel said. "You might catch this bug too!"

"We'll be careful," Caleb said. "We'll take the milk and eggs up to our home and tell your customers to come up here to fetch them."

"Well, okay," Rachel said. "But please stay out of my house. It's full of germs." She began coughing.

"Don't worry about a thing," Caleb said. "Whatever you need, we will get. If you feel too bad, we'll take you to a hospital."

"Okay. But you stay safe!"

"Don't worry. We're getting lots of fresh air and sunshine and taking vitamin D and zinc."

J. J. stood in Caleb's large shed, looking around at the plant set-up. "So, you want to expand this?"

"Yes. I'm currently growing only enough for us and for Rachel. But our town may need more fresh fruit and vegetables soon. I've noticed the store is running short most days. Shipping has affected deliveries. We need to step up production."

"Okay. Show me what to do."

Together, Caleb and J. J. began constructing more shelves and installing grow lights at each level.

J. J. looked around and grinned as they began working. "We may be able to feed the whole town with this setup."

"I hope we can grow enough to make a difference."

"That may be necessary, if things continue falling apart like they are now."

"Most families have wild meat in their freezers, but there are a few who don't. I may have to butcher a few more cattle to help if food shortages continue."

While Caleb was working with J. J., Dad called me. Joshua was down for his afternoon nap.

"Lily, Mom has COVID. I took her to the hospital this morning, and they admitted her. I'm in quarantine for two weeks. The hospital won't let me see her. They said I can call her, but that's it."

"Oh, Dad! I'm sorry. Do you want me to come home?"

"No, honey. California is completely shut down. The highway patrol isn't letting anyone in. Only trucks bringing food. You might not be able to leave if you did manage to get in. Stay there ... and pray for Mom."

"I will, Dad." I felt anxious about him. "You've been exposed too. We'll be praying for you too."

"Thank you, honey. I'm not afraid to die, though, because I have Jesus now. No matter what, I trust him. Your mother chose to believe in Jesus too, remember. I told you last time we talked. We're both trusting in him. You stay safe up there with your family in Montana."

"I will, Dad. I love you!"

"I love you too, Lily."

After our brief conversation, I walked out to the shed where Caleb and J. J. were working.

"Caleb?

"Yes?" He finished placing the last shelf on the frame and looked up.

"Dad called. Mom is in the hospital with COVID, and they won't let him see her. She was sick this morning when she first woke up."

Caleb straightened and thought about it for a minute. "I'm sorry, Lily. Do you need to go home for a while?"

"No. California is shut down worse than Montana. We need to pray for my parents. Dad's very worried about Mom, but he doesn't want me there. He said to stay where we're safe."

Caleb and J. J. walked over to me. I leaned into Caleb's embrace. "Let's pray right now," he said. "Father in heaven, we lift Lily's mother up to you in prayer and ask for your healing power to touch her and heal her. We thank you for touching her heart and bringing her to Jesus. It's a comfort to us all. Keep her dad well."

"Yes, Lord," I prayed softly. "I ask for Mom's healing too. I trust you to do what is good and best. Please keep my dad safe!"

J. J. cleared his throat and placed a hand on my shoulder. "Lord, please heal Lily's mom, comfort her dad, and keep him well. Put your peace in Lily's heart right now."

"In Jesus's name we ask this, amen." Caleb wrapped his arms around me in a warm hug. "We will trust Jesus to take care of your mom, Lily. He is in control."

I nodded and included J. J. in a glance. "Thank you for praying with me."

Caleb and I helped care for Rachel's livestock all week. I made fresh soup for her every day as well as small treats to tempt her appetite. Caleb took a card table down and set it up by the back door. When I took food down to her, I'd call her and let her know it was there, then move away and wave from a distance when she came out to get it.

Gradually, Rachel recovered. By the end of the week, she was well, but still a little weak.

The news from California, however, was not good.

"Lily," Dad said, his voice raspy, "I have COVID too. But it's not so bad that I need to go to the hospital. Just coughing and sneezing, like a mild cold."

"Did you see the doctor?"

"No. I can't risk being cooped up in a hospital if your mother needs me."

"Dad!"

"I'm not going, Lily." He was firm. I knew better than to argue.

"How's Mom?"

Dad said nothing, but I heard him sigh.

"She's worse, isn't she?"

"Yes. They've put her on a ventilator."

"Oh." In the silence, my heart reached out to Dad.

"Before they did, your mom said to tell you she is sorry she slapped you and pressured you to abort the baby."

"Please tell her I forgive her!" I said quickly, my heart going out to her.

"I will. I'll let you know how things go." I could hear the sadness in his voice.

"We're praying for you and Mom, Dad."

"Thank you, honey."

"Dad?"

"Yes?"

"Rachel had COVID too."

"Is she okay now?"

"Yes, but she's still weak. Jesse, our nurse at the clinic, is keeping an eye on her. Anyway, you should pray for Rachel too."

"Of course. I will do that."

That night, I tossed and turned, praying for my parents and for Rachel's recovery. I felt helpless, though I prayed off and on all night. Would my parents live? Would Rachel recover completely?

CHAPTER 20

Two days later, Dad called, his voice husky with grief. "Lily, your mom passed away last night."

"Oh, Dad! I'm sorry!" Tears rose in my eyes, tears of grief for Dad's loss. For myself, I felt only sadness. It would have been nice to explore my relationship with Mom now she was a believer. But I'd never get the chance.

That's not true. I will have a chance to have that relationship with Mom in heaven, for she gave her heart to Jesus. We will meet again.

"Dad, how are you doing?"

"I'm better today, but I feel dragged down with grief."

"Oh, Dad. My heart hurts for you. I wish I could come out there to help. When are you having the funeral?"

"I'm not. The mortuaries are full and cannot take more bodies. The ambulance drove Margaret's body to the funeral home. They had caskets. The cemetery staff will bury her tomorrow. I can be there if I keep my distance from the staff. I'm still coughing a lot. But I'm not struggling as much to breathe."

"Oh, Dad." I sighed in grief. "I wish I could come down there to help you."

"I'm glad you aren't here, honey. I wouldn't want you to catch COVID from me. Stay there."

Caleb walked over and put his arms around me. Taking the phone, he spoke to my father.

"Will, I'm sorry for your loss. What can we do to help you?"

"Thanks, Caleb. But for now, just pray for me. Once I'm well and finish a few things here, I will come up there to see you all."

"We would love to have you, sir."

"Call me Will."

"Yes, Will." Caleb cleared his throat. "We look forward to your visit. We have a guest room, so don't plan to stay anywhere else."

"Thank you, Caleb. But I'm looking forward to staying at one of the cabins at the lake and doing some fishing. I'm not ready to be around people much yet."

"I understand. But know that you are welcome here."

"Thank you." He paused. "How's Rachel? Is she better?"

"She seems to be growing stronger every day, Will. Don't worry."

"Thanks for telling me, Caleb. I'm glad to hear she's better. I'll have to get some things settled here before I come to Montana. I'll let you know more in three or four weeks. I'm looking forward to seeing you and Lily. My grandson too."

Rachel recovered quickly from COVID. Her healthy outdoor lifestyle had made her strong and resilient, much to my relief. I'd felt anxious about her after my mother's death. Would I lose Rachel too?

Caleb had kept my heart from despairing with his encouraging words and prayers for Rachel's recovery.

"But Caleb," I asked anxiously, "we prayed for my mom to be healed too. But she died. How can we count on prayer if some people die anyway?"

Caleb bowed his head and thought about my question. "I think it comes down to trusting God for the answer to our prayers, Lily. Sometimes, he heals, and sometimes, he allows death. For the Christian, that is the ultimate healing, for we are with God in heaven. But whether he heals or not, we can trust his answer is for our ultimate good. When we pray, we present our requests, then we leave the matter at Jesus's feet to answer as he sees best."

Caleb drew me close to his heart. "If being a Christian meant we would never suffer or die, *everyone* would choose to be a Christian. Jesus asks us to trust him for all things. We live by faith in a world separated from God. And for the believer, this life is the only hardship we will ever suffer. For those who do not put their faith in Christ, this is the only heaven they will ever experience. So, we trust God to work all things out for our eternal good and for his glory."

"Trust. I'm learning to do that." I relaxed in Caleb's arms. In the days ahead, I thought about what he'd said often. It was a new way of seeing life.

The day finally came when Rachel called us to say she was well. "Thank you for helping with the animals. I think I can take it from here. I'm full of energy today."

"Well, don't wear yourself out!" I protested.

"I'll be fine, Lily." I could hear the smile in her voice.

"Rachel, I'm glad you're well! Be careful not to do too much."

"I will. I'm just going to take care of the cow and the chickens. Then I'll go inside and relax. Don't worry about me, Lily. I still need some space to make sure I'm no longer contagious. So, keep your distance for another few days."

"Okay," I said, still anxious. "But if you need anything, just call."

Two weeks later, Caleb and I both had a touch of COVID, but it wasn't nearly as bad as it had been for the older people in our community. The first day was the worst, but by the second day, we were feeling much better. Joshua didn't suffer from it at all, though Caleb and I sniffled and coughed for a week afterward.

Rachel came up to help with Joshua while Caleb and I battled COVID. "I'm sure I have some natural immunity now, since I've had COVID too. Don't you worry about me. Let me take care of you all."

Gratefully, Caleb and I accepted. What a blessing Rachel was.

J. J. had continued working in the shed while Caleb was sick and had almost finished the shelving. Within a week of Caleb's recovery, the two men planted the first seeds of the crop they hoped to harvest for our town.

Our side of the lake was blessed not to have any COVID deaths, though many were affected by the virus.

Dad called soon after Caleb and J. J. finished planting.

"I'll be there in another couple months," he said. "It's taking longer than I expected because I'm getting rid of almost everything here at the house, and I'm putting the house on the market soon."

"What about your job at Grandpa's bank?"

"Your grandpa understands. He's grieving over Margaret too. I think he will retire soon. I have enough money in savings to start over in Lake Thechihila where I can see you and my grandson often."

"Dad! You're moving *here?*"

"Yes, Lily. I'm coming home."

"That's wonderful, Dad!"

"Thank you, Lily. I think it will be easier to get over losing Margaret if I can relax and fish and hike the mountains again. Seeing you and your family will be rewarding too. It's what I need to do now."

My thoughts went to Rachel after talking with Dad. How would she feel about having him back in town? Would she feel uncomfortable? Or would she be pleased?

"Miz Rosa," Laura said. "What am I to do? I do not have enough money to stay in my cabin now the restaurant is closed."

Rosa sat across the dining room table in her home and poured coffee into their cups, a faint frown on her face.

"Laura, we must leave our home too. The bank is taking it and the restaurant. We will move into the forest. We know of a good place where there is water and plenty of wood. You can come with us. We have a tent and a camper."

"Are you sure?"

"Yes. We will help you and Mesa."

"I have a tent and sleeping bags. I hope we'll be okay during the winter." Laura looked anxious.

"Oh! We make sure you are okay with us and find a way to stay warm. By winter, we maybe can rent a house. You can live with us."

"Thank you, Rosa."

"It is as it should be. We will take good care of you. We will be in forest when my baby comes. I show you how to help me when my time comes in June."

"Are you sure?"

"Yes. I'm sure."

"I've never delivered a baby before."

Rosa nodded. "It is okay, Laura. We go to mountains in two days. On Wednesday. Can you come then?"

"Yes."

"Then we stop here at noon so you can follow. Okay?"

"Okay."

The two women sat quietly, sipping their coffee. Mesa had fallen asleep on the couch. Rosa's children were playing at the park across the street next to the lake. A peaceful spring breeze puffed the curtains at the windows. Though nights were still cold, the daytime temperatures were warmer than they'd been in April, the month before. Laura feared Mesa would not do well camping in this weather.

It will be cold in the forest. Mesa and I may have to sleep in the car until things warm up. We will be cramped, but we can do it. I have sleeping bags. Those will help. With summer coming, we should be okay. Maybe the pandemic will end before cold weather returns.

I can put most of my things in storage for now. I can keep my post office box at the general store so I can receive unemployment checks once my application is processed. If I save most of it, maybe I can afford an apartment in the city when the weather gets cold again. There may be jobs available by that time.

Wednesday came quickly. Laura had managed to squeeze all her possessions into a small storage unit in town, keeping out only the things she and Mesa would need for living in the forest.

At noon, Manuel, Rosa, and their three children drove up to Laura's place and waited while she buckled Mesa into the car seat in her old, gas-guzzling Chevy Impala. The car was dented, and the seats were ripped in places, but it was big enough to hold the basics she would need. The car was also big enough to use for sleeping.

"I'm ready," she said, smiling and sliding behind the wheel.

Manuel slowly started down the road, the small camper trailer in tow. Laura fell into place behind him. Together, the two cars wound their way up the valley and out onto the highway. A few minutes later, Manuel turned off onto a dirt road and drove back into the forest. Two miles in, he stopped in a small clearing.

Pulling in behind him, Laura stopped.

"Come on, Mesa," she said gaily, climbing out of the front and helping her toddler out of the car seat in the back. "Let's go for a walk."

Mesa looked around, her eyes wide with apprehension.

"I see a lake," Laura said, pointing through the trees. "Let's go look."

"We come too." Rosa took Carlos by the hand. "Diego, Julisa, help your father, *por favor*. I be back soon."

Together, Laura, Rosa, and Carlos walked through the trees to the lake, which wasn't very big, but looked clear and clean.

"There is creek coming into lake too," Rosa said, gesturing toward her right. "It come from spring bubbling from ground. There is pump near where we park. The water, it is good."

Laura nodded. "This looks like a good, safe place."

Carlos ran ahead to the water and waded into it.

"Carlos! *Quidado!* The lake can be deep!" Rosa hurried toward the little boy.

Mesa tugged at Laura's hand. "I want to play with Carlos."

"Only if you hold my hand, honey. Rosa is right. The lake is deep. Too deep for you to play here alone. If you want to play in the water, you must ask me. Okay?"

"Okay."

"Promise?"

"Yes."

Laura led Mesa to the water. "Wait here, Mesa. I want to check how deep the water is in this place." She waded through the freezing water. "Brr! It's cold!"

"Can I go in the water?" Mesa hopped from foot to foot.

"For a minute."

Mesa removed her shoes and put her toes into the water, instantly snatching them back. "Too cold, Mommy."

Walking back out of the water, Laura agreed. "Yes. But this summer it will be warmer."

Carlos waded up to the shore to join them. "Brr!" He rubbed his feet in the grass to dry them.

"Maybe we could go for a little walk and explore?" Laura lifted Mesa into her arms and turned to Rosa.

"Yes. The children will like it." Rosa took Carlos' hand and led the way. "There is outhouse back in trees by where we park. This place is good for staying."

"Thank you for bringing me here with you, Rosa. I feel better already."

"Good. It will be okay, yes?"

"Yes."

"God is with us. We will be safe here."

Laura had piled blankets behind the front seat of her car, building it up to seat level to make extra sleeping space for Mesa. That night as she lay next to her sleeping child, she looked out into the starry sky and thought about Rosa's trust in God. With everything that had happened, how could she have such confidence?

She remembered attending a Bible club in a neighbor's back yard one summer when she was about ten. Her family lived in Oregon at the time. She'd heard about Jesus for the first time there. Oh, she'd heard his name before. Her parents used it as a cuss word. But that summer she had learned who Jesus really was. When the teacher had asked if anyone wanted to ask Jesus to come into their hearts, she had raised her hand. She didn't know a lot about this, but she wanted to be close to this man Jesus.

Since that time, she had been moved from town to town as her dad looked for work. She'd attended many schools, always finding herself on the outside socially. Her parents never wanted to go to church, so Laura had not learned more about Jesus, though the hunger for him remained in her heart.

When she was sixteen, Laura met Pete. He was good-looking and had tons of charisma. She'd fallen for him. A few months later, she discovered she was pregnant. Her parents were angry. She was too young to support herself, and they couldn't afford another mouth to feed. But they didn't believe in abortion. Laura was allowed to have her baby, but her parents were not at all pleasant about it.

After Mesa came, Pete, who was twenty, found a job working in the oil fields of eastern Montana and North Dakota. He asked Laura to bring Mesa and come with him. Her parents were only too happy to see her leave. Let Pete feed and house their daughter and granddaughter. They were his responsibility after all.

Elated, Laura walked away from her family, glad to escape the constant nagging and negativity. But once in eastern Montana, she found life with Pete nearly unbearable. Sure, he smiled and joked a lot. But after working all day, he'd buy a six-pack of beer and get drunk. The drink made him mean. He'd take out his anger on Laura, beating her frequently.

The day Pete grabbed at Mesa and screamed in her face, though, Laura's protective instincts kicked in. She knew Pete would hurt her baby too. So, she packed up her things and left in the old, battered Chevy, heading for central Montana to look for work. She read an ad in a newspaper for waiters at a lakeside town and checked it out. That's how she met Rosa and Manuel.

The small-town environment next to the peaceful lake was perfect. Laura and Mesa had thrived there. Mesa was three now. Laura thought she could settle down at Lake Thechihila forever. Then COVID hit. Now she was sleeping in her car with her child, wondering if her life was doomed to be like this always.

Jesus, I don't know much about you, but I need you. Please show me what to do. Help me provide for my little girl. I have no skills to make good money, but I believe you have a way to rescue us from this poverty. Help me, please!

A tear trickled down her cheek. Laura scrubbed it away and sniffed, but something inside her began to relax. Maybe that was Jesus bringing her peace. Her breathing grew even, her eyelids closed, and she fell into a deep, restful sleep.

In her dreams, she was a lamb, lost on a mountain, caught in a thicket. Jesus, the Good Shepherd, lifted her out of the tangle and held her close to his heart. Safe at last.

CHAPTER 21

Our Bible study group had resumed meeting at Rachel's house after she and our family had recovered. All the members of our group had caught and overcome COVID by that time and figured we had some natural immunity to it now.

We were all supposed to wear masks to stop the spread of COVID, but most of us only wore them when we shopped or did business in town. We lived a rural life, with lots of fresh air and exercise, plus we'd already had COVID. At Rachel's house, we didn't bother with masks.

As soon as we arrived at the Bible study, Rachel swooped in and gathered Joshua into her arms. "Come to me, my little lambkin." She smiled into his eyes, and he waved his tiny hands at her, gurgling with joy.

Handing the diaper bag over, Caleb grinned. "There's a warm bottle in the bag when you're tired of playing with him."

Rachel laughed. "He'll get sleepy long before I tire of him." She waved at the kitchen table. "Help yourself to snacks."

"Mmmm. Is that carrot cake?" It was my favorite of all Rachel's recipes.

"Yes. Help yourself, Lily girl." Rachel moved around the room greeting the young people.

"I've been teaching online since school was closed, but some of my students need extra help. I'm not sure how well this method of teaching is going to work." Colleen bit into a piece of carrot cake.

"Some of the parents have switched to home schooling, I've heard." Misty said over her shoulder as she led Elijah to Rachel.

"Come along, Elijah." Rachel reached down for the little boy's hand. "Let's go play with the toys in the bedroom." Content to stay with our little ones, Rachel led them away and closed the door.

"Yes, I've heard some are home schooling, which should work well if their parents can stay home and feel comfortable teaching. Some of the parents don't know how to teach, and they get frustrated. There are several children in my class who are floundering under these conditions."

"J. J., how's the work going?" Gage shrugged his coat off and hung it on the rack by the door.

"I'm surviving between work at Caleb's nursery and yard work here and there. We've started harvesting some crops at the nursery, and we sell some of the produce to the local store. But it's tough without having the income from the marina."

"I've noticed there have been more boaters at the lake this spring."

"Yes. Since people aren't supposed to gather in public, families are spending more time outdoors on the lake. I think it's a healthy alternative to being stuck in the house."

Gage smiled. "I agree. I've had lots of paint ballers in the national forest this year too."

"Has anyone seen Rosa and Manuel?" Jesse looked around the group. "Rosa's baby is due in June, and I haven't seen her recently."

We exchanged glances.

"Laura Sanders disappeared too. Her little girl was sick last week. I checked up on her, only to discover she had left town."

"I noticed the Thompson family's house down by the lake is empty." J. J. said "They have two youngsters. Does anyone know what happened to them?"

Caleb frowned with concern. "Why don't we try to find out where they've gone. They may be safe, but maybe they aren't. We can at least ask around. Someone might know."

Murmurs of agreement rose around the room.

"Maybe Laura and the Thompsons have family they could go to."

Colleen pulled out her notebook. "I'm putting them on our prayer list."

Later, we sat together at home in front of the fire after Caleb had carried a sleeping Joshua to his crib and covered him with a warm, puffy blanket. Caleb's dog, Molly, curled up at our feet, her tail thumping occasionally. She had taken on the job of watching Joshua's every move, like he was her puppy. But she was off duty since he was now in his crib.

"I don't think Manuel and Rosa would have any place to go. I'm surprised they left without leaving word. Rosa was very close to her delivery date. I'm worried about her."

Caleb wrapped his arms around me. "We'll find them, Lily."

"I hope and pray we do. With Rosa's baby coming in a few weeks, we need to make sure they're all safe. And I doubt Laura had anyone to take her in. Her family doesn't approve of her situation, and she said they don't have any money to help. She's on her own."

"I'm afraid we're going to see more and more people with housing problems in the months ahead." Caleb stroked my hair. "This shutdown has messed up everyone's finances, and some people are already being evicted because they couldn't pay their rent. I'll bet that's what happened to Manuel and Rosa. Maybe Laura too. Didn't she work for them?"

"Yes."

We sat in troubled silence, watching the flames fly up the chimney.

"What can we do, Caleb?"

"We have room here for a few people." He offered the thought tentatively, not sure how I would feel about it.

"Yes. We have the spare bedroom and the loft."

Caleb nodded. "I'm glad you agree. Sharing our home may be uncomfortable, but we should help our friends through this time."

"*If* we can find them."

Gage approached J. J. the day after Bible study. "J. J., I'm going to need extra help part time with all the people now recreating in our area. Nate already works weekends and days when I can't. But we still need help. My department has agreed to hire another fish and game warden. Are you interested?"

"Absolutely. In about two weeks."

"Then you're hired. Just come over to the office and fill out a few papers." He paused. "Will Caleb be okay at the greenhouse if you're not there?"

"I'll talk with him about working with him during my off hours. Now that the plants are up and growing, there isn't much to do these days. I should be able to do both jobs. You know he's getting ready to build a small log home starting next week. I promised to help with that, but the hardest part should take about a week. I'll need to be free to help when the logs come. Once the walls are up, I'll just be working for him part time again."

Gage relaxed. "Good. I wouldn't want to short Caleb's staffing on anything."

At church Sunday, Jesse asked me a favor. "Lily, Ben and my sister, Tara, and their kids will be coming over in two days when Ben delivers that last load of logs for Caleb's house project. I'll be at work until four, and Gage is out until five. I was wondering if you could feed them lunch?"

"Sure, Jesse. I'll just add a little more to the menu."

"The kids' names are Marc and Holly. Liam, my brother, will be with the work crew too."

"Great. I'll look forward to meeting them all again. Last time we met was at your wedding, and I didn't have a chance to say more than hello."

"Thanks, Lily. I appreciate your help."

"Make sure Tara knows to come up to the house with the kids."

"I will. See you after I get off work."

A couple of days later, Ben Farley delivered the last load of logs for the 960-square-foot cabin.

Jesse was still at work. I'd prepared lunch for the men, knowing they would probably be hungry soon, and had told Caleb to bring them up to the house when they were ready for lunch. Two casseroles of hamburger, rice, and mushrooms baked in a cheesy sauce stayed warm in the kitchen oven, while a tossed salad stayed cold in the fridge. A covered basket of rolls, a dish of butter, and a bowl of grapes were already on the table. Plates, cups, and silverware stood ready at one end of the counter.

I watched as the men started building. Ben and Liam placed the logs, each one numbered, on the side of the house where they'd be used. This would streamline the building process. Caleb and J. J. measured and cut the saddle notches into the logs with careful precision while Ben and Liam set the prepared bottom logs on the cement foundation.

Tara drove their pickup to the house. I walked out to greet them as they arrived. As soon as the truck stopped, both Holly and Marc had their doors open and were climbing out. Looking toward the construction, Marc started down the hill.

"Stay up here!" Tara called. "You can't be at the work site. You'll be in the way."

"Aw, Mom," Marc pouted.

I laughed, knowing Joshua would be saying the same thing in a few years.

"Kids!" Tara shook her head. "They want to be in the middle of everything."

"Of course. You must be Tara."

"Yes. And you're Lily?"

"Yes. Come on in. And tell the kids I have cookies for them."

Joshua was excited to see our visitors. A little over three months old now, his personality was showing. He loved people and made lots of babbling noises at them, trying hard to communicate. Konnor had been like that too. Always wanting to be in the thick of things.

Holly wanted to hold him immediately upon seeing him. I had her sit on the couch and showed her how to hold him properly.

"If he gets too lively or your arms get tired, let me know."

"Okay."

"Is there anything I can do to help you to get ready for lunch?" Tara asked.

"I have lunch under control, but I could use some help washing potatoes and wrapping them in foil for dinner. I'm doing baked potatoes and steak for dinner. Jesse and Gage will be coming up then too."

"Sounds delicious. Show me the potatoes."

Together, we scrubbed and wrapped russets, chattering as we worked.

"Jesse told me you came out here from California?"

"Yes. Santa Rosa. But my dad was raised here at Lake Thechihila."

"Really?"

"Yes. And he plans to move back here soon. My mom died recently from COVID, and Dad wants to come back to his roots."

"I'm sorry about your mom."

I shrugged. "I'm just glad she turned to Jesus before she died. Our family wasn't one to attend church, so we didn't learn about how much God loved us until I came out to Montana to live with Rachel. My fiancé had told me a little about Jesus before he died, and I was already interested because of what he'd said. But Rachel ... well, Rachel showed me so much more. I love her. She's become a dear friend."

"I'm glad. God put her in your life at just the right time."

"Yes. What about you, Tara? You don't sound like you were raised in Montana."

"No, I'm from Texas. I brought Jesse and Liam here after our uncle murdered our grandmother, and we needed to get out of his way before he hurt us."

"Oh!" I blinked and turned to her. "When did this happen?"

"When I was eighteen and a freshman in college. Jesse called me and told me what had happened. I drove home, took the kids and our horses, and fled to Montana. Gran had a ranch here which she'd left to me in her will. God brought Ben along to help us then. We fell in love and have been raising kids and horses ever since."

My phone buzzed.

"Lily, could you bring some cold water down to us?"

"Sure, Caleb." I slipped the phone back into my pocket. "We need to take water down to the men. I have a case by the door."

"Let me help you."

"Okay. Let me put Joshua in his playpen first." I gathered him up and placed him in the play pen. "Holly, would you mind keeping an eye on Joshua while I take this down to the crew?"

"Sure. Glad to." She was instantly by the net playpen.

"Can I help carry water?" Marc asked, eager to see the action up close.

"How about you bring one of those folded trash bags on the counter?"

"Okay."

Together, Tara and I carried the case of water to the truck and slid it onto the floor of the backseat. In less than a minute, we were at the work site and the men were gathered around the water, sweat dripping from their faces, shirts sticking to their bodies. Marc jumped out of the truck and ran over to the log Ben had just finished, examining the log, and looking around.

"I like the full scribe Scandinavian saddle notch best," Caleb was telling Ben. "Thanks for putting the notch into the bottom side of the logs. It's the best way."

"I agree. I added onto Tara's log cabin and used the same technique. The original cabin was just chinked. I built a small mill to process logs after building the add-on. I'm putting together log home kits for people now."

"Did you build the add-on yourself?"

"Some friends helped me. All the equipment I had at the time was a winch, so building took a long time."

"Yes. That's what I have too. Building this house won't be quick work, but I have friends to help me."

"Hi, Ben." I'd been listening to Caleb and Ben discuss the work. I'd met Ben earlier when he'd brought other logs.

"Hi, Lily. Thanks for the water."

"No problem. Lunch will be ready up at the house whenever you guys are ready."

"Great."

"Come on, Marc." Tara called. "Let's go."

"Can we go down to the lake?" Marc obviously wasn't eager to stay inside.

"Sure. But let's get Holly first."

"I'd go with you, but I need to feed Joshua and put him down for a nap."

We walked up the driveway together. A few minutes later, Tara and the children were walking toward the lake following the shortcut from the church grounds.

I carried Joshua onto the porch and pointed to the work crew. "Look, Joshua. There's Daddy!" Holding Joshua on one hip, I pointed toward Caleb. The men were using a wheel loader to move the logs off the truck.

"Da-da," Joshua pointed happily.

Caleb is the only father Joshua will ever know. There is a strong bond between them already. Someday, when he's older, I will tell him about you, Konnor. But for now, we're both very happy. God has provided well for us. And though I miss you, I do love Caleb too. He is different from you, but he is a great husband and father. And he loves Jesus will all his heart. I know you would approve.

CHAPTER 22

"J. J., there's been smoke rising over by the old Paulson place. Nobody lives in the abandoned house, which is falling apart. But there's a lake and campground on the north side of the property. Could you go over and check it out?"

"Sure thing." J. J. eagerly stood up from his desk. He hated paperwork, especially when the sun was shining.

"I've heard people have started moving out into the campgrounds around the state after being evicted. This COVID shutdown has been hurting a lot of people. I don't know what you'll find there. Be careful."

"Okay. I'm used to all kinds, what with working at the marina."

"Call me if you need help."

"Will do." J. J. grabbed the keys from the wall and headed for the company jeep.

Rosa stirred the pot of beans cooking over the fire and dumped a small can of spicy tomatoes into it. The spice helped her family feel full sooner. Mesa lay on a blanket nearby taking a nap, her teddy bear clutched tightly in her arms.

"Rosa, here's the water." Laura sat the bucket down next to the campfire. "I'm sorry I took so long. There were some men getting water, and I didn't want them to see me. They sounded rough."

"Oh, this is not good." Rosa looked up in alarm. "With Manuel and the children in town, we must be careful." She looked at the direction the smoke was drifting. "If we are quiet, they may not find us. The wind is blowing the smoke away."

"We must get into our cars and drive away if they come this direction."

"Yes. Is good idea."

"Well, lookey here, Chuck. Two pigeons!" A tall, unshaved man stepped into the clearing followed by another equally rough companion.

"Ah, ain't they cute." The second man was by Laura's side in a moment.

"Leave us alone!" Laura yelled, backing toward Rosa, who had stood, holding a big spoon in her hand.

Laura ducked down and grabbed a small branch from the woodpile. "Get away!" With her other hand, she pulled the phone out of her pocket and started to hit 9-1-1.

"Now, that ain't gonna do you no good, missy." Chuck grabbed her phone and tossed it into the forest.

Mesa sat up and screamed.

Laura struck with her stick, straight at Chuck's stomach. Her dad had taught her that. "Never swing. Just shove straight at the stomach." His words echoed in her brain.

Chuck gasped, buckled, and took a step back.

"Now that wasn't friendly." The first man stepped toward her warily.

Rosa grabbed another stick and rushed up behind him, beating him over the head as hard as she could.

The man collapsed to the ground.

"Now what'd ya do that for?" Chuck demanded, staggering forward.

"You come any closer, and I'll give you another something to think about." Laura backed toward Rosa, who stood behind her, ready to defend her friend.

The sound of an approaching engine split the air as J. J. roared over the ridge.

"Come on, Gary!" Chuck went over to his friend, still holding his stomach. "Let's get out of here. Someone's coming."

Gary moaned and pushed himself up from the ground.

J. J. pulled up and stopped in a cloud of dust. Taking the situation in at a glance, he jumped out of his truck and drew his service gun.

"Halt! Raise your hands!"

The two men stopped and cautiously raised their hands in the air.

"Now get on the ground and put your hands behind your head."

J. J. grabbed cuffs off the truck's seat, keeping his gun on the two men. Cuffing them, he put the attackers into the back seat of his truck and locked them in. Turning back to the women, he holstered his weapon.

"Laura—Rosa. Are you okay?"

"Yes." Laura nodded and hurried over to Mesa. "But you sure turned up at the right time."

J. J. shook his head and stood arms akimbo. "We've been looking for you and your families. What are you doing out here in the forest?"

Laura shrugged. "We didn't know what else to do. We were evicted because we couldn't pay rent." She glanced at the tall, lanky game warden and lifted her chin. "We didn't want to be a burden to anyone, and we didn't have anywhere else to go."

Rosa nodded. "Yes. The bank take our house and La Cocina del Lago. We cannot pay. So, we must leave."

"Where are Manuel and the kids?"

"They'll be back soon. Rosa sent them into town for supplies," Laura said.

J. J. sighed, still shaking his head. He reached for his radio and called Gage. "I found Rosa and Laura. They're here at the lake by the old Paulson place. Manuel and the kids are in town picking up supplies. There were two men in camp harassing the women. I cuffed them and put them in the truck. Call the county sheriff, will you?"

"Will do. Good work. Stay with them until the sheriff gets there."

"Of course. Do we have anyone in town who can take the Gonzales family and Laura and her toddler in? They're out here camping because they were evicted. It isn't safe."

"I'll check around."

"You might ask Rachel. She may have some ideas."

"Good idea. I will."

J. J. put the radio down and turned to the two women. "Once Manuel gets here, we're gonna talk about getting you back into town."

Rosa put both hands on her stomach and grimaced.

"Rosa? Are you okay?" Laura carried Mesa over to where Rosa stood, while J. J. strode over and took Rosa's arms.

"Ma'am, I think you should sit down."

"Yes." Rosa moved toward the small patch of grass and a rumpled blanket. There she lay down.

252

"Are you in labor?" Laura tucked Mesa's pillow under her head.

"I do not know. It is time. It was pain, but we must wait to see if it happens again."

J. J. went back to the truck for his radio. "Gage, Rosa may be in labor. We need to get her to the clinic. Tell Jesse."

"Will do."

"Laura, you must stir beans." Rosa motioned toward the bubbling pot.

Laura looked around for the spoon and found it on the ground near the cooking pot and washed it quickly before stirring the food Rosa had been cooking for lunch.

Manuel and the children returned a few minutes later. Alarmed to see Rosa lying on the ground, he hurried over to her.

"Rosa! *Que pasa?*"

"I'm okay, Manuel. I just have small pain. Maybe baby coming."

J. J. knelt next to Manuel and Rosa. "There were some bad men here. I have them locked in my truck. I'll hand them over to the county sheriff. But the women are okay." He glanced up at Laura, who was stirring the beans. "You know, Manuel, these women are tough! They hit one man in the stomach and the other over the head."

Manuel looked fondly at Rosa. "She is always a brave one."

"I've called Gage, the lead game warden. He's checking around to see if we have a place in town for your families. They shouldn't be out here—too many homeless people, and some do not behave well."

"I am happy if you can help us." Manuel looked at Rosa anxiously. "For me to be in forest is okay, but not Rosa and children. Not safe."

"I agree, Manuel. When we learned your family was gone, we began praying for you and checking around to see if anyone knew where you were. We want to help."

"Gracias, mi amigo. Thank you."

"Caleb, Rachel called and told me J. J. found Manuel and Rosa and their family. Laura was with them. They've been camping out in the forest."

"What? Why didn't they come to us and ask for help?"

"They are used to doing for themselves. But now that we've found them, we need to help. Rosa can't be in the forest. J. J. said she's in labor. They've taken her into the clinic. I told J. J. to bring the children up here."

"Good. We have plenty of room for the family. But what about Laura and her toddler? Caleb asked.

"Rachel said she'd take them in."

"Good."

"I'll get the spare bedroom ready, and if you could put a couple air mattresses in the loft, we can put the boys on them. Julisa can have the bed."

"Okay. Do you need help with the guest room bed?"

"No. I just need to air it. The sheets are clean."

"I'll get the air mattresses from the storage shed."

J. J. arrived with the three children as Caleb carried the air mattresses into the house.

"Look what I have here," J. J. called, helping the kids out of the forestry truck.

"Come in," Caleb said, smiling at the children, who turned large brown eyes toward him. "We'll take good care of you while you wait for your parents. Do you want to see your new bedroom?"

"Yes." Julisa stepped forward. "I do not like sleeping in the forest."

Diego laughed and poked Carlos. "I liked it. We went fishing every day."

"It was cold at night," Carlos complained.

"Well, we will make sure you're warm now," Caleb said. "Come with me. J. J., could you grab the door?"

"Yep." J. J. held the door open as Caleb carried the air mattresses inside, followed by the youngsters. "I have a pot of beans in the car. I'll put it in the kitchen."

"Thanks, J. J." Turning to the children, Caleb told them, "Your bedroom is in the loft. Follow me." He climbed the stairs, leading the way into the open room with a window looking out over the valley.

"Oooo! Nice." Julisa threw herself on the bed.

"I have air mattresses for Diego and Carlos." Caleb dropped them onto the floor. "Let's inflate them."

Hearing the children, I climbed the stairs with a load of sheets and blankets. "These should keep you warm." Three pairs of dark eyes looked at me, and three faces lit up in smiles.

"You have a baby, don't you?" Julisa asked.

"Yes. He's taking a nap right now, but he'll wake up soon."

"Let's get these beds ready." Caleb was already inflating one mattress, so I started on the second.

Ten minutes later, the room was ready, and we could smell the beans downstairs on the stove.

"Come and get it," J. J., who had stayed in the kitchen to prepare lunch, called.

The kids sprang to their feet and rushed downstairs, where J. J. had dished up three bowls for them. Chairs squeaked as the children pulled them out and settled into them. Bowing their heads and folding their hands, the children recited a short prayer of thanks together. *"Padre Dios, gracias por esta comida. En el nombre de Cristo Jesús, amen."*

While the children ate a belated lunch, J. J. took us aside and told us what had happened.

"We can't let them go back to the forest. It's too dangerous out there with all the other homeless people. I'm not sure what we can do about other families who may show up. Gage and I are going to keep an eye on that spot and try to keep it safe."

Jesse called from the clinic later that night after the children were in bed. "Rosa was in labor when she arrived. She had a girl. Rosa and the baby are fine. J. J. said you're taking the family in. Is that true?"

"Yes. I have the guest bedroom ready for them. Can Manuel drive them over here? Or should I send Caleb to pick them up?"

"Yes. Manuel will bring them there. What's happening with Laura?"

"She's staying with Rachel."

"Perfect." Jesse said.

"Now all we need to do is find the Thompsons."

"Gage is checking with the other fish and game wardens and the rangers to see if they might be at another campsite."

"Okay. Keep me posted."

"Sure thing. I'm sending Manuel and Rosa over now."

"See you in a few minutes." As I ended the call, I turned to Caleb, who was standing across the room, hands in his pockets, with a curious smile on his face.

"We don't know how long this pandemic will last, or how long everything will be shut down. Are you willing to add to our household for the long haul?"

"Yes, Caleb. How could we let the Gonzales family live in the forest when we have plenty of room here?"

"I agree. I think it's what Jesus would do."

"Yes. Do you think Manuel might be interested in working for you in exchange for housing and food? I know he would not want to accept our help if he couldn't repay it in some way."

"I don't know if he can do that type of work, but I plan to ask."

"Good. I know we don't have a lot of money, but we will find a way to stretch what we have." I walked into his arms.

"You are the most surprising woman I've ever met. Most women would have been a little flustered at the thought of opening their home to people they hardly knew."

"Oh, but we *do* know them. We met them at Rachel's for Thanksgiving. We know they belong to Jesus. That makes them family, doesn't it?"

"You bet. We are brothers and sisters in God's family."

Manuel's truck worked its way up the hill slowly, J.J. following him in case they needed help at the house. Caleb and I went out onto the porch to welcome our new guests.

J. J. took the new baby while Manuel helped Rosa climb down from the truck and carefully climb the steps to our house.

"We're glad you're here!" I reached out and touched Rosa's shoulder. "We have a room all set up for you."

Once inside, Caleb said to J. J., "Okay, let's see this baby." He gently moved the blanket aside. "Beautiful."

I led Rosa to the couch, and J. J. placed the baby in her arms.

"Would you like something to eat?" I turned toward the kitchen. "J. J. fed the children some of your delicious beans, and we still have some left if you want some."

"Yes, please." Rosa sounded timid and started to rise.

"No, stay there. I'll bring it to you."

Caleb cleared his throat. "Manuel, Lily and I would like for you to stay with us for now. I'm going to need help in my greenhouse and on my log home project. I'd be grateful if you could help me with the work."

Manuel looked anxiously at Caleb. "But we do not want to—how you say—*imponer.*"

"If you mean impose, you are not imposing. It would be a pleasure to have you and your family stay with us."

"If I can work with you, then yes, it would be very good to have a place where my family is safe. I do know some things about houses. I build them in Mexico. We use adobe for walls there, but I work with roofs and other things too."

"Good. Then we'll consider it a privilege to have you as our guests. In God's family, we are all brothers and sisters here."

"*Gracias*, Caleb. *Muchas gracias!*"

Caleb and I were beginning a grand adventure and were setting the standard of hospitality firmly at the heart of our marriage. First, Rachel had taken me in, now I was taking in others who needed a place to stay for a while.

CHAPTER 23

The next few weeks were busy. Since Ben and Liam had helped put up the log walls, most of the heavy work was done. The house was not complicated, and with J. J. and Manuel working with Caleb, the roof went on fast. They soon had a good rhythm going.

Rosa wanted to help me around the house, but I insisted she rest until she could walk without pain. Julisa helped with the babies and ran errands for us. Diego fed Caleb's horses and made sure they had water every morning, a job he thoroughly enjoyed. Carlos helped with smaller chores around the house.

Joshua was excited to see another baby, but they were both too little to play. Whenever I put Joshua in his playpen, he wasn't happy unless he could see Rosa and her new baby girl.

"I've named her Bella." Rosa stroked the cheeks of her sleeping baby. "Bella means beautiful."

"That is a great name for her. Yes, she is beautiful." I sat next to Rosa. "She's so tiny and delicate."

Molly came over to where Rosa sat and sniffed the baby, wagging her tail gently. Then she walked over to the crib where Joshua had fallen asleep and lay down. She was turning into a great protector for our little ones.

"Laura is at Rachel's house now. I stayed with Rachel until Caleb and I married. She is very special to me."

"She will be good for Laura too." Rosa nodded. "Laura has bad boyfriend who beat her up. She leave him and bring Mesa here. We hope he do not find her."

"If he does, we will protect Laura. Rachel and Caleb protected me from an old boyfriend who came here to bully me into going back to California with him. Caleb told him to leave, and he did."

"Good."

"Why don't you go lie down for a while, Rosa? I'll look after the older children."

"Yes. This is good idea." She carried her sleeping baby into the guest room.

My phone rang.

"Hello?"

"Hi Lily. This is Rachel. I'm in Bozeman with Laura. She needed a few things, and I wanted to buy some more cloth for a quilt for Mesa. I think there is enough red cotton cloth in my collection at home to go with what I'm seeing here at the fabric store. But would you mind going down there to check? You know where I keep my cloth."

"Sure. I'll go."

"Thanks, honey."

"Rosa, Rachel needs me to check something for her. I'll be right back."

"Is okay," Rosa assured me. "Diego make sure children are good."

I grabbed a tape measure and walked outside. Julisa, Diego, and Carlos were playing on the lawn below the house.

"I'm going down there to Rachel's house to check on something. Will you be okay here?"

"Yes, Miz Lily. We will be fine. I'm old enough to watch over Julisa and Carlos." Diego smiled up at me from the lawn.

"Okay."

I hurried down the path to Rachel's place, entering through the back door. The kitchen smelled of fresh banana muffins. Ah. There they were. A covered basket sat at one end of the counter.

Smiling nostalgically, I went upstairs to Rachel's room and to the cupboard where she kept her cloth. Pulling the plastic tub out and setting it on the bed, I carefully lifted the pieces until I found the red one. After measuring it, I called Rachel.

"You have a red piece with yellow and white flowers on it. Was that what you wanted?"

"Yes. How much is there?"

"There's three-quarters of a yard left."

"Oh, good. That's what I'd hoped. Thank you, Lily."

"Sure. I'm glad to help."

"See you later."

"Bye."

I slipped the phone back into my jeans pocket and lifted the tub of cloth into the cupboard. Turning to go, I froze. There, on the shelf on the other side of Rachel's bed, was what looked like a scrapbook. And on its spine was a picture of me when I was about four years old.

What? Why ...?

I didn't know what to think. Walking around the bed, I reached for the book, lifted it down, and sat on the edge of the bed to look at it.

Inside, on the very first page, was a birth certificate. *The name of the baby was Lily Annette Carson.*

I gasped. The mother's name was Rachel Carson. *And the father's name was Will Mains.*

I just stared at it for a few minutes, unable to take it all in. The birth date was my birthday.

But my birth certificate in my files lists Margaret Mains as my mother! This cannot be.

I turned the page. On one side was a picture of me at about a year old. The other page had a one-page letter pasted on.

> Rachel, I hope you are well and able to walk again by now. Here is a picture of Lily. She is happy and is growing like a weed. Margaret and I have told our friends we adopted her, but only Margaret has done that. I will not lie and say I adopted my own daughter. There was no need for me to do so. Our friends think she is beautiful. I do too. And I love her with all my heart.
> Sincerely, Will

Turning the page, I saw another photo of me, this time from when I was about two. A note was pasted to the opposite side.

> Rachel, Lily is walking and sometimes running these days. She likes to walk with me in the garden and look at every flower. Her favorite flowers are red roses. She puts her nose into them and sniffs whenever she finds one. Yesterday, she tried to sniff a dandelion and got yellow pollen all over her nose. She is talking in short sentences, and she sings her favorite songs. I think she will do well in music.
> Sincerely, Will

A letter dated a year later—another photo. This time, I was hugging my favorite doll.

Rachel, Lily loves the doll you sent to her. She named it Marigold. I think she likes the way the name has so many syllables. She pronounces each one carefully. We started her in preschool two days a week. Margaret said she is shy and being with other children will help her socially. She colored a picture at school. I'm sending it to you. I think she has talent.
Sincerely, Will

On the following page there was a careful drawing of a round duck, with an oversized bill and very big feet.

Every year, my father had sent Rachel one photo of me, and a brief note. When I was seven, he sent a story I had written and illustrated. At age ten, I was holding my first guitar. A copy of my high school diploma and a photo of me at graduation—a picture of Konnor and me from college with Aaron and a few others—a program from college when I'd played and sung *Scarborough Fair*—a picture of Konnor and me at the lake.

Dad had kept Rachel informed of my life once a year.

"Lily?" Caleb's voice called from downstairs. "Where are you?"

"I'm up here." I wiped away the tears sliding down my face.

Caleb came upstairs, covered with dust from work. "Lily? Rosa sent me down to get you. Joshua is awake. What's wrong?"

I closed the scrapbook and turned the spine so he could see it.

"What's this?"

"A scrapbook of my life. My father sent Rachel a picture and a note every year since I was a baby."

"Why?"

I opened the book to the first page, where my birth certificate shouted the truth, and turned the book for him to see.

"Rachel is my mother!"

Caleb knelt on the floor, not wanting to get dirt on the bed. His arm propped on one knee, he reached for the scrapbook, examining the birth certificate, then briefly scanning the photos and notes in a quick perusal. Afterward, he looked up at me, a light sparking in his eyes.

"Well, that explains something I've noticed," he said.

"Explains what?"

"Your face is not like Rachel's, but some of your expressions are identical. Sometimes, I've been startled to see the two of you side by side, looking at me in the exact same way. You walk like her. Your hair is the same color. You're both artists. You think alike." He shook his head. "I've often wondered if there might be a family connection, but I never guessed you were her daughter."

Caleb paused, a slow smile spreading across his face. "This also explains why Rachel is so happy these days. For as long as I've known her, Rachel has been pleasant but sad ... until you came. Now she's genuinely happy."

"Oh!" I stared at Caleb, thinking of our wedding day.

"What?"

"At our wedding—when Pastor asked, 'Who gives this woman,' Dad said, *'Her mother and I.'* I thought it was strange at the time, but he meant *Rachel!"*

Caleb threw back his head and laughed. "Oh, wow! He really said that, didn't he?"

I laughed too. "I'm sure Rachel understood what he meant."

"I'll bet she did."

"Caleb, what do I do now? How do I tell Rachel I know she's my mother?"

"Well, I guess we'll have to pray about it and ask God for wisdom."

I put the scrapbook on the shelf and smoothed the bed where I had been sitting.

Caleb stood too. "Let's go home. We can talk about it later tonight." He held out his hand to me and pulled me close.

Standing there encircled by his arms, I thought back to Mom and how we had not done well together. I thought of the many times I felt she hated me. "I understand Mom now."

"How's that?"

"She was forced to raise her rival's daughter after only a year of marriage. No wonder she didn't like me. No wonder I felt she hated me at times."

"Yes, I can see that." Caleb against my hair, considering the situation.

I sighed and shook my head. "I never knew she wasn't my mother. But I *felt* it in my bones."

We walked up the hill slowly, considering the unexpected discovery.

"I've loved Rachel since the day we first met. She was warm and loving, and I felt welcome. I never felt that way with Mom. No wonder Dad sent me here after I learned I was expecting Joshua. *He sent me back to my mother!* He knew I needed her. He knew Rachel would welcome me with open arms and comfort me."

"By the grace of God. Yes. You were faced with a very similar situation to the one Rachel faced. But your dad knew Rachel would not let you suffer the loss of your child like she had. Wow. What a beautiful story!"

"And Dad is moving back here."

"Yes. He is." Caleb thought about it for a moment. "This will be very interesting to watch."

I laughed with delight. "It will indeed."

The next morning when I saw Rachel head out to gather eggs, I slipped down the pathway to the chicken coop.

"Can I help you, Rachel?"

Her face lit up. "Why, Lily! How nice. Yes. I've already gathered the eggs from this side of the coop." She motioned with her right hand while holding the basket on her left arm.

Together we searched the nests, gathering the eggs into the basket. Laura wasn't up yet when we entered the cozy kitchen.

"Would you like a muffin?"

"I'd love one."

Rachel reached for the basket of muffins and sat it on the counter between us, smiling sweetly over at me.

"Rachel," I said as I took her hands in mine. "May I call you Mother?"

She was speechless. Her eyes blinked rapidly, and her cheeks grew bright red.

"I saw the scrapbook in your bedroom yesterday. I looked at it. I know you are my real mother." I smiled into her eyes.

"Oh, Lily!" she blushed and clutched my hands in hers. "I've wanted to tell you, but I didn't know how."

"It's okay, Mother. I'm just glad I know now."

She sighed in relief. "I'm glad you aren't upset, honey."

"Why would I be? I already love you like a mother. I'm pleased to know you really *are* my mom. Now explain. Why didn't Dad tell me all this?"

Rachel shook her head helplessly. "He couldn't. Margaret said she would not agree to let him bring you home unless she could present you to their family and friends as their adopted daughter, not Will's daughter with me. She wanted Will and you to be totally cut off from me. As the years passed, she refused to let Will tell you that you were adopted. You see, she adopted you and had your birth certificate changed to an adoption birth certificate, which names the adopted parents as the birth parents."

"I see. But Dad wrote to you anyway?"

"Yes. He told me he would keep me informed about you secretly once a year. I couldn't bear to let you go without any news of you, honey. You have always been precious to me."

I nodded. I understood. I knew I could never let someone else take Joshua from me.

"Your dad made sure I kept the original birth certificate. I don't know how he managed that. But I put it in the scrapbook with all your pictures."

"I know. I saw it." I squeezed her hands.

"Margaret couldn't have children. Will said she'd had an abortion a couple years before he met her, and it left her sterile. You were his only chance to have a child of his own."

"I see. Well, I love Dad a lot. He made up for what I lacked from my adopted mom."

"Good. I'm glad. He has always been proud of you and has loved you dearly. That is what made it bearable for me, knowing you were with the father who loved you."

"He was always on my side." I smiled remembering all the times he had gently managed to make sure I was happy.

"Two years after I was in the accident, I was able to walk again. Then my aunt died and left me this farm. I think she was upset my parents had made me give you up. Anyway, it helped me stand on my own, finally. But I have missed you every day we were apart."

"I never felt my adopted mom loved me. She was proud of my achievements, but she had no warmth toward me."

"Now you know your true mother has always loved you."

"God has blessed me greatly." I smiled. "And Joshua will always call you Grandma." I stood, walked around the counter, and hugged my mother.

Rachel held me and laughed with pure joy.

After our guests were in bed that night, I walked outside with Caleb. We sat together on the porch swing while I called my father.

"Dad, this afternoon I found Rachel's scrapbook with all my pictures and all the letters you wrote to her. I know the truth now."

"Yes. Rachel called me and told me."

"She did?"

"Yes. It's time you knew. I wanted to tell you, but I was waiting until I would be with you in person." He sounded regretful.

"Dad, it's okay. I think this way was best. It gave me time to process everything before talking to either of you."

"Are you all right with this?"

"Yes, Dad. I am thankful you sent me here! Rachel is wonderful. I'm glad she is my real mother."

"Good." Dad sighed with relief.

"When will you come to Montana?"

"As soon as the house closes. I found a buyer. The closing date is in three weeks. You can look for me then."

"Do you still plan to stay at a cabin on the lake?"

"Yes. I have one reserved."

"Well, we will look forward to seeing you soon, Dad."

"I love you, Lily."

"I love you too, Dad."

CHAPTER 24

Will finished signing the last document. The house was sold. The money would go straight into his Montana account which he had maintained over the years to somehow stay connected with his roots. Now he would return to his hometown and start over.

His father-in-law, Bruce, had wished him well and said goodbye. His heart was crushed by losing his only daughter. Mavis, his wife, had died several years earlier.

"Bruce, I hate the thought of you living here all alone at a time like this. If you want to come to Montana, I'll help you find a place. Lily and her family are there. I'm sure she would be a comfort to you."

Bruce shook his head. "No, I'm too old to move away from here. Besides, Dave and his family are still here, and Michael will bring his family for Christmas. I still have my sons. I'll be okay. But I will come up for a visit once in a while."

"Yes. I understand. You have plenty of family here. But we'll welcome you if you decide to come for a visit. I know Lily will want to see her grandpa. You'll want to meet your great grandson too."

"Thank you, Will." Bruce held out his hand and the two men shook hands.

Will's thoughts turned toward Rachel as he drove north. He remembered the stern phone call he'd received from Rachel's mother.

"You left Lily pregnant when you went to college, Will. She had a baby. A little girl she named Lily.

"What?" He was incredulous.

"Yes. And now Rachel has been in a car accident, and we don't know whether she will live. The doctor said if she does live, it will take her a long time to recover. We think it's time you step up and show some responsibility toward your daughter."

He cringed at the bitterness in her voice.

"We want you and your wife to take Lily. She's half yours. It's your turn to share the load, Will."

He'd told Margaret about the baby. She had been furious. But after arguing about it for days, she said she'd agree to raise her, with conditions.

"The only way I'll agree to this is if Lily never knows she was adopted. We can tell our friends we adopted her. Once we've left college, we'll move back to Santa Rosa, and nobody will know. Plus—and you must promise this—you cannot see Rachel ever again once you've brought the baby home."

"Fine."

"Promise me!"

"I promise."

He remembered the day he'd seen Rachel in the hospital. Her beautiful hair had been shaved to allow the surgeon to stitch the cuts on her head. It had grown back a little since the accident and now covered her head with a short crop of gold interspersed with jagged, red scars. She had been pale and listless, her left arm and leg in casts, her eyes huge and full of tears when she saw him.

"Rachel. I came as soon as your parents contacted me."

"Oh, Will. I'm sorry." Tears ran down her face.

Reaching for a tissue, he wiped the tears away. "Why didn't you say something? Why didn't you tell me you were pregnant?"

Rachel shook her head helplessly side to side and murmured, "You were in love with Margaret. I had lost you. I didn't want to hold you back or cause trouble."

"I would have stayed if you'd told me."

"I wouldn't have wanted you to stay. You didn't love me anymore."

"Rachel, I've seen Lily. I'm taking her back to California with me. Margaret won't let me bring her unless she adopts Lily and I cut all ties with you. But I promise I will send you pictures and letters once a year so you will know Lily is doing well."

Rachel nodded. What else could she do?

"I'm sorry, Rachel." Will bowed his head and held her hand gently.

"It's all right, Will."

"Goodbye, my sweet darling." He kissed her hand and left.

He didn't see Rachel again until Lily's wedding, and then only for a brief chat. Rachel had seemed quiet and a bit sad when she was around him. Now he was going home. Home to Lake Thechihila. He didn't expect anything to be the same with Rachel. How could he? He had unintentionally betrayed her once. He'd promised to love her forever, only to leave her for Margaret. One cannot cut love out of one's life for over twenty years and expect a resurrection.

Two days later, Will walked off the flight into Bozeman, Montana. Caleb met him inside the terminal.

"Welcome back, Will."

"Thanks for coming all this way to pick me up."

"No problem. What are you going to do about a vehicle once you're in Lake Thechihila?"

Will shrugged. "I'm not sure yet. There may be someone in the vicinity with a car to sell."

"You're probably right. If not, we can come back to Bozeman to buy one. Here. Let me help with your luggage."

During the drive back to the lake, Caleb told Will about the Gonzales family and Laura Sanders. "We're letting the Gonzales family stay with us in exchange for Manuel's help with building the log cabin I've been working on. I'm going to use it as a rental for people who want an authentic Montana experience. More people are recreating here in Montana since COVID hit.

"We'll have Miguel and Rosa stay with us until we can find a place for them to live, which may be a long time. But Lily enjoys having them with us. She has a real gift for hospitality. Like her mother." Caleb grinned. "Rachel has taken in Laura Sanders and her little girl."

"Yes. I remember that about Rachel." Will remembered back on those high school years. Rachel was always inviting other girls over to her aunt's house for a meal or to stay overnight. She had the reputation of being a comforter.

"We've found the Thompson family too," Will continued. "They went missing about the same time as Manuel, Rosa, and Laura. Pastor Peters and his wife took them in. This shutdown has really done a job on the economy here in Montana. But it is also stretching us as Christians and helping us grow spiritually."

Will nodded. "California is in trouble too. We're locked down tighter than a drum, but it hasn't stopped the spread of COVID."

"I'm sorry about your wife. How are you coping?"

Will looked out the window at the forest with mountains beyond and sighed. "Margaret and I lost touch with each other's hearts years ago. The final straw for me was when I saw her slap Lily and demand she get an abortion. But later, after I sent Lily here, I met a friend who invited me to a Bible study, and the Lord started warming my heart toward my wife. I felt pity for Margaret and tried to rebuild what we'd lost."

Another sigh. "We were starting to make progress when she contracted COVID. I'd been telling her about Jesus, and she finally gave her heart to him. I know she is with him now. But my main grief is it took me so long to reach out to her and try to salvage our marriage. Things could have been very different if Jesus had been part of my life earlier."

Caleb nodded. "I understand."

"Now I just want to watch my grandson grow and enjoy Lily and you."

"We're glad you can be here, Will. Lily has baked your favorite lemon cake." He grinned. "She's so excited, you probably won't be able to get a word in edgewise for a few minutes."

"Good. I haven't seen her excited in a long, long time."

Caleb was right about his prediction. Lily was excited and happy to see her dad. She thrust Joshua into his arms before he'd taken five steps into their home. Joshua smiled up at his grandpa and patted his face while Lily introduced the Gonzales family. Never before had Will been so thoroughly welcomed by so many people at once. His heart lifted, and he laughed as he swung Joshua up to look him straight in the eye.

"Hi, Joshua. I'm your Grandpa Will. We're going to be very good friends."

Joshua crowed happily and kicked his feet.

Later that night as he slid into his bed at the cabin by the lake, Will sent up a prayer of thanksgiving to God for his family, and dreamed of days ahead when he would teach Joshua to fish.

At the break of dawn the next morning, Will arose, dressed, drank a quick cup of coffee, and walked from his cabin up the road toward Rachel's house. Best meet her when she was free, he thought, for he knew she would be fixing breakfast for her guests later. There were things which must be said between them.

Seeing a light in the kitchen, he went around to the back door and knocked.

Rachel looked up from the eggs she was putting into cartons and smiled. She opened the door and simply walked into his arms, laying her cheek against his chest in the way she'd done back in high school.

"You make it too easy for me after all I've done to hurt you, Rachel darling," he whispered into her hair, his arms holding her close, his tears running down and mingling with the tears on her face.

"There can be no shadow between us, Will."

She lifted her face to him, and he kissed her, the years of separation and longing fading away to nothing. They were boy and girl again, with the sweet smell of lilacs filling the morning air, and a long summer day ahead. She had taken him back into her heart and life with no pouting or tears or recriminations. Just warm, accepting love.

Thursday evening, Dad joined our Bible study group, much to my delight. He helped Rachel set out the plates and the baked goodies she had made. He let me introduce him to our friends and told them how pleased he was to meet them.

Dad held Joshua until it was time for the little ones to leave, then handed him over to Rachel. I saw a flash of love pass between them like the first ray of sun in the morning, and I smiled to myself.

Our topic for the evening was the story of Ruth and Naomi, the story I'd discovered earlier on my own. We were reading the first chapter that evening. I loved hearing those immortal words of Ruth to Naomi again. "Don't ask me to leave you and turn back. Wherever you go, I will go; wherever you live, I will live. Your people will be my people, and your God will be my God. Wherever you die, I will die, and there I will be buried."

I glanced up at Dad and saw him brush a tear from the corner of his eye. Yes, the words moved him too.

After our time together, Caleb and I were the last to leave but one. Dad. He stood behind Rachel, his hand on her shoulder as she handed Joshua over to Caleb.

As we turned to go, we heard my father ask, "Rachel, will you walk to the point with me? I believe we have some things to talk about."

I glanced up at Caleb, who drew me close to his side, a soft smile on his lips. We turned to look back as we climbed the pathway back to our home. We watched Dad and Rachel walk together hand in hand toward the lake, taking the shortcut leading to Thechihila Point.

I remembered the first time I'd seen Rachel praising God through her loss and tears as she gently smiled and raised her hands to God while we sang "Blessed Be Your Name."

God had smoothed the path before these two star-crossed lovers and had drawn them together at last.

Remembering the words to the song Rachel had cherished down through the lonely years, I said softly, "Blessed be the name of the Lord, indeed."

ABOUT THE BOOK

The story of unmarried pregnant women who have been helped by churches is one which I've seen lived out several times. Our church in Montana, and other evangelical churches where I've attended over the years, decided long ago to be actively pro-life. We believed we should reach out to these desperate mothers and their babies through the love and grace of Jesus. We loved those whom God brought our way and taught them about our Savior. Some of these young women married men in our churches. Most went on to become strong Christians. This book, though it is fiction, is a representation of what we and other churches have accomplished through the powerful love and grace of Christ.

I wanted this book to cover the COVID pandemic, for we learned some important things during that time which may help us in future emergencies. The actions taken by the little church in Lake Thechihila are similar to the actions our church in Montana took. We stayed in touch and united, as much as we could. Our younger families continued meeting in homes. Our pastors provided online services. I was teaching young people when COVID hit.

I kept in touch with my class, providing weekly written lessons and encouraging ongoing participation in helping others. I was impressed by the continued Christian service carried out by those young people. In a time of great stress, the love of Jesus continued to flow through our church to each other, to our community, and to those in need.

In chapter eleven, I wrote about a battle in Nuevo Victorio, a small town in Mexico. Though the name of the town is fictitious, this kind of battle is real. These events happen often in Mexico. Yet the church remains strong and faithful to Jesus. At the time of this writing, many are trying to escape Mexico because of the violence there.

As I write fiction, I want to keep the stories as true to life as possible, for in doing so, I can communicate truth in ways nonfiction cannot.

I hope you have enjoyed *Legend of the Lake*. Although this book is written for adults, it is a sequel to my New Adult book, *Before You Find Me*, a romantic suspense featuring the Webster family, which is also set in Montana. *Before You Find Me* was a finalist in the 2023 Golden Scroll Awards by Advanced Writers & Speakers Association.

ABOUT THE AUTHOR

Sheri Schofield is a Bible teacher and award-winning author/illustrator. Colorado Christian Writers' Conference named her Writer of the Year in 2018 because of her writing ministry to children. She and her husband, Tim, lived in the Rocky Mountains of Montana surrounded by wildlife and the challenges of blizzards and wildfires. They now live in the Cowboy State—Wyoming.

After many years of teaching children about Jesus through her classes and books, Sheri now writes for adults as well, both fiction and nonfiction. In her fiction books, she writes about life in Montana and Wyoming, sharing the lifestyle and struggles faced there. *Legend of the Lake* is her second contemporary western romance. The first was *Before You find Me*. Though these books are complete in themselves, some of the same characters are in both books, which creates a sense of continuity and familiarity.

Sheri is a member of Advanced Writers & Speakers Association (AWSA). In addition to her books, she writes for Arise Daily Devotions (www.arisedailydevos.wordpress.com), along with a great team of Christian writers. After a year of writing for Arise Daily Devotions, Sheri was named Writer of the Year for her contributions, which highlight life in the west.

Along with her husband, Sheri has developed the ministry *Faithwind 4 Kids,* which provides Christian books for children and families in their town.

"I see myself as a planter, throwing seeds out into a field. The books are the seeds. The people around me are the field. God waters the seeds, which grow in people's hearts and eventually become his harvest. My job is to plant the seeds of the gospel, then pray for God to work," Sheri says. "I want to do my part in helping others meet Jesus."

If you've enjoyed *Legend of the Lake,* please write a line or two about the book on Amazon, Goodreads, or Barnes & Noble. Reviews mean the world to us writers—they're what keep us writing!

Contact me at https://sherischofield.com I'd love to hear from you.

www.ingramcontent.com/pod-product-compliance
Lightning Source LLC
Chambersburg PA
CBHW070444030726

47503CB00004B/884